Second Chance

against the

Third Reich

U.S. Army Colonel Rescues His Daughter from the Nazis

By Kent Hinckley

ALSO BY KENT HINCKLEY

Hearts, Minds, and Coffee

Publisher's Note

This is a work of fiction. Names, characters, places, and incidents are the product of the author's imagination or are used fictitiously, and any resemblance to actual persons, living or dead, events, locales, or business establishments is entirely coincidental.

Copyright © 2021 by Kent Hinckley

ISBN- 978-0-9915453-5-3

Library of Congress — pending –

Published by: Reyall Corporation
5666 La Jolla Blvd. #200
La Jolla, CA 92037

Printed in the United States of America

See also www.kenthinckley.com

to Sharon,

Chapter 1

June 29, 1944
Meersburg, Germany

There's always a way to do the impossible. After thirty years in the army and three wars, Colonel Dirk Hoffman followed this saying as he braced to attack the Nazis.

Twenty-six years before, in the Great War, Lieutenant Hoffman saw combat as a platoon leader. One night in the Argonne Forest, hissing bullets surprised his squad and his best friend died in an explosion of blood as Hoffman stood stunned at Zach's mutilated face and vacant eyes. The young lieutenant vomited, glanced again at Zach, and escaped with five wounded survivors. Hoffman never spoke of that horror but remained scarred with nightmares ever since.

Hoffman's current mission against the Third Reich differed from his combat experience. It took him weeks to infiltrate through enemy lines to reach this most dangerous moment for the rescue of his daughter, Caroline. Zero hour of 5:00 a.m. was four hours away.

The seminary, that imprisoned Caroline, was a fortress, the contact with German Resistance unreliable, and the escape into Switzerland had a small chance of success, yet the only part that worried Hoffman was the SS Major General whose obsession was to hunt him down and kill him.

Hoffman knew the SS expected him, but saving Caroline seemed attainable. His main concern was finding her without many soldiers guarding her.

1

Chapter 2

Seven years earlier . . .

Major Dirk Hoffman, group head for the supply section of the 7th Cavalry Brigade, Fort Knox, Kentucky, sat at his battered desk and reviewed requisition forms. His brown uniform, with medals from the Great War displayed on his left chest, impressed soldiers who dealt with him but his weathered face, solid body, and military swagger intimidated even the tough ones.

In the hallway, a corporal moved an old metal filing cabinet on a squeaky hand truck when a hurried messenger entered and bumped into it. The filing cabinet fell off the dolly and crashed onto the floor with a loud bang. A few heads turned, saw the mess, and returned to work.

Major Hoffman, however, went on alert, eyes wide and heart pounding. He was back in the Argonne, October 1918. He bent forward in the chair, dropped his head under the desk, and closed his eyes. Once again, a vision of his buddies getting killed appeared on his mental screen.

His lungs heaved as he pulled for air. Sweat beaded on his forehead, and arteries on his temples pulsated, He craved for shots of whiskey. He looked beyond the steno pool and wondered if a machine gun nest waited outside the window. He leaned back

3

in his chair with his eyes closed, and his body unknotted steadily, He breathed slowly.

These torments struck at random times, and many tried to comfort him; they counseled patience: "Don't worry, time will heal." But almost twenty years had elapsed since this affliction started without improvement. Hoffman prescribed his own antidote: detachment from his family and isolation from friends except those few in the Officers' Club bar. In his world, safety ruled. His only comfort was to associate with army guys who had experienced wartime combat.

After a few minutes, the mental terror subsided, and he took another deep breath while pulling his shirt away from the right rib area as though it stuck to his skin. He saw the messenger, a staff sergeant, standing at the doorway to his office. The sergeant ignored the awkwardness of facing a field-grade officer and said, "Sir, the commander needs the report by seventeen hundred hours."

An embarrassed Major Hoffman regained his composure and replied, "Tell the colonel I'll have it ready by then."

He buckled down to the paperwork and heard his name called by his secretary who pointed to the phone. "Your wife is on the line."

Hoffman answered. "Yeah, what do you want?"

Kaye omitted greetings. "Be prepared when you come home. Caroline wants to talk to you."

"Does our spoiled child want more money for her singing? She's twenty-two and should fend for herself. I was sixteen when I lied my way into the army."

Driving home, Hoffman thought about all the funds he paid for her singing lessons and outfits since junior high. Singing did not interest him, but her musical lessons did keep her out of his hair. Her jazz group won awards which emboldened her to continue and to appear on stage, and at eighteen she became the lead singer.

He didn't understand girls, but admitted that Caroline took after him. She was clever, stubborn and had a temper. Fortunately, she had her mother's looks: good figure, medium height, brown hair, blue eyes.

Hoffman knew his daughter yearned to escape the tedious life at an army base and reach for the glittery world of show biz. He didn't blame her because his own life seemed dreary as he watched clerks, secretaries, and bookkeepers flit about the room in the endless minuet of paper processing.

When he drove into the driveway, he decided that he would hear her plea and then say no.

The Hoffmans resided in a bungalow at the fort's housing subdivision. As a major, he qualified for a detached cottage with two bedrooms and one indoor bathroom. Most other houses had an outdoor toilet. His home was older than other base housing with a three-foot gap between the next-door unit, and all of the houses were painted in khaki brown. That was life in the military, and it seemed adequate, especially during the Depression.

As Hoffman stepped into the living room, Caroline rushed to him. "Sir, I'm so excited. You'll never guess what happened."

Kaye said, "Caroline, settle down and let your father relax after a busy day," as she brought out an old fashioned. He went to his leather chair that squeaked as he sat down. Kaye parked herself on the sofa next to him while Caroline sat on the floor. She smiled, trying to keep the thrilling news inside.

After two sips of his cocktail, curiosity got the better of him. "Okay, Caroline. What are you so excited about?"

"Sir, the Germans love jazz, and their representative in New York saw our performance and raved about it. He invited our troupe for a five-week tour to sing in Germany!"

She paused, waited for his reaction, hoping he might jump up or clap his hands. When he said nothing, she continued, a little less confident. "Wow. I can't believe it. We leave next week." She stopped, looked at her mom for support, then glanced at him, but

5

her father remained silent. She added, her voice trailing off, "Barely enough time to pack."

Kaye said, "Isn't it wonderful? All her hard work has served her well."

Hoffman took a hefty sip and his face reddened. "Sing in Germany? Are you nuts? They're our enemy."

Caroline's eyes narrowed, lips pursed, cheeks burned. "Our enemy? Are we at war with them? Americans love Germany. We're German. We speak German to your parents. The Olympics in '36 were a huge success that showcased Germany's prosperity while the rest of Europe and the United States are in a stinking depression."

Hoffman interrupted. "Germany violated the Treaty of Versailles. They are building up their military and have reoccupied the Rhineland. It's only a matter of time until they stretch their might to other countries."

Caroline countered, "But Hitler said that the Rhineland belongs to Germany. He only wants peace for Europe. Anyway, why would America get involved? It's a European problem."

Hoffman cracked his knuckles and said, "We'll get drawn into it just as we saved Europe's ass in the Great War." He stared at his drink and repositioned himself in his chair. "Besides, I don't have the money to send you."

"That's the beauty of it. They pay all expenses."

Hoffman bristled and said, "Why would they pick up expenses? Something fishy is going on."

"Germans love jazz but have few groups, and America has most of the jazz musicians and singers, but Germany wants white singers. Otto saw us perform and said we will have great appeal coming from America."

"I don't like this trip." Hoffman turned to his wife. "Otto? So now it's Otto?"

"Sir, you've never seen me sing. How can you make any judgments? You don't know anything about the popularity of jazz in Europe."

"I can see it now. You will get into trouble and beg us to send you money."

Caroline said, "Sir, I've saved money to buy anything I need. I've squared it with my boss at the store for my absence. He thinks it's a great opportunity."

Hoffman's jaw tightened and the lines between his eyebrows narrowed. "I won't permit it. I can't have my unchaperoned daughter gallivanting around with the enemy across the Atlantic Ocean thousands of miles away."

Her eyes could not compete against his stare; instead they became watery. She looked down at the floor and felt helpless. She had tried to reach him for so many years only to receive morsels of acknowledgment, and now, with her future ahead of her and no support for her dreams, she couldn't talk, couldn't fight. She came to her final point. She mumbled while she looked at her feet, "Sir, I'm twenty-two. I don't need your permission."

Hoffman's neck arteries bulged and he pulled at his shirt again always at the same place—on the right side of his torso. "You don't understand how rough and tumble warlike Germans can be. They're killers. They killed my best friend."

"I know the story, and I'm sorry. In fact, you constantly remind me about your dead buddies instead of paying attention to me—who's alive. Don't I count?"

"So, you think you can go out on your own now, is that it?" Holding the glass, he swirled the ice around, then pulled rank and yelled, "Where will you live when you return?"

Caroline and Kaye looked at each other. Caroline said, "That's all you do, control, control, control. I have my own life. You never pay attention to me. Don't you want me to have fun, learn about the world? Few groups are given this chance."

Hoffman stood up. "End of discussion." He went outside to his toolshed.

Kaye looked at her daughter. "I'm sorry, honey. I'll talk to him."

"It's no use, Mother. What he needs is a good war to keep him away from here."

"Caroline, that's not fair."

"Oh, Mother. I thought you were on my side." Caroline ran from the room in tears.

The next morning, the overcast sky prevented any sunlight from entering through the windows. Hoffman came down the stairs five minutes before the start of the ritual breakfast at 7:30. He saw Kaye cooking eggs in the big iron pan.

Clad in his pressed army uniform with his shoes shined and his brass polished, Hoffman followed a routine of a family meal before leaving for the fort. Three place settings were precisely arranged with orange juice glasses filled, coffee pot in the middle of the table, and white bread stacked by the toaster. A folded newspaper was placed to the right of Hoffman's plate at the head of the table.

Kaye served scrambled eggs and bacon and sat down opposite her husband. Hoffman read the paper, and they waited for Caroline.

Hoffman said, "She'll get over it. She'll see it's for the best."

Two more minutes passed. Kaye went upstairs. After more silence, she ran down and burst into the dining room. "She's gone. Her suitcase and clothes are gone."

Hoffman remained in his chair. "Caroline never listens to me, never did what was right. I'm going to kill Otto!" Hoffman threw the coffee cup against the wall with coffee staining the wallpaper.

Kaye glared at his childish behavior for the umpteenth time and said, "All she wants is your approval." Kaye walked around the table and looked down at him. "She's gone and you kicked her out."

"What do you mean?" Hoffman tilted his head to face her with a sheepish look.

Kaye's face flushed. "I've stuck up for you. I've seen you wake from your nightmares, resent everybody and everything, duck at the sound of a loud noise, and give me the silent treatment." She started to leave then turned around. "Your body is here, but you are still in France. We're your family, but you push us away, and we're on your side." Kaye paused, gathered herself, and took a deep breath. "She means everything to me. Everything. Might as well kick me out, too."

Hoffman offered no response. He wanted to head to the Officers' Club and have a few beers.

Five weeks on the concert tour became five months as Caroline's troupe joined a German ensemble. After a seven-city tour, the group returned to Berlin for a long-term run at the glamorous Hotel Kaiserhof. Caroline became the headliner and received ample proceeds from gate receipts. Kaye went to visit in 1938 and became a show mom and chaperone.

At the end of 1938, Hoffman received a phone call from Berlin. Caroline spoke in a monotone voice. "Mom forced me to call you with my news. I'm getting married. She thought you'd like to know."

"Who's the guy?"

"He's in the army."

"What's an American army guy doing over there?"

"Konrad belongs to the Wehrmacht, you know, the German army. He's wonderful. Aren't you happy for me?"

"What rank is he?"

"I knew you thought that would be important." Caroline waited and said with frustration, "He's a captain."

A long pause ensued as Hoffman absorbed this information. He finally broke the quiet. "What side are you on?"

"You can't stand losing control. It's my happy moment, and you question my loyalty. What about your loyalty to me?"

When Hoffman didn't say anything, she added, "I love Konrad. Don't worry, sir, I won't bother you anymore."

Chapter 3

Six years later . . .

While Colonel Hoffman was domiciled in London to oversee logistics and supply, he spent much of his time at the Portsmouth Dockyard, Britain's large naval base and repair facilities located fifty miles southwest of London. He and his group coordinated the assembly and delivery of landing craft to British, Canadian, and American forces who were in the final stages of Operation Overlord, the invasion of the French coast.

He inherited an inefficient group one-and-one-half years ago, but Hoffman succeeded by reorganizing the Quartermasters Corps and pressuring the military and civilian workers to expedite their timetables. Since he fought bureaucracy, his methods invariably antagonized people, but the results enabled Overlord to be ready one month earlier than projected. Thousands of landing craft rested in ports along the southern part of England ready to advance across the English Channel, and Supreme Command planners had secretly made Portsmouth the departure point for Sword Beach during the Normandy landing.

During a meeting with majors and captains in the naval yard, Colonel Hoffman shouted, "I don't care if a general or admiral gives you excuses or delays, get these boats to the designated ports right away! Our job is not to please the higher-ups but the fighting men. Got it?"

In unison, the officers said, "Yes, sir."

"Any delays, get hold of me immediately."

"Yes, sir."

Generals and admirals knew that Eisenhower would support Hoffman if push came to shove, so no one ever pressed Hoffman further.

He returned to a cluttered office where an American army captain with an envelope in his right hand stood up.

"Colonel, you received this summons from headquarters. You are to report to MI6 in London tomorrow at 1400 hours."

"What do they want?"

"You'll have to find out, sir. The higher-ups approved the meeting."

"They must need a briefing." Hoffman had never spoken to MI6 before.

The next morning at 8:30, he took a train from the dockyards to London, almost a three-hour trip. The unknown purpose of the meeting nagged at Hoffman and kept him awake. As he relaxed in the coach, he looked out the window at the city of Portsmouth and saw the streets jammed with trucks and troops as they followed the hand signals of the military police that directed them to various staging locations. The British people had to remain at home preferably inside their houses while this traffic nightmare inched forward. When Hoffman arrived in London, he went to his office and two hours later, walked to MI6.

Secret Intelligence Service—better known as MI6 or Military Intelligence, Section 6—was charged with the collection and analysis of overseas covert intelligence to support national security. They provided important findings for the planning of the coming invasion. MI6's mystique made many officials nervous when they entered its quarters, let alone undergo its questioning.

The rain and wind and made navigation of the sidewalks difficult as he entered the nine-story building at 54 Broadway Street with a brass sign in front, MINIMAX FIRE EXTINGUISHER

COMPANY in black letters. He passed through two checkpoints to arrive on the fourth floor.

A man came into the lobby and said, "Colonel Hoffman? I am Commander Ambrose Bainbridge, MI6 Deputy Director of Covert Activities in Germany." Without any greeting, he added in an imperious tone, "Follow me."

Hoffman thought his host looked like typical British gentry: conservative suit, no smiles, stocky, thin gray hair combed over, and an uppity manner; yet his serious eyes and tightened jaw belied a warrior not to be taken lightly. "Would you like some tea?" Hoffman declined the offer, so Bainbridge with a dour expression picked up his pipe, tamped down the tobacco, and relit the bowl.

He spoke in an educated British accent. "Colonel, let's get right to the point. When did you last communicate with your daughter?"

Hoffman sat up straight and wide-eyed. "My daughter? Has something happened?"

Bainbridge ignored the question. "Just a query. An American married to a Nazi is not an every day occurrence, and we have to follow up every lead."

"I haven't heard anything, but my wife received a letter from Caroline that was mailed from Spain, which was then forwarded to the States. It took three months to get to her." He paused. "Caroline said that as a foreign alien, she was not sent to an internment camp for foreigners because she was married to an SS officer. She says she's fine."

"When was the letter received?"

"About one year ago." An unlikely thought suddenly occurred to Hoffman. "Does she work for you?"

Bainbridge forced a grin. "If she only could, but unfortunately no." He played with his pipe and said, "We have recently become aware of her presence in Berlin but know nothing about her. Our agent there informed us that she is an American, and our analyst here found out that she is your daughter. I need to know about her and you."

13

"Me?" Hoffman hesitated. "All right, I understand. The last time I spoke to her was in 1938. She called me from Berlin to tell me about her engagement. She was a jazz singer in a group that traveled throughout Germany. She married a German army officer, a captain, I believe, named Konrad Frolich. Caroline and I haven't talked since, and she hasn't responded to my letters. As you can tell, we aren't close."

Bainbridge said, "Her husband is a major now and belongs to the SS, the elite German force. He works for SS Major General Bruno Bachmann." Bainbridge whacked his pipe on an ashtray. "Ever heard of him?"

"No, I only know the big shots like Hitler, Himmler, and Goering. That's all."

"We are keenly interested in Bachmann. He's an ambitious thug with a huge temper. He has street smarts and no morals, which describes all Nazis except most of them aren't very bright. Bachmann's in charge of security for Berlin and for penetrating the German Resistance. He's rooted out some of their leaders much to our dismay. We hate losing anyone." Bainbridge packed more tobacco into his pipe. "One of our agents inside his headquarters picked up that Bachmann suspects that your daughter might be a spy and put surveillance on her. He expects to uncover her clandestine activity, real or made up, and then jail her. Our agent estimates that Bachmann will act in thirty days." Bainbridge stopped to see Hoffman's reaction before lighting his pipe.

Hoffman shook his head and looked down. "How can she be a spy? She's married to a Nazi."

"As I said, Bachmann doesn't care that Caroline is married to his intelligence chief who happens to be Konrad Frolich."

"My son-in-law works for him?"

"We wondered if you heard anything about her situation? I gather you haven't."

"Caroline? A spy? She likes Germany and hates me."

"Maybe she changed her mind . . . about Germany anyway."

Hoffman said, "Is her husband protecting her?"

"He probably has no say in the matter. Bachmann is ruthless and will likely force Frolich to do his bidding, regardless of his feeling for your daughter."

"Can we do anything to get her out?"

Bainbridge said, "We don't have the manpower to contact her given the imminent invasion. We work with the German Resistance, but they're not as strong as their French counterparts. It's impossible for us to move commandos into Berlin, and she probably doesn't want to be reached. She's had plenty of time to leave Germany if she wanted to."

"Is there anything I can do?"

"I'm afraid not unless you get any news about her or know someone who can warn her."

Hoffman exited the building in a daze only to be greeted by the rain storm. He was angry at Caroline. *You're messing up my life. If anything happened to you, Kaye would suffer a heart attack.*

He sloshed through the water on the sidewalk oblivious of the puddles while his anger at the Germans intensified. Hoffman wanted to scold Caroline for disobeying him in 1937, and because now in 1944 she needed rescuing and there was no way to rescue her. How dare she upset his life and put herself in the jaws of the Third Reich. Her irresponsibility meant that he needed to devise a way to save her, which posed huge problems since he knew little about what commandos are supposed to do behind enemy lines.

In the midst of his anger, Caroline's image as a young girl surfaced. She was so adorable in her pink dress as her short legs ran around the yard, and when she stopped, she looked at him and said, "Daddy." His heart melted. What power she had. Then he went off to war and never recaptured that connection with his little girl. The more he thought about those innocent times, the more he missed them.

He regretted his behavior after he returned from the Great War. He spent more time with a beer or whiskey than with her. He wanted some beers now to stop thinking about this awkward situation, but he couldn't submerge the past any longer. Because he ignored his daughter, he believed that Caroline wedded Major Frolich out of spite for him. It was Hoffman's fault his daughter went to Germany, his fault that she married a Nazi, and his fault that he couldn't now protect her. Anger dissolved into sadness as he thought about the effect on Kaye if she knew her daughter might be killed. He'd lose Caroline and Kaye at the same instant.

As he walked in the puddles and rain, he suppressed a cry in his voice but a tear escaped from his eye. The thought of Caroline's death grabbed his chest. He turned away from the sidewalk and found shelter underneath a building's overhang. He leaned against the wall, head down. He took deep breaths as he contemplated Caroline's death. He couldn't fathom it or accept it. She was such an innocent child. A life without his daughter? Without his wife? Impossible.

He left the wall and shook his head to scatter these ugly thoughts. Come on, Dirk. Time to take action. No more sentimentality.

The rain and wind picked up and pelted his face and jacket, but Hoffman kept his stare straight ahead, blind to the inclement weather. He had to get Caroline out of Berlin, out of Germany, but could not come up with any solutions.

Colonel Hoffman walked in a trance to the Supreme Allied Headquarters at 20 Grosvenor Square in the Mayfair District, still in thought about his daughter's plight. He reached the Supply Department on the third floor, removed his damp jacket, sat at his desk, and thumbed through his mail.

Colonel Max Goreki, also in supply and a close friend from their days at Fort Benning years ago, entered the office and approached Hoffman. With bushy eyebrows pushed together and eyes darting left and right, Goreki glanced over his shoulder out of caution, which alerted Hoffman that bad news was coming.

"Dirk, did you hear the scuttlebutt? After eighteen months of planning and enormous funds spent to get ready, some drunken brigadier general at an embassy party blurted out that the invasion would occur in June."

Hoffman dropped his jaw. "That stupid general has just jeopardized Overlord."

Chapter 4

May 3, 1944
London, England

Goreki continued, "Everyone's shocked. Even though very few know the date, his outburst takes away the surprise that is necessary for this operation. Only high-ranking officers and guests heard, so we don't know if the information went beyond the party. The brass is trying to stop the rumor mill. Ike demoted the general to lieutenant colonel and reassigned him to the States. Everyone is panicked, and the planners have spoken with the infantry commanders to assess the current strategy."

Hoffman hadn't known the date or place of the attack but expected Operation Overlord to commence soon, as did the British and the one million American soldiers stationed in Great Britain. The Germans expected the invasion to occur in June or July and be led by General George Patton. Over the previous two years, the Wehrmacht erected hundreds of miles of fortifications that extended from the border with Spain around the Atlantic tip at Brest and up the English Channel northeast to Denmark, the so-called Atlantic Wall. Hitler believed it could not be breached.

The Supreme Command guarded the date and landing site with extreme secrecy because the assault on France was a tactical gamble—establishing a beachhead was not a certainty. The Germans could thwart the invasion by deploying thirty divisions, some 500,000 soldiers, plus nine more divisions, approximating 100,000 men in reserve, to deny the allies a foothold on the continent and throw them back into the sea. German intelligence estimated that the Allies' chances of a favorable outcome approximated fifty percent. If the Allies failed, the war would grind on for years.

After Colonel Goreki departed, Hoffman looked at the letters on his desk. Months and months of exhorting and pushing to get men and machines ready, now blown apart by one sloppy drunk. He grabbed the pile of letters and hurled them against the wall. He looked at the mess then fell back on his desk chair and pushed it back till the casters hit the wall behind him. What a day. Everything under his control was now shot to hell. He rubbed his eyes, letting his head fall back as he stared at the ceiling. Unconsciously he kept pulling his shirt away from his right side.

He scooted himself and his chair back to the desk, pulled out a key, and opened the bottom drawer. His pistol sat inside along with a map of Germany and old letters from Kaye. He fixated on all three, grabbed the gun and map, and placed them on top of his desk. His personal war against Germany had begun, but instead of conjuring a plan to save his daughter, all that emerged was anger at the situation and frustration that he couldn't come up with a solution, so he decided to visit the Officers' Club and clear his mind.

The O Club was located in the basement of an old four-story office building. The lower-level structure stayed intact while the upper floors showed scars from the three-and-a-half month bombing raids in 1940 by the Luftwaffe, the German air force. As he walked the three blocks, he passed by large chunks of fallen masonry on the side streets and the battered buildings that had been evacuated.

When Hoffman entered the crowded bar, soldiers withdrew from his path because no one wanted to catch one of the colonel's broadsides resulting from a short fuse, whether drinking or not. The pub wasn't fancy but catered to military, friends, and female companions; one could hardly hear over the clanking of glasses, music, and the roar of the patrons. The haze from the smoke and odors from perspiration prompted Hoffman to stake out a place at the end of the bar at the far side of the room to avoid the throng.

Hoffman found a stool and gestured for the bartender to come over.

He said, "Good to see you, Colonel. What can I bring you?"

"Hey, Basil. Get me a bottle of the hard stuff, quick."

"My name's still Chauncey."

"If you say so, Basil."

He was surprised that Hoffman opted to drink whiskey before beer, different from his usual. Chauncey shoved a full bottle and glass in front of the colonel and retreated to a safer part of the bar because he had enough hassles with juiced officers without adding Hoffman to the list. The colonel looked different, and Chauncey thought something had changed in his life.

Hoffman poured a large portion of whiskey into his glass and gulped it down. Then he poured himself another.

Major Albright, who sat next to Hoffman and observed the rapid downing of the liquor, said, "What's the rush? Afraid you'll miss the war?"

Hoffman looked at his seatmate and noticed that the major belonged to the Judge Advocate General Corps, which meant he was a lawyer. Normally the colonel would criticize admin types, but a lawyer in Fort Knox saved him from a lawsuit, so he backed off. "Just thinking about my daughter and wife. Can I pour you a drink?"

"Yeah, sure. Where's your family now?"

Hoffman didn't want to go into details, so he answered, "Fort Knox."

The two army men talked shop while Hoffman drank the amber fluid. During a break from talking, Hoffman reviewed the MI6 meeting and the prospect of Caroline being imprisoned. He dropped his eyes. Poor Caroline.

More people kept coming into the club, and one captain accidentally knocked over a chair that scared Hoffman and prompted him to fill up his glass from a now quarter-filled whiskey bottle. His unsteady hands guided the potent liquid into his glass but small spills still resulted. He thought about Kaye. He tugged at his shirt once again and took out a photo from his wallet taken ten years before. When he saw the two women in their innocent poses, his eyes moistened even after he put the picture away. More anger appeared as he recalled Bainbridge's talk about Caroline's plight, and Hoffman wanted to unleash his fury but held himself in check.

Hoffman resumed his conversation with the major who seemed to know everyone at the bar and told funny stories about many of them. As the colonel surveyed the room, he noticed a loud-mouthed Brit who had a fancy blue uniform with garish ribbons and medallions and a big gut. He asked the major, "Who is that overstuffed dandy? He dresses like a peacock."

Major Albright said, "Oh, you mean His Royal Pain in the Ass, Major Percy Dankworth? Isn't he pretty?"

"He's a show-off. What's his story?"

"He's aristocracy, a bully, and exploits the fact that when his father dies, he'll become the Earl of Shrewberry. He's not worth a damn but uses his bloodlines to get preferential treatment such as admittance into college and an assignment to a noncombat position as a major in the British army. He browbeats enlisted men and junior officers, and the higher-ups let him get away with it."

Hoffman started to slur his words. "That fake duke or whatever he is could use a few manners." Hoffman fumed. "This twit may soon experience combat for the first time."

Soon Major Dankworth staggered over to the bar in search of more drinks, so a wobbly Hoffman stood up to confront the peacock. As Dankworth stumbled toward the bar stools, he collided with Hoffman.

Dankworth said, "You're in my way."

Hoffman shouted, "You crashed into me. I was here first."

"Yanks always have to be right, don't you?"

"Clear your ass out of here," said Hoffman.

"You move into our country, think you run the show, and take our women. Who needs you?"

"You obviously can't fight Hitler on your own. You Limeys use our money, our equipment, and our men. Why are you complaining?"

"You're a dimwitted jerk. Don't you know who I am?"

"A jackass?"

Dankworth readied his fists. "You should respect your betters."

Chauncey moved around the bar to separate the two. "Save the fighting for the Germans."

But both wanted satisfaction. Percy swung first and missed. Hoffman tried to maintain his balance and countered with two swings. Both caught air. Plastered, the two tried to anchor their footing, but neither could mount much offense. Chauncey raced out to find the MPs.

Hoffman grabbed the bar rail with one hand to keep himself upright just as Dankworth unleashed a left hook. Its force caught Hoffman on the side of the head, and he used both hands on the bar rail to remain standing. The hit brought a bit of clarity to Hoffman whose cheeks flushed, nostrils flared, and fire emitted from his eyes.

Yanks and Brits massed around the bar and egged both fighters on as each soldier cheered for his countryman. "Come on, Percy, knock 'em out."

"Okay, Colonel, make us proud. Take him."

"Percy, hit him in the balls."

"Don't waste any time, Colonel. He can't even take one punch."

When Dankworth followed with a right-hand punch, Hoffman used his left to block it and threw a right fist into Dankworth's nose, then another to his cheek. As Dankworth fell to the floor, Hoffman pummeled him with a third punch to the chin and a fourth to the other cheek. He leaned over but couldn't stop his momentum and fell on top of the bloodied and unconscious Dankworth.

A few soldiers rushed in and helped Hoffman up, but he fell backward and took two with him. When he tried to push himself up, his eyes rolled and he passed out. The MPs dragged the combatants to a vacant room where Hoffman and Dankworth lay sprawled out cold.

Chapter 5

May 3, 1944
London, England

Major General Joe Machinski, logistical operations head of Supreme Allied Headquarters, sat with colleagues in the far end of the Officers' Club when he heard the ruckus. The MPs informed him about the drunken brawl between an American colonel and the helpless British major. This incident could undermine relations between the two allies and needed to be addressed immediately.

Machinski went to the room where both comatose bodies lay. He spotted Colonel Hoffman and identified Major Dankworth. Machinski remembered that the Brit was distantly connected to Churchill's family, and they would demand an inquiry. Machinski used to be friends with Hoffman, understood him to be a contentious soul, cursed from his combat experience in the Great War. Given the colonel's many medals during the Great War, Machinski showed compassion and wanted to get him out of the Officers' Club. He ordered the MPs to carry Hoffman to his apartment.

When Hoffman awoke around noon, he put both hands on his head and winced from the hangover made worse when someone knocked loudly on his door. An MP entered, saluted, and informed Colonel Hoffman about his behavior at the club. Hoffman shut his eyes and groaned. The MP, a corporal from Idaho, said that Hoffman was to report to Major General Machinski in his office that afternoon at 1500 hours.

At 1500 hours, Hoffman sat in a sparsely furnished foyer and waited for two hours. His foot tapped the floor, his body fidgeted, he pulled his shirt out from his scar, and looked constantly at the clock and hoped for a firing squad to put him out of his misery. Hoffman and Machinski served together in the 1920s. Hoffman held a higher rank during most of the years until his ill-tempered personality alienated those on the promotion board. They did not reward hotheads, and their standards allowed Machinski to advance more rapidly.

Hoffman slouched in the anteroom's chair waiting for the tongue-lashing he deserved. He wondered how he could defend himself when he had already condemned himself to jail and hard labor.

Finally, at 1710 hours, the general's aide summoned him.

Machinski said, "Dirk, you've done it this time, and I can't bail you out. The Board of Inquiry meets tomorrow and takes a dim view when Americans beat up our ally and host. Ike can't overlook this blunder."

"Joe, I don't even remember doing anything," he paused to rub his forehead, "but that's no excuse." He shook his head. "What's next?"

"You'll probably be demoted and sent back to the States. The board can't show any favoritism, and Ike can't ignore the board's decision in his position as commander of all Allies. You clobbered a British army major with royal connections, which is a serious offense."

The Board of Inquiry met for fifty minutes in a closed hearing and heard the arguments of both sides. It submitted its findings to Major General Machinski to carry out its decision: Hoffman would receive a demotion to major subject to army approval and immediate repatriation to the United States for further assignment. His military career, while not over, had ended. One drunken outburst erased his previous achievements, but thoughts about his disgrace went to Kaye, and the shame his behavior put on his family.

Now he wouldn't be able to participate in the amphibious expedition to France that was expected to be the greatest battle of the war. And he yearned for one more chance to smash the Third Reich.

As he sat in his apartment and examined the meager choices for his future, he remembered what MI6 said about their lack of resources for a clandestine undertaking to Berlin. He also recalled the worry that spread through Supreme Headquarters about the slip of the tongue by a brigadier general that erected more stumbling blocks into Operation Overlord. He considered schemes, even those with high risk, that might allow him to get to Berlin and go after Caroline. One idea struck him.

He called MI6. "Commander Bainbridge. Can I meet with you?" Then he arranged for a second meeting with Major General Machinski.

As he settled in a chair in front of Bainbridge's teak desk, Hoffman kept his attention fixed on the Brit. "You mentioned that you couldn't get anyone into Berlin given the demands of Operation Overlord. If someone managed to reach Berlin, could the German Resistance provide support?"

Bainbridge raised his thin eyebrows. "What do you have in mind?"

Hoffman leaned back into his chair and rubbed his ear. "With MI6's help, I can end up in Berlin, and then with the aid of the Resistance, I can get my daughter to Switzerland."

Bainbridge looked at Hoffman as though he should wear a straitjacket and return to the asylum. "Is this an American joke? Has it been a slow day at Supreme Headquarters?"

Hoffman ignored the sarcasm and proceeded. "Everyone knows the Allies will attack the French coast, but they don't know the place or date. You have German double agents, right? If you convince one of them to recommend to German intelligence that I know the landing location, they may want to kidnap me, take me to Berlin, torture me until I release a false site, and voila! I'm in Berlin."

"Is part of your plan to survive the torture?"

"They won't kill me. I'm too valuable a source. They'll kill me after the real invasion, but the Resistance can rescue me before that happens. Then I get my daughter, and with the escape route mapped by the Resistance, we'll reach Switzerland. The Nazis won't worry about us since they'll be preoccupied with the Allies in France. I speak fluent German and won't stick out as a foreigner."

Bainbridge took out a flask and poured its golden contents into his tea cup and sipped it. "This mission will likely end in your death. Does your plan have official approval?"

"I'm meeting with my boss, Major General Machinski, shortly. I'll request him to authorize you to work with me. This mission will be confidential. No one is to know about it."

Bainbridge shook his head and said, "I heard you encountered a sticky wicket recently. Is this plan your way to make up for your mistake?"

"That's why I see Machinski tomorrow. But I need to inform him that you will assist me."

"If Machinski approves your lunacy, we'll do our best to help an ally."

Machinski originally didn't want to meet with Hoffman given his hectic schedule but acquiesced under Hoffman's insistence. The general would allow Hoffman ten minutes.

That night at his apartment's small dining table, Hoffman reviewed the day and agreed with Commander Bainbridge. The plan was sheer idiocy, but Hoffman had to redeem himself, and if he could escape the Nazi torturers, then he could save Caroline.

For the next day's meeting, he worked to prepare a convincing sales pitch since he had to overcome Machinski's reluctance to go against the board's decision. Hoffman decided not to mention the part about rescuing his daughter since it might cause Machinski to reject the plan. For the rest of the night and into the early morning, Hoffman rehearsed his brief presentation, and his nerves got the best of him as he stumbled over words and stuttered. He couldn't eat, sleep, and at times fell short of breath.

In past leadership roles, Hoffman gave stirring talks to his men, briefed generals with confidence and cadence, but at this moment, he could not muster self-assurance when he would plead his own case.

That morning, with an ashen face, tired eyes, and bent posture, Hoffman departed his apartment and made his way to Supreme Allied Headquarters.

Chapter 6

May 11, 1944
London, England

Colonel Hoffman arrived at the main lobby, climbed two floors, and stood outside Machinski's office. Hoffman straightened his shoulders and took a deep breath, exhaled, tucked his service cap under his left arm, and opened the door. He checked in with the receptionist and sat ramrod straight in the reception area ready to be called. In the quiet of the foyer, he went over his spiel, fidgeted, adjusted and readjusted his tie, pulled at his shirt on the right rib, picked at his fingernails, and squirmed in the chair. The delay helped his composure. The longer the wait, he found his tension eased.

Sweat dripped down his back and forehead, which undermined his combat-ready bearing. The meeting would be the toughest of his military experience. He was not sure how to overcome the Board of Inquiry's verdict since he had alienated many people with his tirades during his career. Machinski was the only person who would give him a fair hearing.

An aide came out of the office and waived his arm toward the office door. "The general will see you now, sir."

Hoffman walked on the concrete floor and looked straight ahead past the aide, entered the large office, stood at attention, and saluted while Machinski remained in his chair, motionless.

Hoffman scanned the austere office anchored by an oak desk behind which was a map of Europe flanked by the American flag on the right and his two-star general's banner on the left. The

31

discomfort reminded Hoffman of facing his father before a beating for playing hooky.

Machinski looked up from his desk. "Dirk, you asked for the meeting. Go ahead."

Without waiting for the at ease order, Hoffman said, "Sir, I know what action you must take, and I deserve it. I have an alternative that might help. I request permission to offer it."

Machinski said, "You've put me into a thorny spot, and I have no choice but — "

Hoffman interrupted. "Please listen."

The general leaned back in his chair, took a deep breath, and frowned at Hoffman. Ten seconds passed in silence. Given his many weighty issues, dealing with this personnel matter did not rank high on his to-do list. Machinski clenched his jaw. "I'm listening."

"I have a way to negate the breach of the invasion date uttered at the embassy. Appoint me to chairman of a committee called Invasion Logistics or some sort."

"Is this a joke?"

Hoffman persisted. "Hear me out, sir. Hold one meeting loaded with false information, so it will be etched in my brain."

Hoffman's words left Machinski stunned. Had his friend fallen over the edge? As Machinski raised his hand signaling for him to stop, Hoffman raised his voice. "Permit me to continue, sir."

Machinski gave a sigh of exasperation and grudgingly nodded.

Hoffman proceeded. "After the logistics meeting, have MI6 contact one of the German spies that have turned to our side. Tell them about me and my vital knowledge. Have them set up a kidnapping. They'll take me to Germany, torture me, and eventually I will let slip the false location of the landing."

Machinski calmed down and looked at his friend differently. "That's a suicide mission."

"I know. Death is better than shame."

Machinski stared at the colonel. He saw a sorrowful, nervous, and contrite man, very different from the robust soldier with whom he served.

Hoffman continued. "MI6 will help me. No one in supply will miss me since my duties are finished."

"Dirk, you don't have to do this. You screwed up, but I'll bring you back after a while. You're too valuable."

"I let myself and others down. I've also quit drinking."

Machinski rose from his chair and walked around his desk, looked at Hoffman, then went to a side table and poured himself a glass of water. He stood there in thought, looked at the glass, put it down, then went back to his desk.

"If you go through with it, no one can know. No records will exist. Do you understand?"

Their conversation followed a military formality that Hoffman understood even when friends spoke to each other during presentations.

"Yes, sir. I've thought about it and accept that my death will never be acknowledged." He paused and under his breath as if giving a confession said, "It's the least I can do for my country."

"What do you need to prepare for your mission?"

Hoffman said, "With your authorization, I'll work with Commander Bainbridge at MI6 who will coordinate with German double agents in London to get me to Berlin. After the invasion, report that I am missing in action. The secret will be preserved."

Aware that he used too much of Machinski's time, Hoffman said, "Do I have your approval, sir?"

Machinski remained in his chair and fiddled with a pencil between two fingers on one hand. "Overlord has run many deceptions. This one is convincing." He sat up straight. "I approve this mission but wish you didn't have to do it."

"Thank you, sir." Hoffman did an about face and went to the door.

Machinski got up from his chair and broke the formality. "Dirk, wait." He came over to his longtime friend with a smile.

"I'm sorry about this. We had good times together." Machinski put his hand on Hoffman's shoulder and added, "And your fluency in German?"

"It's rusty, sir, but I can still tell the Führer to jump in a lake ten different ways."

Machinski extended his hand, and Hoffman grabbed it. "Thank you, Dirk, for your friendship for all these years. God bless you."

"I won't let you down." They both saluted each other. Hoffman left with watery eyes.

Chapter 7

May 15–28, 1944
London, England

Following Machinski's approval and set up by Commander Bainbridge, Hoffman attended the first and only meeting of the Logistics Committee in a cold conference room and was duly indoctrinated about a false invasion site. He didn't know where the actual landing was to occur, but "Calais" and "Patton" were key words for him to impart.

Unknown to Hoffman, Lieutenant General George Patton was being used as a decoy heading up the fictional First US Army Group staged in South East England, directly across from Calais. The Nazis believed that Patton would lead the invasion, which meant Calais would be the point of attack, and any other assaults on the coast would be considered diversions. A few senior Wehrmacht officers believed that Normandy was the only other viable site, but Hitler disagreed. He believed without reservation that Calais was the target.

Prior to contacting a German double agent, MI6 decided to simulate torture and evaluate Hoffman's tolerance. The OSS, the Office of Strategic Services, forerunner of the CIA, meted out various Nazi techniques using truth serums like scopolamine, LSD, and other drugs in addition to beatings, sleep deprivation, and starvation. MI6 only administered small doses of drugs, and Hoffman showed stamina to resist and keep his equilibrium.

An OSS doctor told Hoffman, "We've found that truth serums are not one hundred percent effective."

"Any I should watch out for?"

"Some interrogators preferred sodium pentothal because it made people more talkative but not necessarily more honest. Scopolamine and LSD can penetrate one's free will leaving a person vulnerable to the interrogator, but hallucinations usually predominate."

"Will they affect me physically? Hurt my health?"

"The drugs may tire you out. Food will help to counterbalance. If the Nazis starve you, your heart could beat very fast, and you'd tire easily. Get as much sleep as you can."

"Will my mind suffer?"

"You won't be a robot and unwillingly obey their commands, but you may be disoriented." He paused. "To gain time, you can always ask the interrogator to repeat the question or say I don't know, but even better, you can lie or you can tell the truth. You are in control most of the time."

Hoffman said, "Anything else I should be aware of?"

"Your personal issues will likely pour out especially with scopolamine, but with each drug, you will keep your ability to think."

Hoffman asked, "What do you mean 'personal issues'?"

"Any unresolved problems with being beaten as a kid, esteem, or the Great War. They will surface, you will feel their intensity, but on a positive note, you may realize a breakthrough as you go deeper. Emotional baggage gets loosened easily. Just remember that your brain can keep you from releasing sensitive information that you don't want to release."

Hoffman thought about the comments as the doctor added, "The Gestapo has started to use mescaline. The tests we've run are not conclusive, but we have found mescaline's effects to be minimal. Until you are taken, make sure to take the vitamins I gave you, eat good meals, and don't drink any alcohol."

Others in OSS offered suggestions as how to best endure torture, and they hoped to lessen the hardship by educating Hoffman about the torturer's tactics and trickery. Knowledge of various strategies gave Hoffman confidence as opposed to the uncertainty of what will happen next. All of these hints could only go so far. His ability to withstand pain and the chemicals would be the ultimate test of his success.

After Hoffman completed the torture simulations, contact with the Germans took center stage. Bainbridge gave Hoffman his final instructions. "After the torture ends, the German Resistance will somehow contact you. I don't know the specifics about how they will do it, but we've worked with them for the past two years, and we think that they are reliable."

Hoffman said, "This is not very comforting."

"I recommend that you don't go, but since you insist, you need to be aware of one other warning."

"What's that?"

"We think that a spy or spies exist in the German Resistance."

"You're loaded with good news. How do you know?"

"We're not positive about anything. I'm alerting you to be careful. We think the Berlin group is clean but suspect that the Munich bunch may be corrupted. I wish I could be more helpful."

"Do you expect me to reach Switzerland?"

Bainbridge smiled. "Once the Berlin Resistance hooks up with you, your trip should go smoothly. They've escorted Allied pilots with their escape routes for three years. When you cross into Switzerland, your troubles are over. You'll probably sit out the war because neutral countries can't release any soldier, even Germans, to their own side."

"Can I escape and get back to London?"

"If the Swiss catch you, they will lock you up. Besides, escape through France or Italy is dangerous."

"So, what do I do when I arrive in Switzerland?"

"Go to the US Legation in Bern and ask for Allen Dulles or Winthrop Endicott. Allen heads up the OSS for Europe. He does a fantastic job, and Winthrop Endicott is Allen's right-hand man. They make quite a combination especially since both speak German. With their efforts, we Brits and Americans have made successful inroads into the Third Reich."

"But you said the Resistance has a mole somewhere?"

"When you get to Bern, maybe you can work with Dulles and Endicott and find him or her."

"Commander, I'm not in the intelligence area. I'm supply and logistics, remember? How can I identify a mole?"

"You'll have fresh eyes to ferret out the traitor."

Hoffman sat back and asked, "Since I'm putting myself into your trusty hands, how reliable are your double agents?"

Brainbridge grinned and said, "Our sister organization, MI5, handles intelligence on the home front and have seized many German spies when they arrived via parachute, submarine, and mostly as refugees from neutral countries. Upon capture, we ask if they want to be a double agent or not. Those that won't work for us are executed. Those that accept took the next step and transmit disinformation to their Nazi controllers. We monitor them closely and are pleased with their effectiveness."

At the end of May 1944, an MI5 handler briefed a German double agent about Colonel Hoffman. The spy radioed the information, and the German High Command bought it. Two days later, Abwehr, the German Intelligence Service, ordered his abduction.

Hoffman expected to be kidnapped on May 28 or 29, so he prepared by getting plenty of sleep. He thought often of Caroline and what he would say when he faced her. To admit his own parental deficiencies to his daughter was tougher than he realized. It brought up anger, weakness, and remorse. He prayed to survive the torture.

Chapter 8

May 26, 1944
London, England

Hoffman had too much idle time as he prepared for his kidnapping; his reflections about life and death spread throughout the evening. The plan to be kidnapped and the reunion with Caroline did not have the allure it did two weeks ago. The Nazis will break him, kill him, and he'll never reach Caroline. Jumping out of an airplane without a parachute offered more thrills, at least for a short moment, than throwing his life away with the Nazis.

When the fog lifted from his brain, sanity returned and he realized he couldn't leave Caroline to the Nazis and their wickedness. She had to be rescued. It was his duty to protect his daughter even if she hated him. Besides, he would die if he had to accept a demotion and reassignment to the United States.

And then there was Kaye, his long-suffering wife. She didn't sign up for the hardships of living with a basket case of a soldier. He had to make it up to her; he had to get their daughter back.

He loved Kaye's monthly letters. Her last one talked about the neighbors, about a beautiful new scarf she bought, and about the bandages she made at the Red Cross. He was disappointed that she didn't wish the war would end so she could hug him.

Hoffman sat down to write a letter to Kaye. He stared at the paper for half an hour unable to start. He thought of his experiences before the war and the good times. He visualized memories of Kaye and Caroline on hikes, then he and Kaye with friends at barbeques, and his baby girl in his arms at her birth. Afterward, he thought about his detachment every year after his return in 1918.

He couldn't find any words to admit his inadequacy as a husband and father. He started the letter five or six times in his messy scrawl. As his lungs tightened his hand shook, hoping words would flow onto the paper.

On the ninth attempt, he expressed his regrets.

Dear Kaye,

I continue to have nightmares. Now the dreams include you and Caroline. I see you in the front yard and run to you, but you're beyond my reach. The faster I run, the faster you stay away from me. But you don't run. You move effortlessly in a standing position as though you were a chess piece. I get frustrated. I yell at you to stay still. Then I wake, scared that I've lost you both.

I think back to Fort Knox. I should have bought Caroline the spring dress for her class dance. I should have taken you to the movies or a picnic. I missed out. I spent too much time at the base when I could have come home.

I can't say anything about my situation, but I have a new assignment that could delay the writing of my next letter. I'll send it off as soon as I can.

I wish I could see you in your beautiful new scarf. Love, Dirk

He wondered: Would Kaye know if I died? Would Kaye know that I tried to save Caroline? Would this letter be the last communication I would have with her?

Hoffman realized that because of the secret mission, Kaye would receive a telegram: missing in action. His mission and cause of death would be buried by the army for decades. Yet Kaye knew about his bravery, and the MIA telegram would inform her that he saw action, and so she would conclude that he died a soldier's death against a vicious enemy.

As he sealed the letter for tomorrow's mail, Hoffman was ready for the German kidnappers.

Chapter 9

May 28, 1944
Berlin, Germany

Brigadeführer or Major General Bruno Bachmann, head of Berlin security for the SS, returned to his office with a mischievous grin. SS General Hans Juttner, chief of operations, had given him a prize for which he had lobbied. He authorized Bachmann to oversee the interrogation of the American and extract the top-secret location for the Allies' invasion of Europe.

He had clawed his way up the SS hierarchical ladder by absolute loyalty to Hitler and by implementing his radical programs, so Bachmann was now poised to achieve the summit. If he succeeded in this mission, he would most likely become a member of Hitler's inner circle.

Bruno Bachmann grew up in Ulm, a small manufacturing town ninety miles west of Munich where his aloof father was a mechanic and his stoic mother took in laundry. Being the youngest of four children, the pint-sized Bachmann wore hand-me-downs and shoes that were usually too big, which caused him to struggle and walk in an awkward manner. While his schoolmates ridiculed him for his raggedy appearance, for shortness in height, and for his inferior performance in the class room, Bachmann swore to outdo his tormenters and take vengeance upon them.

In 1918, an unskilled Bachmann, discharged from the army, returned to his home and gravitated to local gangs since unemployment reached astronomical levels and hyperinflation damaged the economy. As a con artist and scammer, he fit right in as he learned the trades of robbery and extortion that led to a couple of short stints in the local jail.

His life changed in 1926 when he heard Adolf Hitler speak about Germany's plight caused by the French, British, Slavs, Marxists, and more importantly, the Jews. Hitler mesmerized him and other angry Germans who hated their country being stepped on. Bachmann joined the Nazis the next day to beat up Jews and to torch Jewish businesses.

The Nazis gave him a brown uniform and allowed him to wield his club with impunity. They did not ridicule him; in fact, they praised him for ardently obeying orders. He became the protégé of Heinrich Himmler who headed the SS or Schutzstaffel, Hitler's personal bodyguard. The more brutal Bachmann was, the more promotions he received. In 1938, Hitler made him a brigadier and head of Berlin security. In 1942, Bachmann was elevated to major general.

When he received approval to torture the American colonel, Bachmann raised his arms in glee and called his intelligence chief, Major Konrad Frolich. "Konrad, get me the files of the best Gestapo interrogators. Hitler blessed me with a crucial mission, and I won't fail him."

When Bachmann reviewed the files and selected his choice, he ordered his administrative assistant to set up an appointment. The lieutenant called Major Rolf Gebauer. "You are to meet with SS Major General Bruno Bachmann at ten o'clock tomorrow morning. Be prompt."

The next morning, Major Gebauer arrived early, collected his thoughts, and recalled that Bachmann had saved Himmler's life from an assassin years ago, which would account for the rapid advancement. Gebauer's stomach tightened as he thought about Bachmann's savage reputation. Gossip spread that he was the high priest of manipulation and violence, with an iron heart to go with his Iron Cross.

Gebauer brushed off his uniform, combed his hair with his fingers one more time, and proceeded to the reception area. "Major Gebauer to see Brigadeführer Bachmann."

"The general is expecting you."

With his black cap tucked under his left armpit and dressed in his black uniform with a red armband showing the black swastika, Gebauer knocked and entered the office, stood at attention, clicked his polished boots, and gave the Nazi arm salute. "Heil Hitler. Sir, Major Rolf Gebauer reporting." He felt hot under his collar being in front of a general who could ruin his career if he screwed up.

Major General Bachmann sat at a huge mahogany desk with files and reports strewn over it and never looked up. The air in the room was still. He raised his right arm slightly as a token acknowledgment to the salute and continued to read a memo. He motioned for the major to have a seat while he kept his eyes on his paperwork.

Gebauer looked around the lavishly appointed office with vintage paintings displayed in ponderous frames that seemed like they should belong in a museum, not an army office. Along with elegant chairs and rugs, he concluded that these items were liberated from Jewish merchants.

As he waited for the general to finish, Gebauer noticed Bachmann's black hair slicked down, the thickset but not muscular body, jowly cheeks, and ashen complexion. His tailored black-and-gray SS uniform was covered with medals, ribbons, and medallions.

Finally, Bachmann raised his head. "Do you know why you are here?"

"No, sir." Gebauer felt Bachmann's gray penetrating eyes that rarely blinked.

Bachmann looked around his desk for a missing folder and yelled toward the door. "Lieutenant, where is the Gebauer file I asked for this morning?"

The lieutenant, who sat outside the office, ran into the room and stood at attention. "Yes, sir." Then he went to the right corner of the desk. "Sorry, sir. I put it here." He gave the general the file with shaky hands. Bachmann took the file; the lieutenant saluted and left the room.

Bachmann opened the folder, read one section, looked up and said, "You are one of the best interrogators in the Gestapo, is that right?"

Without modesty Gebauer said, "That is correct, sir."

"Your file is impressive. You are an expert with chemicals although seven prisoners died from an overdose."

"It's how I learned where the limits are, sir. Their deaths didn't bother me."

"And you get results quickly with these chemicals?"

"Yes, sir. My nickname is the Chemist." Gebauer's rotund body, fleshy neck, receding chin, and soft effeminate fingers offered little to indicate he was an expert in anything.

Bachmann looked back at his papers but spoke with condescension. "I'm about to give you a crucial assignment and want results quickly, and the prisoner must not die."

"I can obtain any information you require without killing him."

"I hope you can. If not, you will go to the Eastern Front, understand?"

Losing his confident air, Gebauer said, "Er . . . yes . . . sir."

"Major, the High Command has ordered me to interrogate an American that the Abwehr will kidnap from London. This job has the highest priority. He knows the location of the landing site on the French coast. Your job is to get it within five days if not earlier, understood?"

"Expect it sooner, sir."

"This mission is vital to Germany."

"When do I start, sir?"

"Shortly. His name is Hoffman, a colonel in the US Army. Once you acquire the coastal location, call me. You are not to mention the site to anyone unless I authorize it."

"Yes, sir."

"The High Command has provided someone from the Wehrmacht as your assistant. This interrogation is to be kept confidential, and you will report to me every day about your progress."

"Assistants get in the way, sir. I can handle it without any help."

Bachmann bellowed, "That is an order, Major!"

"Yes, sir."

Bachmann resented having to place someone other than SS in the same room, but German senior officers insisted. The High Command did not trust the brutal Gestapo. The assistant would assure that the prisoner would remain alive, plus, unknown to Bachmann, senior officers would secretly receive a second opinion rather than rely on a fanatic member of the Gestapo.

After Gebauer left, Bachmann decided to celebrate and made a reservation at the Lavish Lodge, a bordello used by SS generals for their aberrant sexual fantasies. The brothel staffed its rooms with good-looking refugees gathered from slave labor workers in German industries and from concentration camps.

Bachmann sat back and envisioned his triumph as he announced the Allies' landing site on the coast of France. Hitler would bestow many accolades for his great accomplishment and might even present him with the Knight's Cross in front of generals and field marshals. How could he fail? The truth serums would provide the answer. The kids in Ulm would envy Bachmann's stature.

On the other hand, if Gebauer didn't extract the location by the fifth day, Bachmann would take his whip and club and flog the American to the bone and get the information the old-fashioned way.

Chapter 10

On May 31, 1944, at one in the morning, commandos snatched a sleeping Hoffman, his satchel, some clothes, and papers off his desk that included a map of Calais. They dispensed knock-out drugs to make him more docile during the trip east to the small English coastal town of Lydd. Normally the drive would take two hours, but due to the wartime blackout, visibility was minimal. The slotted covers on the headlights deflected the light downward on the road causing the van to travel slowly, so the trip took three and a half hours to reach Lydd. The commandos had reconnoitered the piers of small coastal towns and chose Lydd because the boats, while in desperate need of repair, appeared to be able to travel ten miles out into the channel.

The van drove through the main part of the town and headed east to the harbor that moored four medium-sized fishing boats plus thirteen small craft. The group had difficulty walking along the weathered planks on the dock that the fishermen left in disrepair due to limited availability of materials. The pier was empty at 5:00 a.m. and the commandos did not expect any problems in commandeering a boat. The fierce winds slowed the boarding, but after delays, the group left the mooring and one and a half hours later, reached the rendezvous point. They met a U-boat that interrupted its North Sea patrol to pick up the VIP passenger and take him to Rotterdam.

News about the prisoner's arrival in Rotterdam reached Major Gebauer in Berlin as he made his way to the designated building within a hospital complex outside of Germany's capital to set up the torture room. When Gebauer arrived, he entered the first floor and looked for the steps to the basement but stopped in the patient ward and spotted a comely nurse in the midst of wounded German soldiers. He was drawn to her blonde hair, genial face, appealing figure, and sad eyes. She wore a standard uniform of a blue-and-white striped blouse and a white apron plus a nurse's hat clipped to her hair in back with a small red cross emblem stitched on the front. He stopped and asked an attendant the name of this person.

"Freya Rudiger," came the reply.

Gebauer said, "She's quite attractive."

"She already has a boyfriend."

Gebauer nodded and then said, "Hmm. I must introduce myself to her one day." As he walked away, he thought, Yes, we will meet very soon.

He located the basement room where he would perform his trade with a Wehrmacht captain as his aide. The officer stood up, gave a heil Hitler salute. "Major Gebauer, I was selected to be your assistant. My name is Axel Lichterman." Gebauer's salute was less crisp. He disdained the Wehrmacht since most of them did not belong to the Nazi party and had their own military traditions.

He spoke in a condescending manner, "Have you interrogated prisoners before?"

"I started at the POW camps and recently came here to question wounded prisoners. I succeeded with most of my sessions." Captain Lichterman did not say that the Wehrmacht developed a different approach from the Gestapo's torture. Wehrmacht methods preferred to use relaxed settings and treated prisoners with courtesy and consideration. They would often drink coffee with them or take them to the camp's cinema. No appearance of coercion existed, which relaxed Allied prisoners, so they unwittingly revealed information which they thought innocuous, but when put together, yielded a wealth of intelligence to the Germans.

Gebauer asked, "Any experience with drugs?"

"No, sir."

"Then you can't really assist me. Just watch when I administer the drugs, be quiet, and let me follow my routine, is that clear?"

"Perfectly."

A train took the American prisoner on the last leg of the journey on June 1, 1944, arriving at Beelitz Sanatorium, a sixty-building hospital compound about fourteen miles southwest of Berlin. Hoffman was transported to Berlin because the best interrogators, the Gestapo, were located there. These ruffians excelled because they had total allegiance to the Third Reich and were sadists. After nearly thirty hours of transport, the effects of the drugs began to wear off. Hoffman spoke with faltering words, "Have we arrived? I'm tired and hungry."

At 9:00 a.m. Berlin time, Hoffman's guards, the commandos, drove to the southeast corner and reached an out-of-the-way three-story facility that housed severely wounded soldiers. The building's basement would serve Gebauer's purposes since the area had little traffic and could be walled off. At a side entrance, the two guards held Hoffman up by grabbing under his armpits. With a heavy German accent, in English they said, "Move, Colonel. More steps." Hoffman staggered through the side door but had trouble walking, so the two burly men carried him down one flight of dimly lit stairs into a wide, vacant hallway. The dank stone walls felt like a dungeon from centuries ago. At the end of the hall, in the shadows, the brutes stopped at an entry. One guard struggled to open the heavy wooden door. Inside the dark room, a small light bulb hung from its electrical cord provided illumination for Hoffman to make out a table, four wooden chairs in the middle of the room, and scattered debris by the back wall.

On the side wall, he saw another table with a large red candle holder with a candle burned down to the last inch. The wall in back of the table had a small indent that contained a plaster statue of Jesus crucified on a cross except one third of his left arm was gone. Jesus faced the far corner away from Hoffman as if he didn't want to see the pain that would be inflicted. Hoffman heard muffled noises from two silhouettes in the darkness. He smelled tobacco, must, and mold. His cloudy mind wondered if this room would be his tomb, the last place he would know.

When the commandos guided him to the center of the room, Hoffman felt dizzy, so they turned him around and held him at attention. Slowly a bespectacled Gestapo major passed through the shadows and stared at his prisoner. "Guten tag, Herr Colonel."

Then the major slugged him in the gut. He thought, I have until June sixth to get the information. This will be easy.

When news of the kidnapping reached MI6, Bainbridge radioed agents in Berlin to watch for the arrival of "Stork," Hoffman's code name, chosen because it signified new beginnings. The German Resistance had many informants placed in various locations, and MI6 expected that Hoffman's whereabouts would be broadcast back within days.

Bainbridge was a meticulous man, indefatigable, and reliable. He would monitor Hoffman's progress and provide updates as necessary to his MI6 superiors with copies to Winston Churchill and General Eisenhower. When an agent reported the next day that Hoffman was taken to the Beelitz Sanatorium, Bainbridge notified his network and proceeded to get as much data as possible about the complex and the surrounding area.

Chapter 11

June 1, 1944
Berlin, Germany

The sucker punch thrown by Major Gebauer caught Hoffman by surprise. The force from it was not overpowering, yet the effects from the knock-out drug weakened his balance. It threw him backward and he fell to the floor. Hoffman did not try to get up. He rested until the two commandos yanked him into a standing position. Hoffman smiled to himself as the episode showed him that this Gestapo officer could be taken in a fair fight by a sixth grader.

"My name is Major Rolf Gebauer. I'm your interrogator. I've never tortured a colonel before, so this will be fun." He hit him again in the stomach. Seeing him remain on his feet, hunched over, frustrated the major, so with some effort he pushed him down.

After the assistants hoisted Hoffman to an upright position, the major said, "You had your last meal, your last glass of water, and your last moment of freedom. You're mine for as long as I decide to keep you alive." Hoffman remained silent. MI6 agents said that he should expect constant threats from the Gestapo. Scare tactics are one of their ways to break their victims. With a scowl, Gebauer stood close to Hoffman's face. "Your life is nothing. I can shoot you any time I want." He reached into his jacket, produced a silencer from a side pocket, and screwed it on his pistol. "No one will know. Your death will be quiet."

Hoffman thought, *The major won't kill me, at least not right away. He needs me. He may beat me up but not in the face, throat, or head since I need to give him answers. And I won't reveal that I speak German. Maybe it will give me an advantage.*

Gebauer put the gun away and unleashed more blows to the body and a kick to the groin. From the floor Hoffman felt his blood vessels throb. "Why hit me? You haven't asked me any questions?"

"Shut up. I have drugs. You will tell me everything I want to know." Gebauer kicked the fallen American one more time. "Get him up." The two soldiers, who wore dark clothes without military insignias, propped the prisoner up.

"Stand there until I return." Gebauer saw the satchel and papers. He snatched them and left the room. Only the guards remained, but they sat down. The Gestapo inquisition tactic was to fix uncertainty into the prisoner's mind. It worked since Hoffman didn't know what time it was, if it was day or night, or how long it had been since he'd left London. His immediate thoughts dwelt less on danger and more on food and water.

After fifty minutes of wobbling back and forth, Hoffman's rubbery legs could take little more. He took tiny steps to keep his teetering body vertical but finally fell to one knee. This action prompted the assistants to kick him in the stomach and slug him in the jaw. As he tried to cover up, they showered him with their fists, and during the thrashing, Hoffman passed out.

When he awoke he was naked, his wrists and ankles were tied to a chair with a thick rope strung across his body while nearby the two brutes stared at him. Hoffman scanned the room to steady himself and focused on breathing and thinking about a steak dinner with a beer. The OSS told him to keep his thoughts about past experiences to maintain sanity. Despite the tasty thoughts, he couldn't ignore his injuries, thirst, hunger, and fatigue that caused his body to lean against the ropes with his head drooping forward.

The squeak when the door opened broke the silence. Hoffman knew who had returned; he didn't look up and tried to conserve strength. His body strained against the rope, and the ties around his ankles and wrists cut through the skin and left open sores.

He saw the polished black boots and the pressed black pants in front of the chair.

When he straightened his neck, his nemesis appeared with a greedy grin. Gebauer was a small man at five and a half feet, blond hair, pudgy, large ears, rimless glasses, and deep lines between the eyebrows. The flabby skin around his neck pushed over his stiff collar.

Does this jerk represent the master race? All he can do is bully especially if he uses a gun against his tied-up adversary. What a wimp. If I could have five minutes alone with him. Check that. Make it thirty seconds.

"Want to tell me something?"

"Like what?" Hoffman forced the words out in a whisper.

"Where are your forces landing in France?"

"You won't believe me."

"Try me."

"The fact is that I don't know. Only a select few know. Ask Eisenhower. Maybe he'll tell you."

That answer unleashed more hits from Gebauer, which caused the chair to fall down and Hoffman to knock his head on the cement floor. When he regained consciousness, the chair was restored to its normal position, and the thugs and Gebauer had departed. Colonel Hoffman blinked and peeked around and saw that Jesus was still there and a stranger in a gray uniform stood in the middle of the room.

The new foe was younger and dressed in the Wehrmacht uniform of a gray-green tunic and matching pants with dark green shoulder straps. Hoffman shivered and said, "Who are you?"

"I'm Captain Axel Lichterman. I'm not Gestapo. I'm army. In America, you'd call me the good guy to Major Gebauer's bad guy." Lichterman was taller, had dark hair, friendly eyes, lithe physique, and smiled — which seemed out of place.

"I'm not talking to any German whether one is good or bad."

"The Wehrmacht believes that politeness gets better results than torture. And if you don't want to talk, then don't talk. Gebauer disagrees with our civil method. He likes to inflict pain. There are advantages to talking to a good German."

"Like what?"

"You may need a favor."

Hoffman dropped his head. "I know your tactic. Our people in London told me."

"What did they say?"

"You try to pretend you can keep the Gestapo away as long as I give you information. But the Gestapo is here and clobbering me, so your tactic isn't working."

"The Gestapo is here, and I have little influence. I'm an assistant, but as you see, you have been granted time from his torture while Gebauer gets his drugs ready."

Hoffman said in a tired voice, "You speak English well. Where did you learn it?"

"I wanted to travel to England or America, so I studied it hard in school."

"Have you been there?"

"No, but one day I will."

"How long until the bad guy returns?"

"About one hour, so try to rest."

"I'm cold. Do you have a blanket? And what about the bathroom?"

"Do it on the chair, and I'll hose you off." He paused. "I'll find a cover."

"When does Mr. Personality get serious about the questioning?"

"When he prepares his drugs. He loves this part. I wish I could help you."

"But killing people is okay?"

"We are fighting a defensive war. Others attacked us."

"You don't really believe that, do you?"

Lichterman avoided a debate and went to another part of the room. Hoffman's eyes followed him and noticed the pronounced limp. He didn't know what to think about this captain. He definitely couldn't rely on him for anything, but at least the captain allowed him sleep.

Lichterman knew Hoffman didn't trust him. Why should he? The SS and the Gestapo were monsters, and Axel hated them, too. He had witnessed their brutality especially when he was assigned on the Eastern Front. He did not look forward to Gebauer's evil in the next session.

Chapter 12

June 2, 1944
Berlin, Germany

The noise in the hallway prompted Captain Lichterman to remove the blanket from his naked prisoner. He gave the American a quick drink of water and then rushed to a nearby chair. Hoffman sipped the liquid and slowly eased into equilibrium. He forgot where he was until his body rubbed against the rough cord across his chest. The footsteps in the hallway reminded him when he was in that corridor yesterday. Was it yesterday or the day before? The area he remembered was old and needed painting although at one time it must have been a grand structure. Still dazed and sore, Hoffman noticed that the room temperature was warmer but he was still cold.

When the major entered, Lichterman said in German, "He slept. Nothing else."

Gebauer looked at the captain and in a pompous tone said, "Of course the prisoner didn't do anything. I can see that. What kind of assistant are you?" Lichterman ignored the insult.

Gebauer read the papers from Hoffman's desk in his London apartment and noted the map of Calais. Gebauer was confident where this narcotic journey would lead him. He set up his chemistry set on the table. No words were spoken—business as usual at the office. He turned and confronted his prisoner.

"I have chemicals to give you and have all day to get the information." He smirked. "You will give me everything, of that I am sure."

He's toying with me. Thinks he's a big deal but he's scum.

Gebauer relished domination over another human being. In his youth, the roles were reversed when he was the victim of tough boys in his neighborhood who preyed on smaller kids. No longer would he have to endure the torment by students or the beatings by his stepfather because he was top dog and would inflict the pain. He flaunted it, grateful to Hitler for an opportunity to serve the fatherland. Membership in Hitler's Brownshirts changed Gebauer's life. Since the Führer allowed him to pummel Jews and Communists, his cruelty matured. His perverse temperament pleased his superiors who transferred him to the Gestapo.

He excelled as an interrogator against German civilians turned in by their fellow citizens. From that assignment, he graduated to Allied prisoners and developed skills to extract intelligence using chemistry. He learned about the effectiveness of each chemical and how far he could push the prisoners. His conceit, limited intellectual capacity, and absence of scruples so reviled by a civilized society turned out to be the exact attributes desired by the Gestapo. As a Gestapo, he could get anything he wanted like favors and girls. If people objected, he reported them or better yet interrogated them. His confidence rocketed because he had a gun.

Gebauer planned to probe Colonel Hoffman's subconscious and follow normal procedures, except in this case his superior decreed no overdoses and to get the information in five days. He decided to break the colonel in one day and impress Bachmann and other generals. German intelligence expected an Allied invasion in either June or July, but because of the current violent weather, a channel crossing was deemed too difficult for at least two or three weeks. The Germans did not have weather sensors west of Great Britain, for if they had, the instruments would have revealed a pocket of calm between the two storms headed for France in four days.

Hoffman watched Major Gebauer approach with his syringe of volatile serum.

God, help me. Let me survive.

Gebauer planned to start with sodium pentothal to loosen the brain and unearth hidden secrets. He injected the drug and enjoyed the moment of Hoffman's descent to the world of delusion, fantasy, depression, and apparitions. He squirmed in the chair and fought against the rope across his chest. He tried to prevent the drug from moving around his body but couldn't stop its progress.

Gebauer said, "That's right. Keep struggling. It forces the drug to get inside more quickly." Hoffman's eyes sent darts of hate, but he refrained from comment to avoid getting another dose.

After twenty minutes of fluid in his arteries, Hoffman's eyes blurred, and the pupils constricted to pinpoints. He rocked slowly from side to side, felt light-headed, and his heartbeat soared. Electricity raced through his entire body as he hyperventilated. He saw Gebauer sit close to him blocking his view. Hoffman had to move his upper half around to view the rest of the room, check in with Jesus, and observe Captain Lichterman.

"How are you feeling, Colonel Hoffman?"

The words reverberated inside Hoffman's head. The sound of the voice magnified through his overly sensitive ears.

Gebauer repeated the question. "How are you feeling, Colonel Hoffman?"

"Uh-huh," was all he could utter.

"Can you answer questions?"

"I think so."

"Who are you?"

Hoffman paused and thought about the question. He felt as though a piece of gauze had encircled his brain. "My name is Dirk Hoffman."

"Where were you born?"

The words came slowly. "West Bend, Wisconsin."

"Where are you?"

"With you and a captain."

"Do you know what city you are in?"

"London?"

"We are in Berlin, Germany."

When he said Berlin, Hoffman was shocked. "In Berlin? How did I get here?" His world became distorted. He had an apartment in London. What's to become of it? "Do I live here now?"

Gebauer laughed. "Yes, this is your new home. You work for us. The Americans don't want you anymore."

"Don't want me?" Hoffman became silent, looked down, and tears welled up in his eyes. He felt so alone. Abandoned by his government.

Gebauer knew that suggestions could influence the subconscious. He showed patience and asked elementary questions to get Hoffman to talk about his early years. The major discovered that after high school, Hoffman worked at factories, got married, had a beautiful daughter.

"When did you join the army?"

"I rode with Pershing in the Mexican Expedition."

"See any action?"

"Not much. I was a sergeant, but when the unit couldn't get supplies, I scrounged through the villages. Pershing was impressed and promoted me to lieutenant."

"Were you in the Great War?"

Hoffman heard the words come into his ears slowly, and when he was ready to speak, he spoke slowly. "I was a platoon leader in the infantry."

"See any action?"

The question was routine and should have yielded a simple reply. Instead old memories long repressed surfaced, and Hoffman started to cry. Gebauer was surprised at this reaction and continued on this line hoping to gain an advantage from the colonel's obvious vulnerability.

"What happened, Colonel?"

"I was part of the Lost Battalion. We were cut off from the Allied lines and surrounded by Germans in the Argonne Forest for six days. We lost so many men." Hoffman wept and through his heaving sobs added, "I lost my best friend, shot right next to me."

Captain Lichterman felt that Hoffman's emotional reaction showed a definite weakness and was surprised when Gebauer didn't recognize its magnitude.

Gebauer had no sympathy for wartime experiences by enemies of his country and let Hoffman cry without interruption. "What happened after the Argonne Forest?"

"I was wounded and went to a hospital, then they sent me home." With the change of topic, Hoffman composed himself.

Still patient, Gebauer asked, "Obviously you did your job well to become a colonel. What did you do in London?" Hoffman blinked, twirled his head to make sense of the situation. His mind scattered yet struggled to gain awareness of his predicament. He remembered that earlier questions were superficial, but this new question was different. He became more alert as the interrogation surged to more serious topics. From his MI6 simulations and coaching, he realized he could answer in any way he chose. He could lie, he could tell the truth, or he could pretend he didn't hear the question.

His body shook as he recalled the coaching. "What was the question?"

"What did you do in London?"

"I chaired a planning committee for Eisenhower, and part of my duties made sure that we had plenty of landing craft." Hoffman chose to answer this one with a half truth.

Gebauer smiled. He was close to the answer. "Tell me about your duties for the invasion of France."

"I supervised all aspects of the landing craft." Hoffman stopped and looked at the ceiling. Oh, oh. Here it comes. Be prepared.

After a few minutes of silence, Gebauer asked, "What about the landing craft?"

"I ordered them to be built and supervised the assembly in England. Thousands of them." MI6 allowed Hoffman to release the landing craft figures to the Nazis; they might frighten the

Germans with the large totals, but Hoffman decided to increase the boat totals on his own initiative. He would lie.

Gebauer in his excitement with these answers wrote down this important information. "What kind of landing craft?"

"We have LCTs, LCIs, and LCAs. Lots of them." Good answer. I can choose any answer I want.

"What do the initials stand for, Colonel?"

"You don't know? We use initials all the time. LCT for landing craft tank. They are four hundred feet long and can carry twenty tanks and two hundred soldiers. The US and Britain built four thousand." Hoffman doubled the amount of landing craft. The Allies only had two thousand.

"And LCI and LCA?"

"LCI, landing craft infantry. One hundred fifty feet long and can transport two hundred troops. We built three thousand. LCA, landing craft assault, used to carry thirty-six troops from larger landing craft to shore. We have eight thousand."

Hoffman in his ethereal fog decided not to make the totals too high. The Nazis might not believe him. Since MI6 permitted him to lie, he lied.

Gebauer couldn't write fast enough. "Anything else?"

"That's it. That's enough."

"Where will they be landing?" Gebauer waited for this crucial answer.

Hoffman's mind hoisted a red flag through the clouds. Pay attention to your answer. He waited as he considered his reply and then mumbled. "How should I know? Not in my area of responsibility. I'm tired."

The sodium pentothal was losing its bite as weariness began to set in. Hoffman dropped his head and became limp. Gebauer left the room to pass along the figures about the Allies' landing craft. Lichterman also called his supervisor, but his conclusions differed from Gebauer's. Lichterman did not deliver any figures about landing craft but instead told his boss, "Hoffman impresses me. He is tough and has high-level responsibilities for the Allies' invasion."

"Has he revealed anything about the date or landing site?"

"Nothing yet. It's too early."

"How's Gebauer doing?"

"As expected, he grinds away with his chemicals, but I think he misjudges Hoffman's intelligence. Gebauer is frustrated that the interrogation is longer than he expected, and Hoffman is holding firm and won't reveal his secret."

Chapter 13

June 3, 1944
Berlin, Germany

Major Konrad Frolich entered Major General Bachmann's office and saw him smiling—a rarity in the best of times. "Good news, sir?"

"Our prisoner is spewing out important facts. He chaired a high-level planning committee for Eisenhower. The colonel definitely knows where the Allies will land." Bachmann paused and looked at his head of intelligence. Major Frolich had worked for Bachmann for two years and provided reliable work and could keep a secret. "It occurred to me that your wife's maiden name is Hoffman, is that correct?"

"Yes, sir. Why do you ask?"

"Our prisoner is named Hoffman."

Frolich smiled. "Sir, as you know, there are loads of Hoffmans in Germany and in the United States. Besides, her father is in supply and not intelligence. The generals wouldn't release that sensitive information to someone in supply. What's his first name?"

"Richard. What's your father-in-law's first name?"

"Dirk. Besides, if her father was your prisoner, I'd love to spend a few minutes with him. He left plenty of scars on Caroline, and I'd love to do the same to him."

Frolich finished his business with Bachmann, saluted, departed, and wondered if Bachmann's prisoner was related to

Caroline's father. Konrad needed more details and stopped at the secretary's desk. "What's the name and rank of the prisoner?"

The secretary checked her correspondence files. "His formal name is Colonel Richard Hoffman."

Konrad left the office suite and walked down the hallway with eyes staring ahead but without focus. He remembered that Caroline's father's name is Richard though he went by the name Dirk. I wonder if the prisoner could be Caroline's dad. If he is, there's nothing I can do to help him.

After talking to headquarters, Gebauer returned with a big grin and a spring to his step and thought, Bachmann lapped up the data I collected from the American. He'll be ecstatic when I get the location.

The knowledge that he pleased Bachmann primed him for the next session with the next chemical.

In German, Gebauer spoke insolently to his assistant, "Is the prisoner ready? Did you get anything out of him?"

"No, sir. He kept silent."

"Just as I thought. The Wehrmacht are amateurs. You need direction from us. The Third Reich will win the war due to our brilliance and not your incompetence."

Lichterman gave a side glance to Hoffman, shrugged, and rolled his eyes upward.

When Gebauer finished loading the hypodermic with the volcanic drug, he looked at Hoffman and toyed with him again. "Colonel, you can give me the information now or endure the consequences."

"Never."

"I'm happy you declined my invitation. I will enjoy your destruction." Then Gebauer laughed, injected the drug, and watched the prisoner's body vibrate as the scopolamine reached the brain and stormed the gates of withheld secrets. He expected its potency would break Hoffman's resistance and allow the victim to disclose the French landing site.

While the molecules wended around Hoffman's brain, he recalled the simulation with the OSS weeks ago and how he struggled but survived. He expected another ordeal and prayed that he could keep himself together. The colonel didn't realize that Gebauer loaded the needle with twice the dosage he received from the OSS medical staff. They cared about his stamina and health. Gebauer planned for the colonel's body to exist for two or three more days.

After twenty minutes, the American felt a loud humming noise in his head, and his body seemed ready to elevate but the rope held him down. Dizziness replaced clarity, and his eyesight blurred more than it did under sodium pentothal. His torso felt like it undulated similar to a fun house distortion mirror. He vaguely remembered Major Gebauer being nearby but could not see him through the floating furniture in the room.

Words appeared to reverberate from beyond the cosmos, or that's what Major Gebauer's voice sounded like, but Hoffman had problems understanding because the words came to his ears rapidly. He needed a slower pronunciation.

"I can't hear you. Talk slow," said the colonel.

Gebauer slowed down. "Can . . . you . . . hear . . . me . . . now?"

Hoffman pondered the question for a long moment and said, "I think so."

"Who are you?" Gebauer spoke deliberately knowing the prisoner could barely process words.

Hoffman had trouble opening and closing his jaw. "I am an alien from Jupiter."

"What is your name?"

Hoffman turned his head from side to side and tried to answer. Finally, thoughts followed nerve passageways, and he could form phrases. "My name is Charles." This name came from memory cells in his brain that recalled watching The Thin Man movie years ago, and the hero was Nick Charles.

"So, Charles, where were you born?"

His haziness caused the world to spin faster as well as slow down. It impaired his concentration, which collided with a fog bank. He forgot the question. This banter went back and forth for forty minutes: Gebauer asked a question and Hoffman contemplated it and studied it. The major acted in a patient and precise manner knowing the convoluted replies would eventually pass the fuzziness stage.

When Hoffman's mental veil lifted and the stupor partially dissolved, the major asked, "Colonel Hoffman, I will list places where the Allies might land. Can you comment if the location is true or not?"

"I think so."

"Let's start with Bruges."

Hoffman asked in a monotone. "Where is Bruges?"

"In Belgium, on the coast."

"Yes, I remember Bruges. What about Bruges?" A groggy Hoffman pronounced words in an unhurried manner.

"Will the Allies land there?" Gebauer believed that Bruges was too distant and the coast too rocky for a landing, so he watched Hoffman press for the answer. His eyes, head, and body position twisted back and forth in the chair.

Hoffman heard the question. Who were the Allies? Ah, yes. America belonged to the Allies. His next hurdle: How should he respond? He remembered people in London saying he could lie, tell the truth, or pretend he didn't hear the question. He answered without further delay. "Yes, Bruges was the place."

Gebauer didn't flinch and calmly continued. "How about Dunkirk?"

Hoffman wondered how to reply and asked himself where exactly was Dunkirk? He repeated his previous answer. "Yes, Dunkirk was the place."

"How about Cherbourg?"

Hoffman knew Cherbourg's location. "Yes, Cherbourg was the place."

"Normandy?"

He was on a roll now. Just rely on yes, which seemed to satisfy the major. "Yes, Normandy was the place."

"Calais?" Gebauer purposefully put Calais in the last position since the port seemed the logical landing site.

Hoffman strained with Calais. Calais registered a neon sign inside his head. His brain told him to beware of how he responded. His head and body swiveled uncomfortably. "What was the question?"

"Calais. Is Calais the landing site?"

"Where is Calais?"

"On the coast of France."

A confused Hoffman realized that this question was important. "What's on the coast of France?"

"Calais."

"What about Calais?"

"Is Calais the landing site for the invasion of France?"

He needed to decide what to do with this question. His mental powers were taxed. What did the OSS suggest? Should he lie, speak truthfully, or ignore the question? Too many internal voices intervened, so he opted for his usual answer. "Yes, Calais is the place."

"Thank you, Colonel. You may relax for a few minutes." Gebauer noticed how much time the colonel took to answer the last question. His eye movement and rotation of the head suggested something important about the French port city. Clearly the colonel fought the question and knew something about Calais.

The afternoon session spilled into the evening and beyond. Gebauer was tired, so Hoffman must be totally exhausted, and fatigue would make him more vulnerable to additional drugs. Gebauer suspected Calais but needed confirmation. He would inject another drug to expand the colonel's mind. But first he needed to call in the day's results to Bachmann.

While Gebauer revealed his suspicion to Bachmann that Calais was the target, Captain Lichterman called his boss. "Gebauer thinks Calais is the landing site."

"Do agree with him?"

"Hoffman's body language reacted to Calais more than the other cities, so it's the obvious conclusion, but Hoffman's a tough character and I have doubts."

"What bothers you about him?"

"Hearing about his career and high position in London, plus talking with him leads me to believe that he might be lying. Gebauer underestimates him, and I think that is a big mistake."

"Could this be a deception?"

"I don't know. If it is, Hoffman is playing it exceedingly well especially under all the dope he's received. I'll continue to observe him and watch Gebauer, who may try to overdose him to get early results."

"If he does, he will go to the gallows for disobeying orders."

"He doesn't follow orders from the Wehrmacht, only the Gestapo and Hitler himself."

Chapter 14

Hoffman didn't move when his nemesis entered the dungeon and readied the chemistry set for the next injection. Gebauer knew that the amount of chemicals inside Hoffman's body exceeded normal tolerance levels, which meant that his energy was low but his brain would be more susceptible to suggestion. The urgency and importance of his mission dictated that Gebauer press his quarry to the human limits and unearth the location of the invasion. Time had slipped by, and he had two more days.

Lichterman believed that Hoffman neared the brink. "Sir, Colonel Hoffman's body doesn't react. Should I get him water and food?"

"Can't stand pain, can you?"

"And you thrive on it? Are you happy to tear down a human being?"

"You can't handle war. He has crucial information, and I will do anything to get it. German lives are at stake. The colonel can end it all and give me the location. It's up to him."

"But he can't talk coherently. He may lie to you and not know if he is lying, and we need the truth. You'll look bad if he gives you the wrong location. He also believes that you'll kill him after he tells you what you want."

Gebauer said, "I hope he thinks that."

"He needs to know that by giving us the truth, he'll live."

"I'm only interested in his secret."

"The High Command needs him alive to provide answers about other military matters. I have my orders too and won't be bullied by you."

Gebauer yelled, "My own orders instruct me to get the location, and that's what I'm doing."

"So how can he answer your questions if he's comatose?"

Gebauer bent down, squeezed Hoffman's cheeks between his forefinger and thumb, and peeked at his face. His color was turning whiter, and he was drooling. "All right. Give him food and water. Then I'll shoot him up with LSD."

After giving the prisoner buttered bread and water, Lichterman asked Gebauer, "Any adverse reactions by mixing LSD with scopolamine?"

"Maybe, but I don't care."

Hoffman heard the chatter between the Germans but had a difficult time to process it. A hefty amount of the scopolamine remained in Hoffman's body from the last session and kept him jazzed. Exhaustion pervaded his every fiber. He had enough awareness to hear that his next dose was LSD, and it spooked him. He had problems with LSD in London especially with weird hallucinations.

Because of his own tiredness, Gebauer's hands didn't coordinate well when loading the LSD into the syringe. He was hungry, and so decided to take a break. After the major departed, Lichterman, despite his own weariness, fed Hoffman beans and water.

"How are you holding up, Colonel?"

He labored against the rope and muttered, "How did I do?"

"Just tell him the location. Don't put yourself through this abuse."

Hoffman whispered, "Ah, Mr. Good Guy makes a plea? What's the rush? He will kill me as soon as I tell him. Besides I don't know the location, so there." Lichterman spoon fed Hoffman, who ate the beans in a labored manner.

Lichterman suspected that the colonel, in fact, did know the landing site. He admired his determination and expected him to crack under more chemicals, probably once he was jabbed with LSD.

As Hoffman regained a smattering of lucidity, Lichterman said, "Colonel, can I ask you a question?"

Hoffman nodded slowly.

"Do you speak German?"

In a soft tone, Hoffman said, "What prompted that question?"

"When Gebauer and I spoke in German during the last session, I noticed you listened to us, and you seemed to understand. I won't relay your answer to Major Gebauer."

To admit that he spoke German to the enemy did not frighten Hoffman. He thought he could test Lichterman and see if he could keep a secret. "I know a little German. My grandparents emigrated to America and taught us their language when we were kids."

"I thought so. Get some sleep."

Upon his return, Major Gebauer resumed his preparations while Hoffman's body remained limp and cold. After a double dose of LSD, Gebauer expected his prisoner to lose consciousness in four or five hours, which should be enough time to manipulate him.

When the drug raced through the circulatory system, Hoffman experienced a new reality. A euphoria from LSD emerged. He felt no pain, just love. No problems or worries. Hallucinations with friends and togetherness existed in vivid color. He saw halos around everyone's head.

After an hour, the highs retreated, and Hoffman's delusions went to the negative side as the LSD fomented paranoia with its anguish and oppression. He screamed in terror as he saw his daughter, Caroline, riding a broom, but instead of a black witch's outfit, she wore a white wedding gown and yelled at him, "Father, you don't love me. You ruined my life. I never want to see you, ever!"

"No, no, no. I love you. I have always loved you. You are my sweetheart. I'm so sorry."

These words transported his mind to a purgatory of hopelessness. No one loved him. He failed as a father, as a husband, as a soldier. He failed his country. He failed his God. He bawled and wailed. The deeper Hoffman went, he saw Caroline float closer to him and mouth words, but no sound came out.

Gebauer watched the performance and recognized the signs of the highs and the lows. He let the melancholy play through its despondent phases. His prisoner wept for a longer time than Gebauer expected. He noted that the colonel's main weakness was his daughter, and he would use her as leverage during more questions.

Soon Hoffman observed the vivid apparition of his daughter, which then faded and was replaced by the image of his best friend who was killed in the Great War. Sergeant Zachery's lips snarled, his eyebrows narrowed, and fire flashed out of his eyes and nostrils. Zach pointed his finger at Hoffman and chastised him for something that he could not hear. He interpreted that Zach blamed him for his death.

A wide-eyed Hoffman gasped for air and shook his head. It can't be? Zach can't be mad at me. After this scene, visions of other dead soldiers in the platoon covered in blood appeared on Hoffman's mental screen. They glided around the room and shouted at him. The dead men terrified him, and his depression and loneliness launched into a deeper self-loathing. "Stop it," Hoffman shouted, but the LSD would not permit any halfway measures and yanked him back to his misery. "I should have died in France." Hoffman looked at the far corner and sought Jesus. Help me, Jesus. He screamed, "Jesus, let me die! I want to die!"

Gebauer witnessed the emotional blowup but didn't exploit this outburst since death of soldiers didn't hold much value to him. Soldiers on the Allied side died all the time. So, what? Captain Lichterman noticed the depth of Hoffman's grief about his friends, but Gebauer knew that Caroline was Hoffman's Achilles' heel.

When Hoffman stopped yelling and despairing about surviving the war, Gebauer interrupted. "Colonel Hoffman. Come back. I can rescue you. I can save your daughter from being killed. I will bring your daughter to you here, and you both can go home."

Hoffman saw his body free-fall from the edge of a mountain cliff. He couldn't see the bottom but knew it would come into view shortly. When he heard the voice, he thought the ground called him and he answered, "Can you save my daughter?"

"Only if you answer one simple question. Then I'll release you, and you can go home and be with your daughter." Gebauer paused and focused on Hoffman's eyes, which darted in every direction. "Do you want to be free?"

"You can do that?"

"Of course. I'll untie you and you can leave. It's easy and fast."

Hoffman's disoriented mind swayed back and forth, not sure from where the voice came. "Am I in Kentucky?" He thought he was transported to Fort Knox.

"Yes, just a few miles from your home."

Hoffman's jaw dropped, his eyes glazed over, and he mumbled, "What do I have to do?"

"Tell me where the Allies will land."

Hoffman breathed more slowly and waited. He looked down at his arms, which were tied to the chair. He took another breath. He stared at Gebauer, who was a big blur. He knew vaguely that he was being interrogated, but what was he supposed to say? The chemicals couldn't obliterate all of his consciousness. The people in London said the longer one hangs on, the more credible the answer. But what is the answer this man wants? The nerve junctions proclaimed "Calais" and "Patton." These words surfaced again and again.

While his ability to reason slackened, Hoffman held on. He remembered the advice that he can lie, tell the truth, or delay. He would delay and said, "What was the question?"

In his visual field, Kaye hovered over him. He never appreciated all she did as a wife and mother. She grinned at him and said, "You can do it."

As he watched her body sail around the room, he smiled and noticed that she caressed him with her eyes. Finally, she melted into a bright yellow cloud that floated by the Jesus statue and dissipated. He said, "Thank you, Jesus."

Gebauer squeezed his hands and said, "Colonel. Are you here? Jesus can't help you. Only I can help you. What is the answer?"

As he lingered after his wife's presence, Hoffman asked, "Ask me again. I forgot the question."

Gebauer huffed and raised his voice, "Where will the Allies land?"

Hoffman recognized the question and resented that it was asked so often. "I don't know."

Gebauer's patience was exhausted. Out of frustration, he roared, "What's the matter with you? Answer the damn question!" Gebauer stood up and smacked Hoffman in the face, which caused his head to snap back. Gebauer went to find the mescaline.

Chapter 15

The slap caused blood to flow at the side of Hoffman's mouth. His exhausted muscles could barely move an eyelash. He couldn't move his arms and legs even though he tried. The rope held his torso up, and his neck couldn't lift his head. Then everything went black.

"What have you done?" asked Lichterman. "He lasted six hours with LSD. He needs water and food and rest.

"Shut up. Get out of my way."

"He passed out."

Gebauer bent over the limp body and poked it. No response. He tried shaking the colonel awake without success. "All right. Get him ready. This is the last session. I'll be back."

Captain Lichterman forced water and bread into Hoffman's mouth. "Come on, Colonel. Stay alive."

Gradually Hoffman revived. Disoriented from sleep deprivation, and from the drug onslaught, he mumbled, "Did I crack?"

"Not yet. One more session to go. He will give you mescaline next."

Hoffman spoke slowly. "And afterward he'll shoot me, right?"

"I don't think so. He'll keep you around for awhile in case headquarters has more questions."

"Let me sleep."

Despite the minimal calories from the small food portions, Hoffman was barely awake after a nap but regained a semblance of reason with a surplus of fuzziness in his brain and eyes. He perceived his own presence in the room, which felt like a crypt with its usual chill and rotting smells. *Where's Jesus? Don't leave me.* He scanned the room and saw Gebauer at his chemistry set and Lichterman standing behind the table.

Hoffman searched the far wall and found the mutilated statue of Jesus. Jesus remained silent with his own suffering and appeared disinterested in Hoffman. He realized that he had to rely on himself since Jesus was nailed to the cross.

The filled needle of mescaline sat on the table. MI6 did not impart any strategy about mescaline since they knew little about it. The Nazis were the first to experiment with it. Because it contained similar properties to LSD, they thought it would unlock the hidden nerve fibers and release the cache of deeply held secrets.

Gebauer grabbed the syringe and approached his prey. He believed that this chemical would be the coup de grace, the final blow, and his bosses would shower him with praise. He slid a chair over to the prisoner and sat directly in front of him.

Bleary over the past few days of activity, Hoffman viewed his enemy with hate. He recognized the holster carrying the major's handgun that was within arm's reach and eyed the pocket where the silencer rested. If his hands weren't tied, he could seize the gun and then bam. The thought dissolved. He needed to reveal "Calais" and "Patton."

Gebauer said, "This is the last session. You will tell me everything. I've planned a special treat for you: a new chemical." Because the major spoke English to him, Hoffman realized that Lichterman didn't disclose his fluency in German. With a devilish smirk, Gebauer injected the new chemical. His clumsiness made a rough entry into the skin, and Hoffman jerked back in pain. The Germans didn't know how long to wait for the mescaline venom to swirl inside the body, so they allowed thirty minutes.

After LSD, Hoffman found that mescaline offered a mild high that suspended reality. Somehow mixing mescaline with the residue of LSD seemed to neutralize each other because his brain became clearer despite the nausea, excess sweating, and shaking of his hands—all physical signs that told Gebauer the drug was functioning. Hoffman found even with shaking hands and feet he could plan his answers more effectively. Jesus was helping. Thank you, Jesus.

Gebauer said, "Where are you?"

Hoffman looked around the room as though dazed. "With you."

"What city?"

"I don't know. Where am I?"

This repartee continued for a time. Hoffman acted confused, which wasn't too hard, but Gebauer became cross.

"Where will the Allies land?"

"I told you. I don't know."

"We think they will attack at Calais. What do you think?" Gebauer tried a new tactic. Given all indications from Hoffman's past answers, the delays, the facial expressions, the map, and body language, Gebauer concluded Calais was the target, but he wanted an outright answer.

Hoffman realized that here was his opportunity. He couldn't give it away too easily. As a result, he didn't reply. He squirmed and turned his head from side to side and rolled his eyes as though in a trance.

"I want an answer."

"I'm thinking."

"Think faster."

"My brain won't function. I have cobwebs everywhere."

Gebauer's irritation grew. "I'm tired of babysitting you. I'll settle everything right now." He got up and went to his tool kit.

Lichterman braced for something sadistic. He knew Gebauer suspected that the landing area was Calais, but Gebauer's frustration with Hoffman's meant he might kill the colonel. The major pulled out a small vise and approached the naked prisoner. "Let's try this. To hell with chemicals. I want to see how you react to real pain."

Gebauer put Hoffman's right calf into the vise and turned the handle. The pressure shot an immediate stream of agony. He tried to outlast it but the pain was too intense.

"Okay I'll tell you! Stop it."

"Tell me the city and then I'll stop." Gebauer cranked it further.

"Ow, OW! Stop it!"

"The name?"

"I can't with all this pain."

"Tell me and then I'll stop."

Hoffman's body shook every way, but in the end, he sagged his head and screamed, "Calais. Now stop it."

But Gebauer cranked harder.

"I told you—Calais, Calais, Calais. Stop!"

Finally, Gebauer released the handle. "I didn't need the chemicals after all. You can't handle pain. Typical spoiled American."

Hoffman slumped and whispered, "You, Major, are an ass. We had an agreement. I told you, and you didn't stop." Hoffman tried to gather his composure as blood rushed to his lower leg. With a snarly smile, Gebauer said, "Colonel Hoffman. You gave me great pleasure. I will miss our sessions. And now I must pass along this valuable information."

Hoffman looked up with eyes of fire. "Major, you think you are so smart. Patton will kick your Nazi filth back to Germany. You won't stand a chance."

"Well spoken, Colonel. You and your threats are pathetic. The Germans will pummel Patton. He won't be able to land on the coast. We'll sink him in the English Channel and you won't see it. Good-bye, Herr Colonel."

Gebauer gained another insight from Hoffman. The mention of Patton confirmed his suspicions. Gebauer gave a parting slug that knocked Hoffman back, causing the chair to fall over again. The major smiled and departed to make a phone call.

Chapter 16

June 5–7, 1944
Berlin, Germany

Major Gebauer phoned Major General Bachmann. "Along with the chemicals, I used my old-fashioned method: the leg vise."

The general laughed. "Well done." He could imagine the suffering that the Colonel Hoffman felt. "Old reliable, right?"

"Sir, the landing site is definitely Calais."

The general said, "As we expected, but corroboration by an American army colonel carries weight."

Gebauer added, "And in a fit of anger, Hoffman warned me that Patton would clobber us."

"Your colonel made a gross error. Admitting Patton guarantees that the attack will come from the First Army Group. Since it is located in Dover, he can't go anywhere else but Calais. Good job, Major."

"Should I put Hoffman out of his misery, sir? He has enough chemicals in him that he probably won't last the week, but I can rush the process."

"No. Not now. He may be useful later. Come to headquarters and fill us in."

But Gebauer had another priority before his departure. He admired Freya's curves in her nurse's uniform and wanted an encounter. He went upstairs and searched the ward. When he found her at the far end of the room, he marched over and intentionally bumped into her. She turned and gasped in surprise at seeing a member of the Gestapo. He enjoyed the frightened look in her blue eyes, fascinated that she was afraid of him.

Freya said, "Oh, excuse me," and hurriedly made her rounds for the wounded soldiers. After the third patient, Gebauer moved closer and blocked her path.

"Hi, Freya."

"How do you know my name?"

"I would like to introduce myself to you over dinner sometime." He gave a lustful smile.

She put her hand to her open mouth. She wanted to distance herself from this awkward situation and from this vile man. "The hospital doesn't allow breaks for meals. We are quite busy, so if you'll allow me, I'll continue to help the soldiers."

"I can make the hospital grant you time for dinner with me."

"I have a boyfriend, Axel Lichterman."

"I'll take care of that, too." Another cocky grin.

Gebauer glanced at his watch and said, "I have an urgent schedule, but maybe we can dine next time." He thought this girl would make an excellent trophy. In the old days, her class of female would never associate with him.

He left the floor and dashed to Abwehr's headquarters where he regaled senior officers about his genius in wrenching intelligence from a reluctant American colonel. They especially enjoyed the torture and pain parts. He extracted the landing site one day earlier than ordered. Since the High Command made Hoffman a top priority, Gebauer thought that news of his masterstroke would reach loftier echelons, and maybe Hitler himself.

Bachmann called the High Command. "Calais is definitely the target, and Patton will lead it." Bachmann expected to be treated as a hero by the Nazi generals and field marshals. This was his moment of glory, and to celebrate, he would pay a visit to the Lavish Lodge. The message was relayed to Hitler and Himmler, and they reconfirmed the location to all divisions and reserves in and around Calais.

After Gebauer departed, Lichterman rushed to the lifeless body in the chair, cut the ropes, poured water on the lips, provided food, and attended to the mashed calf. After wrapping a blanket around him, Lichterman carried him to a nearby cot.

Hoffman stammered, "He can kill me now."

"Stay alive, Colonel."

Hoffman smiled. "I did it."

When Lichterman saw him hours later and asked him what he meant, Hoffman did not recall that he said anything.

The hospital was shorthanded, and doctors were exhausted and stressed-out. Lichterman had been up for three days and asked his girlfriend, Freya, to bandage the mangled calf and assist the prisoner back to health. She had finished a twelve-hour shift.

"But he's the enemy. We have few supplies and need them for our own soldiers."

"Freya, I'll elaborate later. Do what you can. He is an important person to the Third Reich."

Strain from the hectic working hours and endless demands from the ward's patients, Freya needed a break. She yearned to spend time, idle time, with Axel, have a cup of coffee — not the fake stuff that cafés offered. But where could she go? Berlin and major cities around it were bombed out. Germans had been on rations for eight years, and she couldn't go anywhere to relax and have coffee and a pastry, so she banished her tired thoughts and accepted Axel's request.

Captain Lichterman had his own phone call to make to his superior. "Gebauer finished his interrogation with chemicals and a painful vise. Hoffman finally disclosed the location: Calais. In fact, he yelled it over and over. Then he said, 'Patton would kick the Nazis back to Germany.'"

His commanding officer said, "What's bothering you? Seems to me, under his pain, admitting Calais makes sense."

"Sir, I'm not sure. Admitting Calais, after enduring the torture and chemical effects, seems logical. But when he mentioned Patton, I was surprised. He didn't have to release that information. Gebauer bought it since he lorded over Hoffman."

"Maybe the chemicals finally loosened his tongue. You're too analytical."

Lichterman said, "The Allies have only two places to land that can handle the deployment of so many soldiers and supplies: Calais and Normandy. I think Calais is a possibility, but my gut tells me it's Normandy and that Hoffman is trying to dupe us."

"That's quite a statement. Based on intelligence and reports to the High Command from other sources, credible sources, Hitler swears Calais is the location and convinced that Patton will lead the invasion."

"You asked my opinion. I know Normandy differs from the party line, especially since the SS and Gestapo favor Calais, but my instincts tell me not to believe everything Hoffman says. I know the Wehrmacht opinion carries little weight with Hitler who ridicules the army and its Prussian traditions." He paused. "I would ask Rommel what he would do if he were Eisenhower. Would Rommel prefer Normandy or Calais? I'd bet on Rommel's answer."

The next morning, June 6, 1944, with a full moon and favorable tides against howling winds, rough seas, and thick clouds, the Allies descended upon the beaches of Normandy. The German High Command never expected the assault during gale wind conditions, and accordingly, the Allies surprised the Third Reich with thousands of ships and landing craft with 160,000 troops and tons of supplies over the next few days. German corps commanders at Normandy needed more soldiers and tanks to defend their positions. They requested reinforcements without success because Hitler believed that the attack on Normandy was a diversion; he was certain the main target was Calais. As such, he kept two Panzer divisions and nine infantry divisions in reserve. Those precious days without the Panzers allowed the Allies to establish a beachhead while they pumped in huge quantities of men and supplies that enabled the Allied troops to break out.

On the afternoon of June 6, Captain Lichterman went to the torture room where an ashen Hoffman slept. Lichterman nudged the colonel awake. "The attack has come. Did you know about it?"

Shaking out the grogginess and blinking to gain focus, Hoffman said, "Where did they land?"

"Normandy." The captain looked at his prisoner. "You really didn't know, did you?"

"I told you I didn't know." He waited. "Are the Allies winning?"

"We haven't received any reports. Orders informed us to prepare for more casualties." Lichterman said.

"So, I take it that Gebauer will arrive here to kill me, right?"

"We are told that he is not allowed on the base. That's all I know." Lichterman departed.

Locked in his room and exhausted from his ordeal, Hoffman remained on his cot and thought, Mission accomplished. See, General. I didn't let you down. Ike, annihilate them, especially the Gestapo. Hoffman then peered at Jesus, winked, and fell asleep.

Previously, Major Gebauer had relished the afternoon and evening of June 5 as he briefed select committees of Gestapo and Nazis about his interrogation. At 9:00 the next morning, June 6, 1944, three hours after the Allies streamed across the beaches, news of the attack on Normandy burned the wires of the military radios throughout Europe and the world. On June 7, Gebauer was called before Bachmann. After Gebauer clicked his heels and sieg heiled, he remained at attention waiting to hear the order of "at ease" that didn't come. Instead the general erupted.

"You idiot. You were duped, fooled, played for a sucker. Normandy is the landing site. Nothing has occurred at Calais."

"Normandy is a diversion."

The general pounded on his desk. "Thousands of landing craft are employed at Normandy. The Allies don't have any left. But still Hitler holds back divisions, and no one can change his mind." Bachmann glared at Gebauer. "I'm sending you to the front so you can fight this diversionary force."

After his humiliation, Gebauer's anger soared as he left the building. One thought rattled around in his thick skull: sometime in the near future, Colonel Hoffman will die. Gebauer would guarantee it personally.

Chapter 17

June 7–20, 1944
Berlin, Germany

While Hoffman remained in a semiconscious state, Freya cared for him between her daily rounds. She rinsed him with a towel and fed him. He slept most of her shift while the chemicals exited his system.

After three days, Hoffman opened his eyes. He looked at the room's high ceiling and blinked a few times until the blur ended. He felt someone running a damp towel over his chest, arms, and neck, followed by a towel to dry him off. He saw a young nurse with blonde hair. When their eyes met, she did not smile but continued with her duties in a perfunctory manner. Through the haze, he said to the young woman in German, "Who are you?"

"I'm your nurse. Axel ordered me to take care of you." She uttered staccato replies, offered no elaboration.

"Thank you for helping me. What's your name?"

"Freya Rudiger."

"How old are you?"

"Twenty-six."

"You are almost the same age as my daughter." He then turned over and returned to slumber. Over the course of the next two days, Hoffman gained strength and lost most of the effects from the drugs. Lichterman visited twice per day and they chatted. Hoffman could stand, go to the bathroom, converse, and tried to ignore the pain in his injured calf. Even though

Lichterman assured him that Gebauer and the Gestapo were gone, Hoffman didn't believe him. Hoffman came to alert when anyone walked outside his room and cowered when loud noises reverberated.

The nights provided little rest. The residue from the mind-bending chemicals stifled his awareness. Depression emerged on a regular basis, and memories of his near death in the Great War reappeared. He woke up gasping for air, drenched in sweat. When Freya entered the room to towel his face and upper body, her frown gave him little relief.

"Is something the matter?"

She didn't reply but thought, Just get this task completed and rush out of the room.

Hoffman inquired again. "It's all right to answer. Have I done something wrong?"

As she continued to clean, she said in a monotone, "My patients hurt because you Americans bomb and shoot them."

Hoffman countered with his own fury. "Have you asked the Poles, French, British, and Soviets how they feel about Germans bombing and shooting them?"

Frightened at his outburst, Freya stopped her task and sat back. "My fiancé was killed two years ago in the Soviet Union, and my parents died from bombs at Dusseldorf. I have every reason to hate our enemies."

"I lost my buddy and many friends in the last war. I can hate, too." They stared at each other during a long silence. Hoffman said, "You don't have to look after me. Just leave." He turned away. Freya started to stand but instead sat down. "I promised Axel I would care for you."

Hoffman felt badly that he blamed her for being German. "I'm sorry you lost your fiancé and parents. You must be very sad."

She waited for one minute to compose herself. "I am frightened. When the Allies invade Germany, they will destroy our country, won't they?"

"I believe so unless you surrender first."

"I want the killing to end." She got up and left.

He watched her walk out. Hoffman was surprised that he felt a sadness, too. His sadness had always existed in his head and expressed itself as anger, but now he saw that he ached for his buddies as Freya ached for her sweetheart and her parents. War was painful and senseless on both sides.

That night, Hoffman realized that he experienced the same difficulty with Caroline as he did with Freya—he couldn't speak about what was in his heart. At 4:30 a.m. he awoke and couldn't fall back to sleep. His body relaxed, and his shoulders felt relieved of the heavy emotional burdens. His nightmares didn't provoke fears and panic as they normally did. He liked this new sensation. Commander Bainbridge at MI6 was correct when he said that emotional release could come from the truth drugs.

When Freya showed up the following morning, her cold manner remained as she changed the bandage. He felt healthier except for his leg. To overcome the bad start with Freya yesterday, Hoffman spoke with more sensitivity and a softer tone. "How do you deal with this misery all around you? So many soldiers? So much death?"

No one had asked her this question before, so she decided to be candid since she'd never see him again. "I stop feeling. My heart aches for those about to die, but I can do nothing." She paused to control herself. "The terminal patients make the most demands, but my workload prevents me from spending time with them." She looked down. "I never thought I'd see such suffering."

Hoffman recalled that Caroline possessed the same dedication to her craft. Freya showed a strong sense of responsibility to her duties that accounted for her high stress level, and he wanted to help her as repayment for taking care of him. "I've seen plenty of death. Let me help you with those men."

Despite the protests, Lichterman approved Hoffman's new task and overruled two other nurses including Helga Pohl, the nurse supervisor. Hoffman wore his civilian clothes taken from his London apartment that lay crumpled in his dungeon. This civilian attire enabled him to blend in. He washed bedridden

German soldiers, brought food, applied compresses, washed clothes, and swept floors, all the while limping on a sore right leg. The patients knew he was an American who spoke German, but no one objected.

They asked him, "Why do you help?"

"We are soldiers. You need aid, and I can assist. In the last war, Germans allowed truces for us to pick up our wounded and dead."

The staff watched the results of Hoffman's efforts and appreciated his hard work. On occasion when an amputee yelled or a soldier with head injuries started to take off his bandages, Hoffman contained the problem. Lichterman did not mention that Hoffman was a colonel; the staff assumed he was a sergeant. The patients called him "Yank" or "Herr Hoffman."

Most of the wounded were young because the reserves of fighting men in their twenties and thirties had dwindled. The High Command filled the depleted ranks with adolescents and men over fifty. A sixteen-year-old private who had lost his right leg yelled out in English, "Hey, Yank. Can I practice my English?"

So he and three others nearby spoke in English, which they had studied in school. The words were heavily accented and the usage was not always correct, but the lessons reduced the tensions and the melancholy. Hoffman said, "Where can I practice my German?" Everyone laughed.

Freya envied Hoffman's easy manner with the tough cases. He often remarked, "You men will adjust to a new life. Heck, I'll be in heaven for years before you decide to join me." She wondered if his comment had a subtle meaning known only to him. Only Helga resented his presence and gave him disapproving looks.

During meetings about the patients' progress, Freya sat near Hoffman to hear stories the wounded shared with him. The men never talked that way to her, but she appreciated how they opened up to Hoffman. She relaxed in his presence and spoke to him more candidly but kept her reserved manner since he was, after all, the enemy. The more they chatted, Hoffman found that he enjoyed hearing Freya talk.

"Axel is jealous that you spend more time with me than he does." Hoffman shrugged his shoulders and grinned.

Nine days later, Lichterman took Hoffman aside and said, "Your help is appreciated, so take this key to your room. You are no longer our prisoner."

Hoffman couldn't believe it. "Why? You'll get in trouble."

Lichterman ignored his question said, "Your presence is risky. Guards may come for you, and this may help you to evade them."

Hoffman asked, "This key means that I can walk away from the hospital one night with hope to reach the American lines, and then you'll be in trouble."

"You will stand a better chance here. Germany fights on both fronts and may overlook a wounded prisoner in a hospital."

Bachmann braced at attention as the gusts of verbal abuse surged his way from his boss, Heinrich Himmler. "You upset our Führer and the Third Reich with your failure to obtain the landing site. A private could have extracted the information." He pronounced the next words slowly so they would sink in, "We relied on you." Himmler walked around his desk and said, "I should take back your Iron Cross. If we lose the war, it will be your fault."

Bachmann could only remain at attention, take the insults, and suffer the shame that he let down his mentor. After the fifteen-minute tirade, Himmler said, "Dismissed."

People in the hallways who passed the major general saw a furious and humiliated soldier with his face twisted, his fists clenched, and his jaw rigid. As he returned to his office, Bachmann kicked the wastebasket to the far side of the room and pushed papers to the floor. He paced rapidly back and forth and looked for a scapegoat to blame.

It had to be a conspiracy. Someone set him up. Gebauer said Hoffman's first name was Dirk, yet the agent in London said the man's name was Richard Hoffman. MI6 must have planned the ruse along with the German Resistance. He wondered if he had a spy in his department. Did his intelligence chief, Major Konrad Frolich, play any part in it? Maybe Colonel Hoffman was related to Konrad's American wife. Bachmann went to his lieutenant and yelled, "Get Frolich in here!"

When Konrad rushed to the office, Bachmann shouted, "The man kidnapped from London was, in fact, Colonel Dirk Hoffman and not Richard Hoffman. Is he your father-in-law or a relative of Caroline's?"

Konrad took a breath, regrouped, and asked, "Dirk Hoffman was the kidnapped prisoner? He's in supply and not high enough to know anything about the landing." Konrad composed himself and said, "Sir, he and I have never met."

Bachmann stared at his subordinate, calmed down, and said, "You had no way of knowing anything about his kidnapping. Our intelligence men in Abwehr selected Hoffman because their spy in London recommended him, so, their man must be a double agent. We've been duped by MI6."

Konrad said, "Do you want me to go through my intelligence sources?"

"No, I'll check with Abwehr. Besides, Hoffman might even be dead since Gebauer thought he couldn't last one week with all the drugs in him." He grabbed Konrad's arm and added, "Don't say anything to Caroline."

"Sir, Caroline hasn't spoken to her dad since 1938. Germany is her home now."

"Don't be too sure about that. She's an American. I've ordered surveillance on her."

"Sir, if she's a spy, then shoot her."

"I thought you would feel that way. Keep it a secret for now. I will have my own troops bring Hoffman to me, and will give you five minutes with him." Bachmann released a greedy smile.

"Thank you, sir. After I'm through, Gebauer would look like a saint to him."

"When you're done, I plan to inflict more pain than he could imagine."

Chapter 18

Gebauer despised his new assignment outside of Berlin. He loathed taking the blame for naming Calais as the landing site when other sources had also identified Calais. Besides, having an assistant during his sessions, imposed by the High Command, limited his effectiveness, and to his further embarrassment he had failed in front of him, a Wehrmacht officer. The final insult: Gebauer's stature as a superior interrogator was trashed. Now he hated both Lichterman and Hoffman.

Gebauer planned a slow death for Hoffman and as for Lichterman, Gebauer would conspire with the devil to consummate a wicked revenge: he would ravage his girlfriend, Freya. And the best part? Lichterman could do nothing. He couldn't risk an encounter with the Gestapo without harm coming his way for the irrefutable rule was known throughout Germany that no one messed with the Gestapo, especially the Wehrmacht.

Lichterman and Hoffman completed their patient rounds, ate a late lunch together, and went on a brisk walk before resuming their duties.

Hoffman said, "So when do I get executed?"

"The Wehrmacht will need you for additional questions or for a prisoner exchange. Since the Allies have streamed into France, the High Command has concentrated on greater issues than worry about a single American prisoner."

"Axel, I disagree. As I see it, the Nazis are furious that I tricked them. I won't be sent to a POW camp because Major Gebauer will kill me. I humiliated him."

"If he comes, our staff will warn you. They hate him too, and not because he belongs to the Gestapo."

"Seems to me, belonging to the Gestapo is enough," said Hoffman.

"Major Gebauer has forced himself on unsuspecting women in the hospital. They can't complain or else the Gestapo will put them in prison. The women don't discuss rape with supervisors; they only talk about it among themselves. Freya told me about this problem, so I organized the nurses never to be alone, and if Major Gebauer comes, they know to get me. Other nurses and orderlies will come, too."

"That son of a bitch. Someone should rip his balls off."

Lichterman said, "If he ever came close to Freya, that someone would be me."

Hoffman's face flushed in rage. "Taking advantage of innocent girls. The master race is nothing but horny bullies."

Few Germans had cars since gasoline was rationed, but vehicles for wounded soldiers existed so Gebauer found a truck that took him to the hospital. First on his agenda was Hoffman. Gebauer arrived at the rear entrance unnoticed, followed the corridor to the basement, drew his pistol, and pushed open the heavy door. Upon a quick glance, he found the room empty. Gebauer went upstairs to find out what happened to the the colonel.

He slipped into the ward where Lichterman worked and surveyed the area. No men or guards were present. As he searched the room, his eyes landed on Freya as she tended to the needs of the wounded. Gebauer smiled and advanced toward her.

"We need to talk."

Jolted by his presence, Freya pulled back. She looked around for Axel or doctors or Helga. In a high-pitched voice, she said, "Major, I have to care for the men."

He ignored the excuse and clutched her left upper arm, then guided her to the nurses' office. The patients saw her but could not help. After Gebauer forced her into the small room with four desks crammed together, he saw Helga by a file cabinet, who looked up in surprise. "Leave. I have an important matter with Freya." Freya, in a slight movement, shook her head, but Helga assessed the situation correctly. She had no choice but to withdraw. After she hurried out, Gebauer slammed the door. Helga found other nurses and alerted them to get Captain Lichterman.

Once inside, Gebauer locked the door while he kept his lecherous gaze on Freya. He said, "Don't look so frightened. I want to talk and know all about you. You have captivated me ever since I met you."

Freya stepped backward with her back against the wall and arms crossed in front. She looked down and didn't say anything.

"I know you are shy, which is part of your appeal."

"Major, I am dating Captain Lichterman. Do you want me to introduce you to another nurse?"

"Freya, he's only a captain. I am a major. I can make your life easier and give you more food and luxuries."

Freya kept her eyes down and said, "That is very nice of you, but I like Captain Lichterman very much." Her shoulders shook.

"But I'm Gestapo. He is Wehrmacht. And he has a bad leg. I am virile and can satisfy you."

"You shouldn't talk like that. We are fighting a war and belong on the same side. Axel got shot in defense of Germany. He's a hero and patriot."

Gebauer shifted forward and boxed her in the rear of the room. He stood inches away, touched her blonde hair, and caressed her cheek.

"Don't do that."

"You excite me."

"No, stop it. I have duties to attend."

"You can take care of me. I am a soldier, too." He held the apron strap and slipped it off her shoulder.

"Herr Major. Please."

"Don't upset me." He encircled his arms around her waist and pressed his lips onto hers. Freya knew if she resisted, he could imprison her, and she would be raped multiple times in jail. Her best option was to let him take her. Self-preservation kept her passive, but she wanted to scream for help. The major placed his right hand on her breast. She gagged in revulsion. When his hand probed downward, she pushed it away and turned her head to avoid further kissing.

"This is wrong. I go to church and am a good Christian."

"I don't care." He shoved her on the desk and hiked up her dress.

"No. No. No. You repulse me."

These words infuriated Gebauer. With a reddened face and enlarged eyes, he hit her hard on the left cheek. She screamed and fell backward off the desk onto the floor.

"So, I repulse you. If you don't go along, I'll kill your precious captain."

Chapter 19

Helga couldn't find Captain Lichterman. As she looked through the window, she saw Hoffman outside. While she disapproved of the American assisting with the wounded German soldiers, she loved Freya like a daughter and Hoffman could find Captain Lichterman. She ran as fast as her fifty-year-old legs would carry her.

As she caught her breath, Helga said, "Herr Hoffman. Where is Captain Lichterman?"

"Why?"

"He has Freya in the nurse's office."

"Who has?"

"Major Gebauer. He forced Freya inside. I have to find Captain Lichterman."

Hoffman heard enough. He dashed toward Freya's ward and ignored the pain in his right calf. Helga followed as best as she could. He crashed through the hospital double doors and took the stairs to the second floor where he darted around the beds on the main ward. A few of the patients saw him and pointed to the nurse's office at the far end of the vast room.

At the office, Hoffman kicked the door open and saw Freya pinned down while Gebauer pulled her clothes off.

Hoffman's face and eyes burned. "You ass. Release her."

Gebauer let go of Freya, who wrapped her torn clothes around her nearly naked body and cowered behind the desk as he turned and faced the irate American.

Gathering his wits, Gebauer pulled out his pistol and inched along the side of the room toward Hoffman. "How dare you yell at me. Why aren't you in your cell?"

At that moment Captain Lichterman, alerted by another nurse, burst through the door. He spotted Freya and then the gun. "You swine."

Gebauer shouted, "Close the door!" He pointed the gun at Hoffman but focused on Lichterman.

Lichterman turned to Freya. "Are you all right?"

"He said he'd kill you if I didn't cooperate."

"Why don't you leave the room, Freya." Lichterman gestured toward the door.

"Don't move. Captain, you do not interrupt me or order me to do anything. I am a major, and you are an inferior."

"Real men do not rape. And I don't care what rank you are. You are out of line."

"So, what will you do about it? Report me?" Gebauer glanced at Hoffman. "You let the prisoner loose. I'll court-martial you. You will be shot for dereliction of duty."

Helga reached the door, her lungs on stress. She heard loud noises behind it but thought better of barging in.

Hoffman drifted toward the major, and his muscles tensed as he anticipated the next move. With the American close by, Gebauer said to Lichterman, "Why don't you take the prisoner to the cell where he belongs."

"I will take Freya first."

"She stays here with me. Carry out my order."

Lichterman did not move.

"Don't provoke me, Captain. I'm not afraid to use this gun."

With his eyes, Hoffman motioned for Freya to move away from Gebauer. When her movement made a slight noise, Gebauer twisted his head to see what she did. That was all the time Hoffman needed. He leaped at the major and thrust his right fist on Gebauer's hand that held the gun. The suddenness of the blow caused him to drop the weapon. With the gun on the floor, Hoffman elbowed Gebauer in the head, and he fell to the floor with blood dripping from his nose. Hoffman snatched the loose pistol and stood over Gebauer. "You piece of garbage."

He put the pistol into his pocket and pummeled the major. Gebauer tried to cover himself with his arms as they encircled his head. After Hoffman pulled back, he kicked Gebauer three times. With the gun drawn from his pocket, Hoffman thundered, "Go ahead, try something."

From the floor Gebauer unwound his arms, looked at Lichterman, and ordered, "Captain, just don't stand there. Attack your prisoner." While Lichterman remained motionless, Gebauer trembled.

Hoffman reached into the major's coat and clutched the silencer that Gebauer had flaunted at him during the interrogation. The colonel twisted the silencer on the gun and aimed it at the major's head.

"Don't shoot. I'll give you money, food, anything."

"You don't have anything I want."

Gebauer begged Lichterman, "Captain, disarm him. He is an escaped prisoner."

Lichterman countered. "You tried to rape a German girl, my girl."

"She encouraged me." He breathed rapidly, his eyes flashed between Hoffman and Lichterman, and he crept backward and hid behind a desk chair. In the silence, he pleaded, "She knew I could get her more food."

Freya shook her head.

Lichterman shook his head in disgust. "You can't even lie well. You're an idiot, a disgrace to Germany."

Freya moved away from the desk and pushed herself against the wall far from Gebauer as her hands clung to her torn nurse's dress.

As Gebauer sat on the floor, he regained his composure and made a last-ditch effort. "Captain, you are a traitor. You will be shot unless you capture the American."

Hoffman said, "Major, it is time for you to apologize to Freya."

"It's her job to take care of soldiers."

"You said to me that you would shoot me, remember that threat?"

"I wish I shot you then but was ordered to keep you alive."

"I'm giving you a second chance to apologize."

"She's a whore and doesn't deserve an apology." Freya arched her eyebrows as she heard the slander.

Hoffman fired the gun, and everyone heard the phftt from the silencer. Gebauer grabbed his right knee and doubled up in pain. Freya gasped in surprise, and Lichterman smiled. Helga heard the shriek but remained outside the office.

"You have another knee. Want to apologize?"

Gebauer continued to hold his shattered joint. "All right. All right." He waited, staring at Freya with hostility. "I'm sorry." The tone was insincere.

"Major, you can apologize better than that." Hoffman pointed the gun at the left knee. "Or do you think I'm bluffing?"

Major Gebauer uttered with a clenched jaw, "You're a pig and a Jew lover."

Hoffman said, "I take that last comment as a compliment."

Gebauer modified his voice, but the undercurrent remained the same. "I apologize."

Hoffman turned to Freya and Axel. "Your lives are in danger with him alive. He'll go after you with a vengeance." They looked at each other and agreed. Hoffman then went over to Gebauer, aimed the pistol at his heart, pulled the trigger, and casually walked away. "So, how do we get rid of the body?"

Freya and Axel went to each other and hugged. She stared at the deceased Gestapo officer. She had seen death often in the hospital, but nothing as terrifying as a murder.

Lichterman shifted his eyes from the lifeless form to Hoffman. "Dead bodies are no problem. I take them to the hospital morgue all the time, but we need to remove his uniform and give him a new name."

They suspected that Helga waited outside, and Hoffman asked her to join them. To all three, he said, "Don't mention what happened here even to close friends."

The three Germans tensed at Hoffman's words and looked at each other. "He came in secret to kill me and rape Freya, and if anyone asks about him, you have no idea, you haven't seen him for weeks, got it?" They nodded. "If you say anything, the Gestapo will kill you."

Chapter 20

No inquiries about the whereabouts of Major Gebauer came to the hospital during the afternoon or the next day. With carnage multiplying on the Eastern and Western Fronts the Allies continued to shell Berlin, and no one probed into the absent Gestapo major. Authorities judged that the bombing raids had killed him. Tensions at the hospital ward eased, but Helga, Freya, and Axel worried that Nazi inspectors could arrive at any moment. Every once in a while, Freya would burst out crying, haunted by the attempted rape. Axel would come over and hug her. "It's over. He won't bother you anymore." She couldn't shake the horror, and Axel knew his words offered little relief, so he turned to Helga. "Can you help Freya?"

Helga, also in shock, said, "Oh, my dear. Poor Freya. Come with me."

Helga Pohl, in her early fifties, carried a hefty build with a cherubic face. She assumed the role of hospital matriarch as part of her duties to the nurses and the fatherland. She ran a tight ship and filled out forms efficiently. Her mind was in a quandary: Should she overlook an American—the enemy—killing a German, yet by doing so, save her favorite nurse? Having an American in a German hospital added undue pressure to daily activity, and he should leave their premises, but her priority was Freya. She would keep silent.

The next day, during a noontime walk, Lichterman said to the colonel, "It looks like you're not going to be shot. Gebauer is dead, and no one appears to pursue you, so you can spend the rest of the war here. When it's over, you will be liberated and can go home."

"Liberated. What a thought. I expected to be killed, but now?" Hoffman didn't mention his goal of saving his daughter. His original objective had not wandered from his focus: get Caroline. Did the German Resistance know he was at the hospital? When would they snatch him and transport him to his daughter's house with an escape plan to Switzerland? He had memorized a Berlin phone number and wondered if this was the time to call.

When they returned to the hospital wing, Lichterman saw Freya standing in the middle of the ward, her eyebrows raised and her lips pursed. Something was wrong.

He could feel it and hurried to her. "What's the matter?"

Then the door to the nurse's office opened, and three SS troops stepped out. One ordered, "Herr Hoffman, come with us." Hoffman looked at Helga, who adjusted her mouth into a slight smile. One SS guard searched him and took his pistol, which included the silencer that he purloined from Gebauer.

Lichterman said, "Where are you taking him? He works here." He turned to Hoffman. "I don't know how this happened. There's so much to say."

Another SS trooper said, "He's the enemy, and for your own safety, keep that in mind."

Hoffman stood still and accepted his fate. He didn't want to get his friend in trouble. He could see the distress on Axel's face. Hoffman smiled and said in a calm manner, "See you after the war."

Two SS guards grabbed his arms and forcibly led him out of the building. As Hoffman walked toward the exit, the amputees as best as possible righted themselves in their beds and said, "Herr Hoffman. Herr Hoffman." He looked back and saw that they were saluting him in the traditional German army way with the stiff hand to the eyebrow, not the Nazi arm salute. Hoffman forced back his emotions and told the SS, "Wait a second," stopped and returned the salute and said, "God bless you." As he looked at them for the last time, a guard grabbed him by the shoulders and shoved him forward.

Chapter 21

Outside on the curb, a guard pushed Hoffman into the back of a Kubelwagen and climbed over the side since the military staff car had no doors. Kubelwagen meant "tub car" because of the bucket seats to prevent occupants from being tossed outside if the car bounced violently. The sergeant scaled the passenger side, and the other guard vaulted over the driver's side to assume the driving duties. Hoffman was surprised that the guards seemed older because of the lines on their faces and beginning of gray around the temples. After five minutes, Hoffman asked, "Where are you taking me?"

The sergeant turned to the back and said, "You'll see."

"What are your names?"

Turning back to face his prisoner again, the sergeant said with an impatient voice, "No names, except I am 'Eins', the driver is 'Zwei', and the guard next to you is 'Drei.' No more questions." Eins turned and faced the front.

Hoffman understood. One, two, three. He thought about escape because the guards didn't appear to watch him closely but realized he would be shot. Three-to-one odds worked against him.

They drove on smaller roads that had few autos but plenty of potholes and headed north of the hospital through suburban Berlin's housing sector. He noticed that the buildings weren't bombed but needed repairs and paint, plus the small yards were overgrown with weeds. After a while, Zwei made a sharp turn onto a dirt alley and Hoffman sat up. The vehicle passed the rear of old two-story apartments and stopped outside of an apartment that had more paint peelings than paint. Everyone climbed out, and the guards led him up the stairs to unit three. The old door had strips of wood hammered across the front covering the holes. "Go inside."

When Hoffman entered, he saw four middle-aged men dressed in dirty overalls and a fifth person dressed in slacks and sport shirt. He wore rimless glasses framed by a scrawny body, thin hair, and sallow cheeks that didn't project a tough-guy image, but he carried himself with confidence. "Colonel Hoffman?" He nodded. "London has informed us about your mission. We have clothes and ID for you and will guide you and your daughter to Switzerland."

Hoffman looked at Eins, Zwei, and Drei, and they smiled because they deceived him so well. Then Drei returned the Luger and silencer.

"You guys sure fooled me," Hoffman laughed.

Eins said, "We almost burst out laughing when we left the hospital."

Hoffman turned serious, looked at Mr. Slacks, and asked, "How are the Allies progressing in France?"

He answered, "They are advancing through the stubborn hedgerows and have air superiority. They will take Paris soon and invade Germany after that."

Hoffman grinned. "Great news," and rubbed his hands together and paced back and forth in excitement.

"We need to hurry in order to transport you to your daughter's house. The SS has penetrated parts of our organization, so we can't remain in one place for too long. It's fortunate we nabbed you when we did because thirty minutes after we left, soldiers from Bachmann's SS unit marched into the hospital. We were told that they were stunned that another SS unit had already seized you."

The Resistance gave Hoffman a dark gray suit, white shirt, black tie, dark socks, old leather shoes, plus maps and money. His ID card stated that his new name was Oskar Trautman and he served as chairman of the Aryan Purity Association. The man wearing slacks had Hoffman memorize the address of their safe house where he and his daughter would hook up with two guides plus the phone number to reach the Berlin Resistance if he ran into trouble.

"Who do I ask for when I call? What's your name?"

"Just call. No names are given." Hoffman understood. Mr. Slacks added, "Surveillance has appeared outside your daughter's house, and they leave around five p.m. That's when you should make your move."

In London, Hoffman thought about how he would confront his daughter but procrastinated in developing a strategy. The current moment dictated that he come up with a plan. He had to present himself and in a short time convince her to escape with him. How would he act when meeting her? Would she throw him out?

Zwei and Drei dropped Hoffman two blocks from Caroline's address so he could recon the area before making his way to the front door. He needed time to avoid the surveillance team and to persuade Caroline to leave with him. They would go by bus to the safe house and meet up with the Resistance. Few cars existed in Berlin due to gas shortage and car shortage, so when Hoffman surveyed the area, he spotted the sedan parked three houses away from Caroline's. It was an Opel, a civilian car painted in a brown-and-tan pattern. It had to be a stakeout since no other cars were seen in the neighborhood.

The row houses were plain with flat or pitched roofs following Walter Gropius's modern architectural style popular in Germany in the 1920s and 1930s. They had narrow back alleys that Hoffman planned to use when leaving. Another advantage: the house was located two blocks from a busy avenue where buses plied their routes. He would ride the number 322 bus according to Mr. Slacks, which would head toward the safe house.

At 5:15 p.m., the driver of the Opel sedan started the car and left the area. Hoffman's moment of truth had arrived. He swallowed hard, walked through the hedges where he was hiding, crossed the street still scanning the neighborhood, and walked up the short path to the small porch. He knocked once, waited, knocked again, turned, and faced the front yard wondering what to do next. After one minute, he heard a noise on the main floor of the two-story home, then muffled footsteps on the hardwood in the foyer.

Caroline opened the door and said, "May I help you?" She didn't recognize her father. She only saw the dark suit and the face of an older man.

Hoffman spoke softly. "Hi, Caroline. Can I come in?"

Bachmann met with Major Frolich in midafternoon. "Konrad, my SS squad tried to arrest Hoffman at the hospital, and they said another SS unit took him. I checked and no other SS units in Berlin went there. The Resistance must have grabbed him."

"Now what?" asked Konrad.

With the phone in his hand, he said, "I'm calling security right now." When someone answered, Bachmann got through to his SS contact. "Do you know where the Resistance's safe house in south Berlin is located?" He waited for the reply. "Good, a man and woman will arrive sometime soon." Once again, information from the Resistance's spy provided timely intelligence.

Konrad interrupted the conversation and said to Bachmann, "Sir, other members of the Resistance could be in the area. When your men capture the American and Caroline, they should kill them. We can't take any chances on them escaping."

Bachmann smiled. "Just a minute. Major Frolich says you are to kill them. I agree. Got it?"

The general hung up the phone. "No sadness? Killing your wife?"

"She is a traitor. She used me."

Bachmann said, "We have a trip tomorrow. Jodl's big meeting."

"Yes, sir. I'll be ready. What time?"

"We should be at the train station at seven a.m."

Chapter 22

June 25, 1944
Berlin, Germany

In her wildest imagination, Caroline never thought her father would show up on her Berlin doorstep, and she didn't recognize him at first. Upon hearing his voice, she stepped back in shock, gathered her wits, and said in a loud tone, "What are you doing here?"

Hoffman said, "Let's talk inside." He walked quickly past her into the entrance hall and stopped. She looked outside to the street, shut the door, and glared at him. "How did you get here? Are you in trouble? You can't stay here tonight."

"Caroline, you can't stay here either."

"What does that mean?"

Hoffman glanced around her living room, which was decorated with old, dark brown furniture, a few paintings, and a tan carpet. Caroline looked healthy with her svelte figure and at twenty-nine carried herself with confidence. Her long brown hair was drawn back, her blue eyes clear, and she appeared to be the modern woman, dressed in khaki slacks, pumps, and a patterned blouse.

"Look, I know that I'm not your favorite person and that we have many subjects to discuss, but we need to postpone this fight. You probably want an explanation. Can I sit down?"

With an edge to her voice, holding herself in a stiff posture and tightening her jaw muscles, she said, "Make it quick. Go into the living room."

He sat on the sofa, did not lean back, and looked at the coffee table and nearby lamps. She sat on a chair away from him but close enough so they could talk without raising their voices. She crossed her arms and legs.

He took a big breath. Here we go. "Did you know that you are under surveillance?"

"Where did you get that idea?"

"As I was coming here, I saw a brown-and-tan Opel parked three houses away. The driver focused on this house and wore an SS uniform. I waited for over one hour until he left, which was five minutes ago."

Caroline kept a stern appearance on her face but fidgeted in her seat when hearing this information. "My husband works in intelligence for the SS. I doubt if he'd allow it."

"It was authorized by Major General Bruno Bachmann. I believe he is your husband's boss."

"How do you know this? I thought you were based in London working in supply or something."

"British counterintelligence told me."

"How did they know?" Caroline's face was turning red.

"Through their agent network. They told me over one month ago and think the Germans suspect you of spying because you are an American. With the Allies' invasion imminent, they decided to shore up the home front."

"That's ridiculous. My husband's SS and very loyal to Germany. I wouldn't endanger his position. The British are wrong. I'm as safe as can be."

"Then why the car outside? Surely you must have suspected that something like this might happen?"

"You're crazy." Caroline's tough façade softened. "How did you get here? And make it through German lines?"

"It's a long story and I can tell it to you on our trip."

"So why did you come? You haven't been on my side for some time."

Hoffman sat back and relaxed. "You're right, but I'm on it now, and we don't have much time."

"You may not have time, but I have plenty."

"You don't understand. We need to leave and quickly."

"So where are you taking me?"

"The German Resistance will lead us to Switzerland. We'll depart for a safe house. I've met with them already. They are taking big risks for us."

Caroline uncrossed her arms. "So why you? Can't the Resistance lead me without you?"

"That too is a topic for later."

Caroline still held her grudges. "So, I'm supposed to take everything you say on faith?" she paused. "Fat chance. I'm mad at you. My odds are better if I stayed with my husband. He listens to me. You go to Switzerland by yourself."

"I wouldn't have come here if the Resistance could handle it by themselves. As you know, there's a war on."

"You're manipulating the situation, trying to make up for your failures, maybe get a few medals in the process. You expect me to drop everything and go. Leave my husband, my friends?"

"Caroline, it's us together or not at all." He stared at her and waited for a few moments. "Do you recall when you were a little girl and we lived on Hancock Street? I built you that tree house that you wanted."

"What's that got to do with anything?" She pursed her lips.

"Remember the first time you climbed the tree and got scared about coming down because of the height?"

"Yeah."

"You wouldn't budge, but I said, 'Jump. I'll catch you,' and you trusted me then." Caroline looked away. She had remembered. "This is one of those moments."

As she thought about his comments, the front door opened. "Konrad."

She went to the door leaving Hoffman sitting in the living room. He wondered how Konrad would react. Would Konrad kill him? He decided to stand and remain near the couch while feeling his pistol with a silencer in his coat pocket.

Major Konrad Frolich strode into the living room dressed in his black SS uniform wearing a red armband with a swastika on it and a stern look across his face. Caroline was at his side.

"Did you come to surrender, Herr Hoffman? You are my prisoner."

Konrad carried his six-foot athletic frame with confidence. Contrary to his physical image, his face evoked a bookish demeanor with his white skin and lazy eyes. His brown hair was cut short but not in a Nazi buzz cut that revealed more skin and little hair. His medium-cut mane appeared as though he were a conservative businessman. His temper was aroused at seeing his father-in-law, but he kept himself in control.

Hoffman stood with rigid shoulders. "I came to protect my daughter. I assume you love her and want to protect her as well."

"I can protect her without you." He went to the closet and took out a pistol. "Are you ready for a POW camp?"

Caroline said, "Konrad, listen to him." She faced her father. "Tell him."

All three sat down although Konrad sat across with his gun leveled at Hoffman.

Hoffman said, "Put that away. I'm not a threat . . . yet."

"Stay seated and I'll put it down. Now, talk." He retained his scowl.

Hoffman spoke in German and related his story about Caroline's vulnerability and Bachmann's belief that she was a spy. "We both have the same goal for her safety. I'm not trying to sabotage or attack you or any Germans unless they try to harm Caroline. Do you have information about her precarious position?"

Konrad took a deep breath, looked at Caroline, then returned his focus to Hoffman. "I wondered if I would ever meet you. I never thought you'd have the guts to visit us. I should punch you in the nose for all the pain you've caused her."

"You can punch me now if you wish, but what good will that do?"

Peering down at the coffee table, taking a breath, and looking up at Caroline, Konrad said, "I didn't want to admit it, but Caroline, there is a risk. Hard to put in words. Bachmann authorized the surveillance and I'm not sure what he intends. It hasn't been easy in the SS married to an American even though you have expressed your loyalty to me and Germany."

Caroline said, "Then my father is right."

"I'm afraid so."

Hoffman said, "With the Allies advancing in the west and the Soviets attacking in the east, you must realize that the war is over."

"I can't concede that officially."

"Come with us. Save yourself and Caroline."

"I can't do that either, but I'll let you leave with her."

Caroline asked, "By the way, what are you doing here so early?"

"General Bachmann is attending a big military meeting in Munich with General Jodl, and I will accompany him, so I need to prepare. We leave early tomorrow morning."

"What a coincidence. Gunhild called and invited me to sing at Jodl's birthday party."

"You mean Gunhild Ackerman from your singing days?"

"Who's she?" asked Hoffman.

"She managed my engagements, like an agent," said Caroline. "She thought it would be a big surprise since Jodl and I are friends. It would be like old times, remembering happier days."

Hoffman said, "General Jodl? The army's chief of staff?" She nodded. "You and Jodl are friends?"

Konrad said, "He was a big fan of her singing, especially her signature song, 'Falling in Love Again' that Marlene Dietrich popularized. Caroline's rendition upped the tempo, and she belted out a sexy arrangement. Everyone loved it because she had such a mischievous twinkle in her eyes as she flirted with her audience. It worked on me." Konrad smiled at Caroline.

She interrupted, "Hitler and his henchmen didn't approve of that song and didn't like that Marlene went to the United States and became an American citizen."

Hoffman ran his fingers through his hair. "Kaye will never believe this."

"Mom met Jodl at one of my performances when visiting me in 1938."

"Kaye didn't mention it to me."

"You would have had a fit."

"So, you had many fans in the German army?" Hoffman said.

Konrad looked at Hoffman. "But I'm not a fan of yours. The only thing saving you is that you are her father."

Ignoring Konrad, Hoffman said, "We need to go. And we need money. I have a small amount that the Resistance gave me."

Caroline rejoined, "Just like at home. You had no money when I lived with you, and now you ask me for money to go to Switzerland. How does it feel?"

"We can argue later, but let's get out of here."

While Caroline packed her basics, Hoffman felt awkward next to his son-in-law and asked, "Have you seen any action?"

Konrad said, "Not yet although I've received training."

"What training?"

"I know how to read maps, navigate by the stars, but demolition of bridges and buildings was my specialty. I don't know why the brass taught me this skill. I'm in an office all day. The commando team even asked me to join them to destroy bridges. Imagine."

"Do you expect to use any of that training?"

"I already have and can blow up other things if the moment arises." He smiled and then whispered, "I heard the Resistance got you out of the hospital."

"How did you know that?"

"All I can say is that Bachmann has someone inside the Resistance, so be careful."

Chapter 23

June 25, 1944
Berlin, Germany

At 6:30 p.m., as the late afternoon sunshine broke through the clouds, Hoffman and Caroline left by the back door and walked along the narrow alley at the rear of the house. Caroline carried a small bag, and Hoffman only had his ID, cash, a pistol with silencer, and bullets.

Hoffman ate leftovers in the kitchen while Caroline and Konrad spent an hour together saying good-byes. She said, "I don't want to leave you. Even though we're in the middle of a war, you have made me so happy, and going to Switzerland without you is wrong." They kissed.

Still in an embrace, he said, "You think I want you to go? I want to have more years with you, and if you stayed here, I may never see you again."

She kissed him hard, separated, and said, "Won't Bachmann be mad at you that I left? Can he jail you or something?"

"He knows you have an independent mind and that I can't control you." They both laughed. "I'll tell him you called me from outside Berlin and that someone advised you about the SS coming to arrest you. You couldn't take any chances especially with the Allies moving toward Germany."

Caroline hugged him and said, "You should leave with us. We can ride out the war in Switzerland. We've put away enough funds in our Swiss account to manage."

At the door, Konrad kissed Caroline one more time and said, "You can't call me since my phone is bugged, but if I can help, contact me somehow." He turned to Hoffman without shaking his hand. "You'd better protect her." He watched his wife and Hoffman walk away. Caroline looked back twice.

One block later Caroline said, "The only reason I'm going with you is because Konrad wants me out of danger, so don't get any ideas that you used your charm and family ties to persuade me to escape."

Hoffman looked at Caroline and said, "I like your husband. Good choice." He paused, "By the way, my fake name is Oskar Trautman. I serve as chairman of the Aryan Purity Association. Can you remember it?"

"Yes, Oskar. Of course, I can." She gave a condescending glance that memorizing was not difficult.

"I am a friend of your husband's family who asked me to escort you." She nodded as though not hearing anything he said. The alley ran into Castle Strasse, a main artery with a bus service. They walked another block and stood at the bus stop. Fifteen minutes later, they boarded a local for the three-mile journey to the safe house.

Sitting on an old and frayed seat, Hoffman noticed that four cars behind the bus was a brown-and-tan Opel.

Caroline said, "Do you know where we need to get off?"

He said, "Yes, Dickensweg, but we'll get off at Sensburger Allee, five blocks away and circle back to check out the area."

"Why? The safe house is safe, isn't it?"

"It's an old habit. I don't accept anything until I've checked it out."

"The Resistance are risking their lives for us. Don't you think they know what they're doing?"

"I've learned from the Great War never to trust your own side's intelligence reports. You shouldn't either."

"Sir, you're paranoid."

"And proud of it."

Caroline said, "I've learned that the Germans are reliable, patriotic, and hardworking. If they say something, it's true."

"You willing to risk your life on it?"

While Hoffman looked at the surrounding area through the left and right windows, he also peeked out the back to monitor the Opel. He broke the silence and asked, "How did you and Konrad meet?"

"At a show in Berlin. I was the main act and attracted a following. Plenty of German officers wanted to date me, but they were immature. At a party afterward, I was introduced to senior army officers. One was General Jodl. I sat at his table, and we had an enjoyable conversation. When a staff member, Konrad, dropped by, Jodl introduced us. Konrad had heard me sing before but was so nervous that we didn't talk much. He had a nice smile, was polite, and not full of himself. I liked him immediately. A few coffee dates followed, and we hit it off. Five months later, we were married. Three years later when he signed up for the SS, he was promoted to major and transferred to General Bachmann's group."

Hoffman asked, "Why did he join the SS?"

"He said promotions would come if a person joined the Nazi party. His answer didn't make sense to me then or now, but he's been loyal and hardworking to General Bachmann. He even saved his life last year during a bombing by the Allies."

Hoffman kept looking around the area and said, "Has he adopted the ways of the SS rather than the Wehrmacht?"

"I'd rather not talk about the military. I saw him less once he became SS."

"Have you met his boss, General Bachmann?"

"A few times, briefly."

"Any opinions about him?"

She said, "He worships Hitler, feels Hitler has brought back prestige to Germany. He hates Britain and France for the forcing the appalling Treaty of Versailles on Germany."

"What about all the killing of Jews and Slavs?"

"I don't know much about it. I was sickened when the Reich confiscated Jewish property and sent them to work camps." She noticed her father's raised eyebrows and darting eyes. "What's the matter? You seem tense."

"I'm looking out for our safety." He paused and said, "Here's our stop."

They stepped off the bus and crossed the street. Hoffman noticed that the Opel turned right onto an avenue away from them. The safe house was located two blocks off Castle Strasse, five blocks back from the current bus stop. Hoffman walked along the side streets. Maybe he would lose the Opel. He touched the pistol in his right-side pocket for reassurance.

As he neared Dickensweg, the safe house was three houses away. He searched the area and did not see the Opel.

As they headed toward the residence, Caroline said, "I know where it is. I've been here before." She proceeded to walk more quickly.

"How do you know about it?" She ignored the question and headed up the front walk toward the front door.

Hoffman said, "Wait a minute. Let's check it out first."

"Nothing to check out. This is the safe house, and they guard it well."

"Caroline, we need to be cautious. Caroline." But she didn't hear him.

He quickened his pace but couldn't reach her as she was too far in front. She reached the entrance and opened the door. Hoffman caught up with her at the same time she went through the doorway. He drew his pistol with a silencer, hid the gun behind him and stayed close to her back.

Upon entering, she saw two SS men in black uniforms pointing their rifles at her. "Welcome, Frau Frolich. Come in. And you too, Herr Hoffman." They did not see his pistol because Caroline unknowingly shielded it with her body. She stopped and stared at the SS and then saw two men lying on the floor in a puddle of blood. She screamed.

The sound caught the Germans off guard. Hoffman said, "Who are they?"

Both SS soldiers gave a quick look at the deceased men and said, "Your comrades." Their quick glance enabled Hoffman to move his arm around Caroline and fire twice with the silencer. Phfft. Phfft. Each bullet pierced their skulls. Caroline screamed again as the SS men fell to the floor near her.

Hoffman left the door open and went to the two dead Resistance fighters. He mumbled, "Zwei and Drei." Hoffman hurried to the window and noticed the Opel turning into the driveway. Two SS men got out.

"Keep the door open and stay in the middle of the room with your hands up."

"What?"

"Don't argue. We have company."

He opened a small window and moved against the wall by the curtain so as not to be seen, but had a clear vision of the front. The first man, a sergeant, did not notice the front window. He only noticed Caroline with her hands up, so he didn't draw his gun when he started to enter the house. The second soldier followed five paces behind, carried a rifle, and kept a pistol in his holster. As he walked up the path, Hoffman shot him. The phfft could not be heard outside the room. The sergeant was unaware of his partner's death. As he stepped into the room, Hoffman rushed to the entry, slammed the front door behind the German, and aimed the Luger at his head. In German, he said, "Hands up."

In a panicky voice, Caroline said, "What's going on? Let's get out of here."

"I need a few answers first." Hoffman stripped the man of his weapon, sat him down on a nearby chair, and tied him up with electric cord. He gave the gun to Caroline. "Guard him."

He went out front and dragged the fallen SS soldier into the house, seized his weapons and bullets, which included extra ammo for his pistol, and laid the dead body next to Zwei and Drei.

Returning to the sergeant and reclaiming the pistol from his daughter, Hoffman said, "How did you find out about this place?"

The sergeant said, "You're going to kill me whether I talk or not."

Caroline said, "My father is not like that."

Hoffman interrupted. "I am exactly like that but will reconsider if you give me good answers."

She said, "You would murder him in cold blood?"

"Yes, just as they killed these two Germans who helped me to escape this morning." He focused with squinting eyes. "You either tell me and I won't shoot you, or you don't tell me, and then I'll put one bullet into your head. Your choice." Hoffman spoke in a cool manner without raising his voice. The sergeant saw the steely eyes and knew Hoffman would kill him.

Caroline had never seen her father so intent in this dangerous situation.

With Hoffman standing next to him, the sergeant dropped his head and said, "We have a spy in the Resistance. I don't know who he is. He told General Bachmann's aide. The aide told me, and we set up this ambush. That's all I know, I swear."

"And you were supposed to kill us or take us prisoner?"

"My orders were to kill you both if we found you."

"And who gave the order?"

"Major Konrad Frolich."

Caroline gasped at hearing this answer. "I don't believe you," she yelled.

"Quiet." Hoffman glared at the sergeant. "So, you found us and came to kill us, right?"

"Those were my orders."

"And being an obedient Nazi, you would carry them out."

The sergeant nodded.

Hoffman said, "Do you expect me to believe an SS man?"

"I'm trying to save my life."

Hoffman said to his daughter, "Check the window and make sure no one else comes." Then he turned to the sergeant. "I will not kill you as long as I never see you again. If you or your team try to stop us or show up in our vicinity, I will kill you no questions asked. Do you understand me?"

"Yes, Herr Hoffman."

After he spoke, Hoffman hit the SS man on the back of his skull and knocked him out.

Hoffman then went to the phone and called Mr. Slacks. "You have a leak. Four SS soldiers tried to kill us. I don't know who the rat is, but two of your men were murdered. I don't trust your organization and will go on my own. Tell your people that two of your men were killed by the SS, and they also killed us." Then he hung up.

Caroline said, "Why did you say we were killed?"

"Giving us more lead time. The SS might stop hunting us until they find out we're alive."

Chapter 24

June 25, 1944
Berlin, Germany

Hoffman and Caroline dumped the weapons into the trunk, and Caroline drove the Opel because of her familiarity with the German gear shift and the Berlin streets. She remembered that her father taught her to drive many years ago. The car sped away from the dead bodies. "Konrad would never order me to be killed. That guy lied; it makes no sense. I'm glad that you didn't shoot him."

"Caroline, we're in dangerous territory, and you need to follow my directions without question. We can't make any mistakes. The consequences are unimaginable."

"Still want to be in charge, right? You haven't changed since Fort Knox."

"Tell you what. If I do any singing, I'll follow your lead. Against the Nazis, you follow mine, okay?"

She glanced at him then looked forward and focused on driving.

Hoffman asked, "I assume that taking the train is the best way to reach Switzerland. Do you agree?"

Caroline said, "You can't buy a ticket without a military pass to travel on trains. Buses would be difficult since they don't go far. We'd have to steal a car to get there, but no one can get any gas. So, what do we do now, sir? Hitch a ride? Do you have your army compass?"

He pondered the problem, and then coming out of his trance, said, "Head for downtown Berlin. Tell me about your friend, Gunhild. Would she have extra tickets?"

"Oh no. I'm not going onstage again. She wouldn't let me come on the train unless I promised to sing in Munich. And I can't agree to that."

"You can agree in Berlin and change you mind in Munich, can't you? You've changed your mind over smaller issues before."

"Very funny." She gave a quick pout of disgust. "This escape resembles how we did projects back home: disorganized with plenty of arguing."

"I didn't plan to meet SS soldiers with orders to kill me. Can't you grant me a little slack?"

Caroline's anger was building. "Don't give me that bunk that these things happen in wartime. I understand the mess we're in. I trusted you. You said jump, and here I am, spared from getting killed on orders from my loving husband. And our escape route just disappeared. Where do I jump now?"

Hoffman said, "We need to stop somewhere and call Gunhild. She'll help you. Friends do that."

"Don't lecture me. I at least have some genuine friends, not drinking buddies." She paused, settled down, and said, "I'll stop at a restaurant."

Hoffman waited in a café's parking lot while Caroline went inside, and returned in ten minutes.

"We're in. Gunhild has two tickets, but we have to meet her at the train station at seven a.m."

"Do you have to sing?"

"Gunhild is bringing my old performing gown. I have to sing Jodl's favorite song, and guess what? General Bachmann and my husband will attend the meeting and the banquet. How's our new plan doing now? How do we evade German senior officers and the SS?"

"Not sure yet, but it beats being piled in a pool of blood at the safe house. You can fill me in later about how you knew about the safe house."

"Don't hold your breath."

The Berlin Hauptbahnhof — or Central Train Station — opened in 1871 with its noble Romanesque architecture and a barrel vault with steel supports. The trains were electrified in 1930, and the efficient rail system distributed trains to the vast Nazi Empire. The station remained unscathed from Allied bombs but suffered temporary closing when Polish saboteurs blew up a corner in April 1943.

Hoffman and his daughter dared not to stay at a hotel where the Gestapo or SS might look for them, so they ditched the car and spent the night in the crowded open seating of the station with businessmen, military, and a few families. With more than one hundred who waited for various trains, no one paid attention to them while she slept and he kept alert.

Hoffman also called Mr. Slacks who said, "I apologize for the ambush. I will try to figure out how the SS found out about you. Only a few knew."

"Unless it was you."

"I deserve that, but remember, I was the one who got you out of the hospital, as it turns out, thirty minutes before the real SS came."

"I liked your two men. Sorry about them." Hoffman waited. "By the way, I left the Opel used by the SS with their weapons in the trunk four blocks away from the train station." He gave the street name and house number where the car was parked.

At 6:50 a.m., Gunhild and her troupe of twelve entertainers disembarked from a bus, spotted Caroline, and rushed over. "I'm so happy you will be part of the show. You will remind everyone about the carefree days of the thirties." After small talk, Caroline introduced Hoffman as her escort. "He is a friend of Konrad's who insisted he accompany me since he worried because of the frequent bombing."

After the introductions, Hoffman and Gunhild nodded to each other. She looked closely at him and saw a resemblance to Caroline but decided not to pursue the matter. Gunhild said, "Caroline, darling, you are such a good friend to come. Jodl will give me extra ration cards when he hears you sing again. I have missed our routines."

"How could I not join you. You gave me so many opportunities and guided me when I first arrived. You are an angel."

Hoffman continued to watch the crowd for trouble while listening to the conversation. He inwardly recoiled at the sight of so many SS officers heading toward the train. He interrupted, "Shouldn't we find our seats?"

Gunhild recognized the anxiety of Caroline's escort at seeing German soldiers and yelled at the group. "Let's move. Our railcar is Number Four, next to the dining car, which is Number Five."

Everyone turned and shuffled as a group to board the train, which was painted in camouflage. The coach's seats were squeezed tightly together creating an intimacy similar to being in an elevator. Even those walking down the center bumped into people on the aisle seats.

Once settled, Hoffman inspected the other passengers and the exits. When he looked out the window, he tensed at seeing Konrad talking to a high-ranking officer, whom he presumed was General Bachmann. Two SS guards accompanied him. Impeccably groomed in their uniforms, all four headed to the VIP railcar Number Three. So that's what Bachmann looks like. Konrad looked downcast.

Major General Bachmann spoke softly to Konrad. "The latest report says they haven't found the bodies yet, and I ordered many SS to look for them."

Konrad said, "I don't know why I'm so sad. Caroline was a spy, and spies are executed. Are you sure about the information?"

"We'll find out soon enough."

Major Frolich nodded slightly and kept walking.

During the seven-and-a-half hour trip, everyone relaxed except Hoffman because he kept a tense eye on the steady stream of passengers that made their way to the dining car and back. Caroline fluttered from seat to seat and reconnected with old friends from her singing days and reviewed with Gunhild the staging of her performance.

She said to Caroline, "Your program will be easy, no props or scenery since the dining room at the Braunes Haus—or Brown House—can't handle anything fancy."

"Is that the Nazi Party headquarters? On Brienner Strasse?"

"The very same."

Anything that had to do with Nazi headquarters frightened Caroline, so she was glad to be on the train on the way to Switzerland instead singing there. When Caroline returned to her seat, she rehearsed the lyrics with the backup singers.

After two hours of travel, Hoffman noticed Konrad make his way down the aisle to the dining car. As he neared the door, his eyes bulged when he spotted Caroline. He rushed to her side. "You're alive. What are you doing here?"

In a dismissive and terse voice, she said, "Don't talk to me. You'll draw attention."

Konrad turned to the right and saw her father and went up to him. "This trip is dangerous. Last night the Allies blew up the Munich Central Station. The train will stop prior to Munich to review passes and identification. I don't know how your ID will hold up, but it's risky."

"Where should we get off?" asked Hoffman.

"Any station before Munich. I shouldn't be seen talking to you."

Konrad resumed his trek to the dining car. Hoffman motioned Caroline to her window seat away from the aisle. When she squeezed past him he said, "The Nazis will hold an inspection of all the passengers just before Munich. We need to disembark before then."

They looked on a map and selected Odelzhausen, a small town thirteen miles north of Munich.

Chapter 25

The troupe eventually stopped their chatter and settled in for the long trip. Most relaxed except for Hoffman, whose eyes darted everywhere and back again. When Konrad exited from the dining car and returned to the VIP coach, he didn't gaze at Caroline, and she ignored him.

One and a half hours later, Hoffman saw the VIP railcar doors open, and one bodyguard entered followed by Bachmann, another guard, and finally Konrad. Everyone quieted and stared at the general. The only noise was the loud clacking of the wheels.

Hoffman muttered to Caroline who sat next to him, "Cover your face and pretend you are asleep. Bachmann is walking down the aisle." With Caroline feigning sleep, Hoffman stood up, stretched, and acted as a shield so his daughter would not be seen. Hoffman glimpsed at the SS general's face as he passed to remember it. Bachmann seemed oblivious to the passengers although he occasionally cast his eyes back and forth at different people. Konrad eyed Hoffman without any recognition as he followed the general.

When Bachmann returned to the VIP car, Hoffman breathed more easily and spoke to his daughter. "Okay, tell me. How do you know about the safe house?"

"Can we talk about it later?"

"It's a simple question."

Caroline acted in a cautious manner, inched forward in her seat, and whispered, "I housed some allied flyers. I dropped them off at the safe house."

"How many pilots?"

"I don't know, twelve or fifteen, British and American. Now let's change the subject."

"Does Konrad know?"

"I put them in the basement when Konrad was at work or out of town. He never knew."

"I'm impressed. A singer gone undercover. Did you join British intelligence?"

"I'm not that clever. I wanted to save lives and would have helped German flyers too."

With Odelzhausen station on the horizon, Hoffman and his daughter got ready to leave. Caroline went to Gunhild. "I'll explain later, but we have to get off here."

Gunhild nodded. Her suspicions were correct. "You're going to Switzerland, aren't you? I don't blame you."

"Want to join us?"

"It's dangerous for you here. Go with my blessing and be careful."

Caroline smiled and held Gunhild's hand. "Sorry I won't be in the performance tonight. It would have been fun."

Father and daughter went through the dining car to the gangway connection and disembarked. When the train left the station, the Hoffmans stood alone on the platform. Two members of the Grüne Polizei, the Green Police because their uniforms were green, lingered near the office and observed the two passengers. The Green Police units belonged to the SS organization.

Hoffman went to the ticket office inside the station guarded by the policemen and asked, "We need to arrange for transportation. Are there buses or taxis available?"

The stationmaster, who also handled ticket sales as well as maintenance chores, laughed. "We don't have anything that fancy. You should have stayed on the train. How far are you going?"

Hoffman became cautious at hearing the stationmaster's question. "The Wehrmacht needed our seats, so we got booted. We want to reach a station south of Munich. Any suggestions? We could hire someone local."

Grizzled from forty years with the railroad, the stationmaster greeted the request with suspicion and said, "There's a repair stall down a block or two. They might know someone."

The stationmaster talked with the two members of the Green Police as he watched Hoffman and Caroline leave. Two blocks later, the Hoffmans found the auto shop that had vehicles covered in rust and approached an unshaven mechanic wearing overalls who was working underneath a hood. When he surfaced, they noticed a large tooth gap in his lower jaw. He said, "What do you want?"

"Do you have a car we can rent or someone to take us to the railroad station south of Munich?"

"Got kicked off the train?"

"The military needed more space and they said the Munich station was bombed and closed, which made it difficult for us to complete our journey. We will pay a premium. We need to attend an important meeting."

The man thought about the possibilities. He needed cash and eyeballed the urbanites dressed in fancy clothes. "If you can wait while I put on a brake shoe, then I'll take you, but it'll cost."

One hour later with money handed over and the destination agreed to, the travelers left with their chauffer/repairman on their thirteen-mile excursion. Hoffman noticed that the man took a keen interest in the amount of Reichsmarks pulled from his pockets.

The driver took back roads and kept looking at Hoffman. He pulled over and stopped on the shoulder. "Something's wrong with the engine."

He got out of the car and reached under the seat, and when the man faced them he revealed a pistol that he aimed at Hoffman.

"Get out. I'll take the rest of your cash." As they stepped on the ground Hoffman said, "Can't we pay you a little more and be done with it?"

"I'm planning to take it all."

Hoffman raised his eyebrows at Caroline and turned to the driver. "If you let us go, you can have her gold."

The man perked up when he heard those words. Gold was better than Reichsmarks. "Let's see it."

Hoffman said to Caroline, "Show him the package in your purse."

Caroline followed her dad's eye movement and then tensed seeing the man point the gun at her. She again marveled at her father's calmness while she trembled at the impending danger. "All right." As she opened the clasp, she dropped the purse and said, "Oops. Damn." The man concentrated on the purse with its contents spread over the ground.

Hoffman grabbed his pistol from his coat pocket and pointed the barrel. Phfft. The bullet lodged in the mechanic's skull.

"Do you have to kill everyone?"

Hoffman dragged the body to the side of the road and hid the corpse under thick bushes. "Get in. I'll drive. I saw how he handled the gears and can manage."

As they traveled on the rural road, Caroline said, "Do we have time to talk now?"

"I guess." His stern eyes met hers, and then he resumed his view of the road.

Caroline had waited a long time to unload her anger and how she suffered. "I tried so hard to get your attention and nothing. I couldn't reach you and neither could Mom." She stopped, looked out the window, and brushed the dirt off her slacks.

"I wanted to say. . ." She took a deep breath. "I'm sorry for your nightmares and the loss of your army buddies. I can't imagine how I'd handle the bad affects of the war, but as a little girl, what was I to do? I've been mad at you for twenty years, and now here you are trying to save me. For what reason? Why didn't you save me when I was a child?"

As she looked at him with her pleading eyes Hoffman turned away, embarrassed at the question, a question with which he had struggled. Now it confronted him in the innocent words of his daughter.

He swallowed, kept his vision on the road, and responded in a hesitant voice, "Honey, I don't claim to understand myself either. I didn't feel safe with anyone except fellow soldiers who experienced combat. I know I was wrong, especially with you and Kaye, but I felt paralyzed and got angry at everyone. Even when I erupted, I couldn't control it."

She nodded, glad that they could talk without argument. "If we could have talked about it . . ."

Hoffman straightened his back. "When the nightmares come, I get scared, really scared. I don't know how to deal with them. The ghosts of my men keep coming at me. I was afraid to ignore them. I thought if I ignored them, I would dishonor them." He stopped and thought about what he unveiled for the first time. "It doesn't make any sense, does it?"

"Father, you could honor them," she paused as her eyes welled up, "and you could still honor us. You can do both. We are your family."

"You're right. I could have paid more attention. I was stupid and I apologize. I feel so badly about it." He rubbed his right eye and afterward ran his fingers through his hair. "You and your mother are the best things that ever happened to me." He glanced at her, gave a smile, and squeezed her hand. "We'll get out of this."

"And that's it? All of those miserable years and you only feel bad?"

Hoffman said, "I apologized and admit that I need to correct my past behavior. I took huge risks to save you. What do you want me to do?"

"I don't know what I want. Those years still hurt. My father rejected me."

"I'm not rejecting you now. I want to make a new life with you and with Kaye. We can build on it for the rest of my life, which I hope will be a long one."

A teary-eyed Caroline remained quiet for the next twenty minutes. They found the station and parked the car five blocks away.

As they walked to the depot, she looked at her father with contempt. He was the brute she remembered: being in charge, not helpful or loving or understanding of her. He was an impervious rock. She had to admit that he handled today's pressure situations with skill, but he should be battle-ready and confident after those training courses he took at Fort Knox. He spent too much time at the firing range to earn a marksman badge instead of time spent with his family to earn a family badge. While his training yielded results today, if he came home more frequently, maybe she wouldn't have married a German. This predicament was his fault.

As they reached the train platform, Hoffman went to the ticket office only to find that two SS soldiers walked around the structure and confronted them with a third closing behind them with his rifle pointed. Finally, one corporal said, "Halt. You will come with us."

Chapter 26

When the SS corporal ordered, "Go to the car," Hoffman realized that the stationmaster at Odelzhausen informed the police, and they alerted the SS to capture them. Hoffman also grasped that these soldiers didn't know Bachmann wanted him. Hoffman gave an anxious look at Caroline, turned, faced the soldier, and produced a big smile. "Thank goodness you arrived. We weren't sure our message got through."

The corporal looked surprised at this response. "What do you mean?"

"You're here to take us to the Brown House, right? Or are you waiting for someone else?" Everyone knew that the Brown House was a Nazi annex, and that this weekend it would hold a big meeting.

"My orders are to take you to headquarters."

"You don't understand. Don't you know who this is? Caroline Hoffman. She is the main act for General Jodl's surprise birthday party and homecoming celebration. She has to be there. She and Jodl are good friends. Maybe that's why the SS was looking for us."

This revelation exceeded the corporal's capacity. "I have my orders."

"They may change your orders to the Eastern Front if you don't take us. Call your superiors or check at the Brown House. We have to hurry."

The soldier decided that he would meet with the officer on duty at the Brown House to make sure Hoffman's statements were correct. The other soldiers with the SS corporal agreed with this course of action as long as they didn't have to make any decisions. When they reached the Brown House, the assistant officer in charge of the event, a major in the personnel department, wasn't sure if Caroline should be admitted.

Hoffman said, "Contact Gunhild Ackerman. She'll verify that Caroline is to perform."

Gunhild, when asked about Caroline, rushed outside to answer the major. When she saw Caroline, she understood. "My dear. We worried so much about you. Please come and get dressed. We don't have much time."

After they left, the major said to the corporal, "Watch her. See if she is really part of the act." They followed the group and waited backstage.

As they entered the building and out of earshot of the soldiers, Caroline said, "Thank you, Gunhild. You saved our lives."

"I did it for selfish reasons. I wanted to hear you sing again. Those were good days. We have a buffet dinner for the cast, so help yourself. I imagine you haven't eaten much."

Hoffman faced his daughter. "If you sing, Bachmann will know you're alive and come after you. And if you don't sing, the three SS soldiers will grab us." He paused. "I need to come up with an escape plan over dinner."

Caroline looked backstage and noticed the three SS men staring at her and then peeked from the curtains to see German senior officers sitting at tables ready for the show. General Jodl sat at a large round table in front as the guest of honor. The large room accommodated the brass quite easily as Hitler frequently orated in this same room.

Caroline said, "Father, you're not the only one that has the ability to come up with plans. I have an idea."

"What do you have in mind?"

"I'll let you know at the end of my number."

While the waiters removed the dinner plates and served apple turnovers for dessert, the curtains parted and the emcee walked out to cheers as everyone looked forward to the entertainment. He introduced a group of eight female dancers who were adorned in appealing white satin dresses. They spun often, which exposed their legs and red underwear. The second and third acts contained singers who belted out military anthems.

After they left the stage, the announcer returned. "For the final act, we have a special birthday treat for General Jodl. It is with great pleasure that we welcome Caroline Hoffman."

She was greeted with Jodl's gasp of surprise and a robust ovation. Hoffman had never seen her perform, so when she came on stage, he was spellbound by her fancy blue gown and the flashy hairstyle that makeup artists toiled over. Her stage persona took over as she strutted onto center stage. Jodl clapped vigorously, and Caroline winked at him.

Major General Bachmann looked at Frolich in surprise. "She's alive. My source made a huge mistake."

Frolich, feigning shock, said over the din, "What can we do?"

"We can't do anything until the show is over. Jodl will be furious if we interrupt his birthday party. After it's over, I'll send my guards to nab her."

Major Frolich said, "Be careful. She is friends with Jodl."

"So I understand."

When the applause subsided, Caroline looked at General Jodl who was all smiles and said, "Happy birthday, General. This song is dedicated to you."

The military band started to play the introduction to Marlene Dietrich's "Falling in Love Again." The audience recognized the popular tune and roared with approval, except the SS officers who hated Dietrich because she fled Germany. The Wehrmacht on the other hand loved Marlene regardless of her citizenry.

Caroline stepped coyly down the stairs and approached Jodl's table while singing, "*Falling in love again, never wanted to, what am I to do? I can't help it.*"

She kept her eyes on Jodl and circled the table. All eyes followed her saucy movements and expressions. She teased Jodl and his tablemates, and they relished her playfulness.

Hoffman was astonished and awed. His daughter's talent surpassed his expectations. She sang so well, but her personality warmed the room and the hearts of the audience. He marveled at her transformation from a modern woman to a celebrity.

She turned from Jodl's table to sing to the rest of the audience.

> *Love's always been my game,*
> *Play it how I may,*
> *I was made that way,*
> *I can't help it.*

She walked around other tables while each officer thought she flirted only with him.

> *Men cluster to me,*
> *Like moths around a flame,*
> *And if their wings burn,*
> *I know I'm not to blame.*

She ended the song to wild applause standing in front of General Jodl. She bowed to the acclaim. Then he stood up, continued to clap, and asked her to join him at the table. A waiter quickly brought another chair. He said, "What a wonderful surprise. I had no idea you would come out of retirement. And you did it for me. Thank you, Caroline. This is my best birthday present."

"Thank you, General. How is Luise?"

"My wife will be overjoyed to hear that you sang for me."

Caroline looked around and noticed that her father eyed the three SS soldiers while Bachmann gave orders to his minions at his table. His SS guards headed toward the back of the stage.

After some small talk, she asked, "General, may I ask you for a favor?"

"Anything, my dear."

"For some reason, the SS wants to take me and my friend in for questioning. Is there anything you can do to get us out of here safely?"

Jodl sobered up when he heard her request. "Have you been a naughty girl?" He said it without any smiles.

"Sir, my only sin is that I'm from America. They don't acknowledge all the good deeds I've done for Germany." She gave bashful look and batted her eyelashes.

"They're weird people."

Jodl loathed the SS and the Gestapo. He especially resented that a former corporal ran the war machine with his goons and ignored the expertise of Germany's real army. Jodl had mentioned this bias to Caroline years ago and she remembered it.

With a robust smile, Jodl said, "Caroline, I'd be glad to assist. Stay at my hotel." He summoned his executive assistant, a lieutenant colonel named Hans Lentz. "Hans, take some guards with you and escort Caroline and her companion to my hotel and get a room for her."

"Yes, sir." Hans extended his arm. "Frau Hoffman, this way," and he led her to the rear of the room.

They went backstage, collected Hoffman—known to them as Oskar Trautman—and hurried to the back exit. Before they departed, her group was met by the three SS guards from the train station. The corporal opened his mouth but was interrupted by Bachmann's two SS guards and a captain. "Halt. We need to take these two into custody."

Jodl's aide outranked everyone as a lieutenant colonel and said, "I am under orders from General Jodl. You need to speak with him."

"We are with SS Major General Bruno Bachmann and are following his orders."

The SS corporal was outclassed everywhere, so he closed his mouth and remained in the background not wanting to upset any officer.

Lieutenant Colonel Lenz said, "Fine. General Bachmann can talk to General Jodl, but I need to leave."

The captain, with a lower rank by a huge degree, knew he was outfoxed. "I will inform him right away."

The other three guards remained in place but did not stop Jodl's crew as they left the building. Lenz directed them to Jodl's Mercedes-Benz. He and the Hoffmans and two guards got in, and the car roared to the Hotel Laimer Hof, two miles away. The Wehrmacht commandeered the entire hotel, so there were plenty of extra rooms. In the lobby, Lenz arranged for their quarters and even had room service provide a small buffet for Caroline.

"They're yours for the evening. Tomorrow we return to Berlin."

She extended her hand. "Thank you, colonel, and please thank the general. You both were so kind to help me."

Back at the Brown House, the outranked captain reported the problem to Bachmann who said, "I'll get them. I know where they're staying." He looked at Frolich. "Deploy our troops around the Hotel Laimer Hof. They don't have Jodl's protection any longer and don't have a chance to escape."

Chapter 27

June 26, 1944
Munich, Germany

After they left Jodl's aide, Hoffman and Caroline proceeded to their separate rooms. When Hoffman went to Caroline's, he noticed she had already plunged into the food cart. "I'm famished. I've never had so many near-death experiences."

"The day's not over. We need to move on."

"That would spoil my evening. Usually after a show, performers relax over a drink and absorb the glory of the show and the audience, but not today, right?"

"After we eat, we will depart. Bachmann's men, I'm sure, know about this hotel. They'll find us quickly."

"Don't we get any sleep?"

"Not here."

After a bathroom break and a change from the show gown into her regular clothes, father and daughter took the employee elevator to the basement. They wandered around looking for disguises.

Meanwhile, four SS soldiers parked at the hotel's front entrance while ten others surrounded the building. The time was close to 11:00 p.m.

As he drifted around the basement, Hoffman found papers and a pencil. "Look as though we're inspecting the place." When they came to the laundry room, he found the employee changing room.

151

As he entered, he was stopped by a man who acted as majordomo of the night shift. In a gruff voice, he said, "What are you doing here?"

"And who are you?" asked Hoffman.

"I am the assistant operations manager. And you are?"

"We are consultants hired by the owners to make a surprise inspection. Can I ask you some questions?"

The assistant manager said, "It's unusual to have a woman be a consultant. Who is she?" He suspected a trick and eyed them closely.

Hoffman used his hand to guide the man away from Caroline and into a corner. "She's the cousin of a high-ranking SS colonel. I was ordered to hire her and had no choice."

The assistant manager nodded. "I understand."

Then Hoffman winked and whispered, "At least he said she was his cousin." Hoffman crooked his head and raised an eyebrow.

The operations man changed his expression and laughed. "Oh, of course."

"So, let me continue. When do your employees change shifts?"

The assistant manager said, "The swing shift gets off between ten and midnight unless there is overtime, and a skeleton crew replaces them."

"How well do the washing machines operate?"

"They function well."

"Do most of your employees take the train?"

"Yes."

"How far is the train station from here?"

"The Hirschgarten station is about two kilometers." He pointed to the south. "It's off the main road."

Hoffman looked around after he jotted down notes. "And what would you say is your biggest problem down here?"

The operations assistant rarely got to comment on his department, and in fact, few people took any time to communicate with him. He loved to talk about his responsibilities. His answer droned on, and Caroline had difficulty holding back a yawn. At the end, Hoffman asked, "We'll look around a little longer. Thank you for your help."

They shook hands and now Hoffman had the run of the basement as long as he continued to write on the paper. After the operations assistant disappeared to another part of the basement, Hoffman headed for the employee locker room. He found the hotel uniforms plus employee garb. He appropriated two hats and two jackets, and they put them on over their clothes. They checked to see if the doorway was clear, took the employee exit, and stepped outside. It was cold and misty.

They bunched up with other employees and crossed the street and went south. They saw two SS guards, so Hoffman murmured, "Relax and walk by them as though you do this every day."

She looked at him with terror in her eyes. He started to limp and said as they neared the soldiers, "I am so tired of the steam. It hurts my skin. And our boss doesn't care anything about the people who work there. He's lucky to have us as workers. If I weren't wounded, I'd go somewhere else."

They passed the guards, who ignored the group and stared at the hotel. Hoffman kept up with his gripes until they reached the next block and took a side street.

Caroline took a big breath. "Whew, that was close." She grinned. "Ever thought of a career on the stage?"

"We need to get to an alley and head to the station."

As he spoke, four SS guards with the help of a maid barged into their empty hotel room, ransacked it, and then sampled the food.

After the search, the guards phoned Bachmann. "They've disappeared." He glanced at Frolich with arched eyebrows. "I'll catch them at the border or a town nearby. They won't get to Switzerland, I promise you." He pounded his fist on the table. "Order the SS to cover Lindau, Friedrichshafen, and Meersburg train stations. If they manage to pay for a ride on a truck instead of a train, we'll seize them at the Konstanz border. Have four troops there with the existing border patrol."

"Yes, sir." Major Frolich left the room to phone but delayed calling. Finally he gave vague instructions to SS units to deploy at various locations including the border at Konstanz. He felt conflicted that he had to track down his wife and did his best to sabotage his efforts.

Hoffman and Caroline reached the Hirschgarten train station at 11:55 p.m. and checked the schedule. The next train would depart at 12:35 a.m. for Friedrichshafen, the end of the line, which happened to be twenty miles from the Swiss border. He bought two tickets.

Deutsche Reichsbahn—German National Railway— consolidated the former state railway companies into one. Allied bombs disrupted the rails, but the work crews made fast repairs throughout Germany and kept the system rolling. Because of rationed gas supplies and limited auto use, the country relied on the railroads, and the Third Reich emphasized that trains would operate on a twenty-four-hour basis.

Time couldn't go fast enough for Hoffman. He and Caroline sat far away on the platform's bench and watched as other passengers meandered in and congregated near the tracks. The shivering Hoffmans coveted the people's coats but tolerated the cold and remained silent. When soldiers made their rounds on the depot's platform, father and daughter would engage in a quiet conversation and acted as normal as possible holding their nerves in check.

Chapter 28

Upon the train's arrival at 12:35 a.m., both Hoffmans watched the people board, then they followed them to one of the passenger cars. He was surprised how many people traveled at this hour. When an older lady couldn't sit down because all the seats were taken, Hoffman offered his seat to her. The lady's husband thanked him, and as it turned out, he was a talkative chap.

He said, "Thank you. That was very nice of you, sir. She is tired with all the bombing. Going all the way to Friedrichshafen?"

"Yes."

"Live there or work?"

"I'm on my way to Konstanz to visit relatives."

"That's fortunate. Friedrichshafen is a mess. It was bombed last April. Most of the Old Town was destroyed."

"What's so important about Friedrichshafen?"

"They have four aviation manufacturers. We don't know what they do, but it must be important for the war. Zeppelin is one of the companies. Someone said that the plants use Jewish labor. The workers maintain the railroad line from this area to Munich so manufacturers can deliver parts to companies all over Germany."

"Any problem getting to Konstanz?"

"You can get a local train to Meersburg, and then a bus will take you to Konstanz, but the bus doesn't always run. The ferry

155

across Lake Constance is closed, so the only reliable way around the lake is to drive, so you might try to find someone with a car going that direction."

"Any hotels in Friedrichshafen?"

The elder man said, "A few. They were fixed up quickly to accommodate the workers. I didn't realize how important this place is. We're getting off at the next stop and will see our daughter."

When Hoffman returned to his seat after the couple left, he said quietly to Caroline, "Friedrichshafen is recovering from a bombing raid. When we arrive, we need to find a map and inquire about transportation. If we get separated, let's meet at a Catholic church."

She said, "I hope one is nearby."

The train pulled into Friedrichshafen at 6:25 a.m. and they followed the stream of passengers into the small train station.

Caroline said, "Now what do we do?"

"How far is Switzerland?"

"I've never been in this city before. I think we have twenty miles to go."

Hoffman said, "Let's go to the bathroom and clean up. We've been in these clothes a long time."

After the bathroom break, they proceeded to the front entrance, and Caroline led the way outside. As she opened the door, she saw three SS soldiers coming at her and quickly went back inside and pushed Hoffman into a seat on the bench. "Stay there." She ran to the side exit.

The three SS soldiers followed her and bumped into people along the way while Hoffman trailed them from ten yards behind. Caroline turned the corner toward the downtown and saw at this early hour that few people milled around. Most were intent on getting home as the stores were closed. She looked for escape routes amidst the bombed-out destruction and avoided the scattered debris by running on the streets and not the sidewalks, but the soldiers gained. She saw a small hotel and prayed they had a rear exit.

Out of breath, she asked a desk clerk, "Where's the back door?" He pointed and she headed in that direction. She turned down a hall and slipped into an open maintenance closet and hid. The soldiers also halted at the front desk and asked about a woman. When they heard that the fugitive went to the back, they raced down the corridors. Caroline heard the soldiers pass the hallway and doubled back to the front door and surprised the desk clerk. She went outside, looked left and right, and stopped as straight ahead beyond the downtown buildings appeared a damaged steeple, which had to be a Catholic or Lutheran church.

Hoffman lost all concern for his safety. His daughter ran fast, but he worried that other soldiers in the area would stop a fleeing woman, an obvious sign of a lawbreaker. He followed the chase as other Nazis joined in the fray. He didn't expect the SS to notice him since he wore a workman's jacket and hat.

Caroline honed in on the steeple and arrived at the Church of St. Nikolaus, a Catholic church, with its damaged white façade and shattered Gothic stained-glass windows. She looked around, went inside, and sat on a pew in the vacant nave. She caught her breath and tried to relax. She thought about staying here so her dad would find her. Or did the soldiers grab him?

The thought that the Nazis might capture her father disturbed her. Her affection had grown as she started to relate to him and enjoyed his presence during this perilous journey. What if Bachmann killed her father? Too many negative thoughts. She needed to prepare for the next confrontation. That's what her father would do. Besides, she didn't think the SS captured Hoffman. She smiled.

At that moment, a nun interrupted her reverie. "Is anything wrong, frau?"

She was thin, had a gaunt face, and a pious demeanor. No wonder she was a nun. She seemed close to God.

"Yes, I need help, sister. The SS are after me. Can I stay here?"

"Yes, my child. This is your sanctuary. God is here." She took her to a room to the right of the altar. "I'll get you something to drink. I'll be right back. Make yourself comfortable."

Five minutes later, SS guards entered with the nun standing behind them.

As Caroline passed the nun, who was flanked by the SS, she said in a loud tone, "I was foolish to think God would be here, sister. I hope you find him."

Hoffman saw the commotion and followed the crowd, which led him to police cars in front of a church. People gathered and wondered what happened inside as did Hoffman. Did they capture Caroline? As he waited, the church doors opened. Three SS soldiers and six police came out with a woman in handcuffs— Caroline. She looked around the street but not in his direction. She got into one car with the SS, and the autos accelerated out of the area. Caroline saved his life by shoving him to the bench at the train station. Now it was his turn to save hers.

As he jockeyed through the mob, he trudged down an avenue, his head full of thoughts. He was adrift in a strange city and didn't know how to find her, and if he did, what was the next move? His relationship with her had grown and given him so much meaning as a father and as a person, and now the Nazis captured his daughter, leaving an empty feeling in his stomach.

Chapter 29

June 27, 1944
Friedrichshafen, Germany

Snatched from the church and manhandled into the back seat of a sedan, Caroline sat between two SS guards. No one spoke as the auto sped past the crowd. Caroline did not see her father outside but felt his presence. Two rifles brushed against her legs and gave her a chill.

Where are they taking me? Will I live to see tomorrow? Dad, blow out the car's tires and save me from these thugs. She didn't like the separation from him; they had become a team against the Nazis ever since he bailed her out at the safe house. These past few days showed her that the two of them worked well together. She wished that they could have forged this relationship years ago.

Then reality hit her. How would her father find her? He would make every effort to rescue her as he did in Berlin, but now the SS expected him to come after her. They held the advantage and made her the bait. She prayed he couldn't locate her.

The car drove to a private parking area on the left side of a large castle. She winced at the guard's harsh grip as he pulled her past the ornate foyer on the first floor and pushed her into a dark storage room followed by the click of the locks. Without any light she moved cautiously with her hands out front, found the door, and turned the knob gently in case it might open. It didn't. She then blindly felt around the room locating boxes, chairs, and one table. Finally, she surrendered to the unlit space, reclined on her side, and cried.

One hour later, as she sat on the floor, gruesome thoughts surfaced in her panicky mind about how her captors would torture and molest her. The SS might kill her, and that possibility brought chills to her body. Finally, she collapsed on her right side in a fetal position and fell asleep.

Hours later, the door opened, the lights came on, and General Bachmann entered with two SS guards. "Caroline, so good of you to come. You've evaded me for a long time, but I have you now." Caroline shielded her eyes against the bright light.

"And now you will pay for your undercover activity against the Third Reich."

"I'm not a spy. Where did you get that crazy idea? Your men have followed me, so they have nothing to report, no mystery rendezvous, no clandestine meetings. I don't know any enemy spies."

Bachmann ogled at her with a pompous smile. "Spies use equipment like radios that my men wouldn't be able to find."

"Then search my house. I don't have anything to hide."

"We did search it, and guess what we found? A British-made Paraset Mark XV. We almost missed it since it was small, but it jumped into our hands once we found your hiding place."

"Where did you find it?"

"Why play games? Admit it like a brave soldier." He waited and looked her reaction. "You hid it in the attic inside a storage trunk."

The news struck Caroline like a crack of a whip and caused her to shiver. A spy radio in my house? And in the trunk? Konrad's trunk. I never opened it. It could mean only one thing. Konrad must be a spy. Her composure returned. "Somebody placed it there to frame me so you could call me a spy. And you fell for it."

Bachmann laughed. "You are quick on your feet, I'll give you that, but your excuse is false. For a while I thought it could be Konrad, but since he saved my life last year, I concluded that the only other option is you."

"He didn't tell me he saved your life."

"He pulled me out of my office during a bombing raid. If I had remained at my desk, the explosion would have killed me. So, you see. It couldn't have been him. He demonstrated his loyalty, something you never had for a country that took you in and treated you like royalty."

"That's why I married him. He's heroic." As she paused and swallowed, one thought took over her brain: she had to deflect suspicion from her husband. So she asked, "What are you going to do with me?"

"Don't worry. We'll find a suitable punishment. Right now, you're worth more as a hostage."

Caroline said, "What do you mean?"

"I'm after your father. We will put the word out that you are imprisoned here."

"Why do you want my father? What's he ever done to you?"

Bachmann's face lost its poise. He glared at her and crooked his eyebrows. "I loathe him and will destroy him." Caroline was surprised at the intensity. Then he added, "Let's just say he embarrassed me in front of the High Command, and I will not allow him to get away with it. He will regret the day he messed with me."

Bachmann turned with a clenched jaw and left the room followed by his SS escort. He forgot about the lights, and they remained on. Caroline surveyed her cell. The storage room contained jackets, brooms, cleaning supplies, mops, and a table at the far end. She saw the second door at the rear of the room that also was locked. She decided to sleep under the table because it provided better protection, but it did not protect her from the worry about her father. His stubbornness would not allow him to quit in his search for her.

She shifted her concentration to Konrad and the revelation that he was a spy for the Allies. She was committed to keep his secret, but how could he conceal this part of him from her? First, he gave orders to kill her and now he aided the Allies to defeat Germany. *Does he have other secrets that he kept from me?*

Two hours later, a priest entered her cell with a tray of soup, hard bread, a small amount of canned meat, and a few potatoes. "My name is Bishop Ernst Gruber. I understand you are an American spy and work against my country. Despite being a lost soul, we can still offer Jesus's love to the misguided."

With an edge to her voice, Caroline said, "Father, I am Catholic and not a spy. I'm married to an SS major."

"Frau, I have no military jurisdiction."

"What is this place? If you are a bishop, are you in charge?"

"This is a seminary. We educate men and ordain them as priests."

Caroline relaxed her shoulders. The bishop seemed kindly and brought her food. "Thank you for the food." She ate it while absorbed with his hardened face, not a face she would associate for a pastor or bishop. "I guess as a bishop, you have to protect your flock, your country, my new country. I've lived her for seven years, you know. I don't like death this war has brought."

"I don't either."

"I especially don't like it that the SS are going to kill me."

"Place your trust in God. He'll show you the way."

"I want to get out of this war and get to Switzerland. I don't want to kill anyone or have anyone get killed. So far, God has put up plenty of obstacles to my goal."

The bishop liked Caroline, but she worked evil by spying on Germany. "Follow the Lord's guidance. Your rewards come through your belief in Him and His son."

"You're caught in the middle, aren't you, Bishop Gruber? Of course, you have to side with your countrymen. It's too bad leaders don't follow the Sixth Commandment."

"Rely on prayer. It will guide you. Can I get you rosary beads to help you?"

"I don't use rosaries, Father."

"I will leave you now but will look in to make sure they treat you well."

"You mean before they kill me?" She showed her anger. Maybe she could sway him to her side but realized any effort on her part would be wasted. "Thank you, Father, for the food and the talk. As a captive," she sighed, "it's hard to show my grace. Maybe I can attain it in heaven."

"Go with God, my child."

Chapter 30

June 27, 1944
Friedrichshafen, Germany

Hoffman wandered back to the train station in a daze and stepped over rubble, most of which had been pushed to the side of the downtown streets. He wondered how he could locate his daughter without first confronting Nazis. Then he remembered the phone number he had memorized for the German Resistance in Munich and called from the train station. After five rings, a voice said, "Yes."

"Is Sky Hawk there? This is Stork." A silence continued for almost one minute until a new person came on the line. "This is Sky Hawk."

"I'm in trouble. My daughter was captured in Friedrichshafen by the SS. I don't know where she is nor what I can do. Can you assist?"

"Call me back in two hours." Sky Hawk hung up.

During the interim period, Hoffman scouted the area, had a meal, and then called. Sky Hawk answered, "I'm aware of your plight. Your daughter was taken to a seminary on the hills outside of Meersburg. Where are you?"

"I'm at the train station in Friedrichshafen. I'm trying to evade the SS."

"Stay there. We have someone nearby. The person's name is Werner and will meet you there within the hour."

"How will he know me?"

Kent Hinckley

"The individual knows your code name." Sky Hawk hung up.

Great. What if their guy is a fake as they were in Berlin? Is this Resistance the real thing? I don't have any choice. I have to trust someone. Maybe I can arrange an exchange with Bachmann: me for her.

He sat down on the bench and waited for Werner. Over the next five minutes, Hoffman watched men arrive and depart, but couldn't decide if one of these strangers was Werner.

Twenty minutes later, he fiddled with his shoes and wrenched his hands. Forty minutes passed, and he saw a man exit from the station's side door, but an older woman in tattered clothes interrupted his concentration and tapped him on the shoulder from his rear. He didn't want to be bothered by an old woman but answered with an impatient voice. "Yes?"

"Did you drop this train schedule?"

"No, I didn't." He turned away to look again for the man expecting him to work with Sky Hawk.

She sat down next to him, and he turned away. "Can you help me?"

"I'm busy right now."

She said, "I have a bird photo collection, but I don't have any pictures of a stork."

Hoffman turned around and looked at her. "Did you say stork?"

"Yes, my name is Werner."

Hoffman was shocked. She did not fill his profile of a Resistance member, but he recovered. "You are a brave woman."

She said, "Show me your ID." After she read it, she said, "Mr. Trautman, my cousin is named Oskar, so I'll remember it. Maybe we can go for a walk."

They got up and strolled along the streets strewn with broken concrete. Few people came in this devastated area, so they enjoyed privacy.

Werner said, "I'm sorry about your daughter. We have a colleague inside the seminary, and he can guide you."

"Who is he?"

"We don't know. Sky Hawk contacts him, usually over the phone. Sometimes he sends a coded letter. In this case, he has agreed to meet with you at one a.m."

"Did you say one in the morning?"

"Is that a problem?"

Hoffman shrugged his shoulders and in a soft voice said, "Okay, I'll be there."

"It will be dark, so you won't see him. The late hour allows him to get away from other priests and keep his identity hidden. Together, you can set up a plan."

"Where do I meet him?"

Werner gave him the address, directions, and background about the building. "It's an immense four-story structure built in 1750 with pink walls. The Prince Bishop of Konstanz used it as his residence, but his tenure ended when the religious diocese was dissolved in 1803. Since then, it has been used as a girls' school, a prison, and finally a secondary school. For fifteen years the castle remained vacant. Hitler gave it to the Archdiocese of Munich in 1935. Hitler was raised a Catholic, followed its anti-Semitic teachings, and often confided 'I am doing the Lord's work' to his inner circle.

"Inside Germany, the church hierarchy supported Hitler mainly as a bastion against Communism. This loyalty applies to the priests in this seminary."

Hoffman asked, "How do I get to the seminary?"

"A bicycle. Meersburg is only nine kilometers away."

Hoffman converted kilometers to miles. "So, it's five miles. Where do I get the bicycle?"

"It's parked in the rack outside the station. It has a blue frame with a basket in front. As for the meeting place, go to the seminary's parking lot on the right. Few cars are there. An old table and four chairs are near a big tree away from the building. Sit down and wait. If he doesn't show up at one, come back at three. Good luck, Mr. Stork." Werner walked away.

Hoffman needed to recon the seminary in the daytime and assess its vulnerabilities.

At 2:00 p.m. he biked to Meersburg, located on Lake Constance, and climbed the gentle slopes of the hill. He found the Neues Schloss — or New Castle — where the Priester-Seminar of Munich resided. As Hoffman peddled around, he saw the table and four old chairs in the parking lot on the right side. He also noticed a private parking area on the left side inside a gated enclosure. The chapel occupied the right front of the building. Making his way in the dark tonight would be easy. He wondered how he could sneak into the facility. Maybe the Resistance's inside guy could help him with that problem. After he checked the area out one more time, he rode to the town and secured a hotel room to get much needed sleep.

At 11:00 p.m. he awoke and left early to see how the building appeared at night. He wondered if Werner set a trap or if the mystery man inside the seminary was a Nazi spy that penetrated the Resistance. After he parked the bike in the bushes, he walked to the parking lot staying in the shadows. The tree blotted his view of the seminary, so he sat hidden at the table until 1:00 a.m.

At 1:10, a voice by the tree said, "Stork?"

Hoffman turned around. "Yes."

The man, clad in black robes, his face protected by the darkness, walked around the tree and said without any greeting, "We have bigger problems than I anticipated. It seems that General Bachmann arrived with ten SS guards and a Major Frolich, whom you may know. Bachmann is very interested in your daughter. She is safe for the moment and locked in a storage room with a guard outside."

Hoffman couldn't see the man's face but noticed fancy stitching on the hem of his cassock and said, "Are you a priest? Why are you helping me?"

The man sat down and said, "A priest wants to help his church followers. In this case, my German flock is being destroyed by a tyrant, so I want my countrymen back. Next question."

"Is Caroline in the seminary? And have you seen her?"

"Yes, to both questions."

"Describe her to me."

"I spoke with her a few hours ago. She's around thirty, beautiful, and full of spirit."

Hoffman still suspected a trick. "Tell me something about her that I might verify."

The priest thought about his conversation and said, "She doesn't use rosary beads."

Hoffman breathed a sigh of relief and said, "Sorry for the inquisition, but I had to be sure. The SS have thrown up many roadblocks."

"I understand. One can't be too careful."

Hoffman said, "Even though I'm the enemy, I don't want to kill anyone. I only want to take my daughter to Switzerland." The priest nodded and Hoffman continued. "Any ideas how to rescue her?"

"I have a couple. It is a privilege to assist the sacred relationship between father and daughter."

When the priest mentioned the sanctity of family, sadness crept over Hoffman. He hated to admit his failings. His legs and arms tensed and in a sorrowful voice he said, "I have not been a good father. This is my chance to make up for my inadequacy."

"Did you fight in the Great War?" asked the priest.

"Yes."

"Did your friends die in battle?"

Hoffman's image of that horrible time came to mind. "Y . . . yes."

"I've counseled many German soldiers with this same trauma, and it shows up in the family. You miss your friends and feel that no one's eyes should witness war's carnage. You also have guilty feelings that they died and you lived."

"German soldiers suffered as I have?"

"Soldiers fighting from all nations have this same hurt. War can kidnap one's soul."

Hoffman remembered Captain Lichterman's suggestion that Hoffman confide in a priest or minister to get help. Hoffman remained rigid in the chair and his body had goose bumps. "I can't shake it. Their ghosts come out and surround me constantly. They look so angry."

The priest spoke softly. "They want you to live. They want you to stop the torture and guilt that you have inflicted on yourself." He paused and became more thoughtful. "You will always have those awful memories, but they don't have to control you. Your friends want to assist. They want to help you rescue your daughter, too. Let them do that."

"Father, I don't know how."

"You're doing it right now. Be with them. Feel them. You'll come around. Believe me. You have the power to do it."

In silence, Hoffman called to his buddy, and Earl Zachery appeared as a filmy image with a grin and sparkly eyes. "Zach is here looking at me. He even smiled. Why didn't he smile before?"

"Maybe he was mad about your harsh treatment of yourself."

Hoffman soaked in the beautiful vision of his pal. Then others joined him with grins and soft eyes and gossamer bodies he could see through. "More of my men in the platoon have arrived. We were together so long ago."

"They are always with you."

Hoffman watched their facial expressions. Then they looked at the seminary and vanished.

Hoffman inhaled deeply. The air outside was still, and the moonless night made everything darker. Gradually he composed himself and took a few more breaths. "Father, thank you. Hope may exist for me yet."

Both remained quiet for a brief time while Hoffman took in a new reality.

When his sorrow subsided, the resolve for Caroline returned and he said, "Father, I need to make a plan."

"If you can make it to Konstanz's border crossing, which is seventy-four kilometers from here or about one hour by car, you both can be safe in Switzerland."

Chapter 31

For the next hour, the nameless priest went over the configuration of the seminary where Caroline was imprisoned and where Bachman and the soldiers resided. He mentioned the basement entrances, the chapel, kitchen, the living quarters upstairs for the priests, and the sleeping arrangements for the ten SS soldiers plus the special offices for Bachmann and the bishop.

Hoffman asked, "When is it the quietest in the seminary?"

"About 4:00 or 5:00 in the early morning."

"Any ideas about how to reach Caroline and get away from the SS?"

"Will you use the German Resistance to help you?"

"Yes, but only minor assistance. I think one man can succeed better than twenty. I need diversions, and the Resistance can provide some, but I haven't thought about any specifics yet."

"To distract the SS, you need an entry and an escape route. They have cars and trucks. They can mobilize the local police. What do you have?"

"Nothing like that. I hope my wits will find an answer."

"They have posted guards everywhere. Even if you get her, their fire power is immense. You would need to carry ten machine guns to defend yourself."

"Do you have a key to her room?" Hoffman asked.

"I may be able to get one, but how do I get it to you?"

Hoffman said, "Leave it on the altar in the chapel under a piece of cloth. I can pick it up."

"I'll leave it on the right side."

Hoffman asked, "Can you provide two cassocks and hats? We can disguise ourselves as priests."

"I'll leave them in the basement."

"If I start a fire, can you enlist the support of the soldiers to put it out?"

The priest answered, "I can suggest it, but I don't know if Bachmann would agree to it. Don't ignite anything valuable. What else do you want me to do?"

"What entrances can I use to get into the chapel?"

"I'll open a basement window in the front to the right of the drain; the SS doesn't know it exists. You can use it at night without fear of being caught. No one goes into the basement at night."

Hoffman released a huge sigh. "Lots of variables I need to think about."

"When will you make your move?"

"Probably in two days." He paused. "How is Caroline?"

"As I said earlier, I gave her food and blessed her. It's an awkward situation since I don't condone her capture and can't influence Bachmann. He has an obsession about you and won't be deterred."

"Are they torturing her?"

"No. She is locked up, and Bachmann expects you to rescue her. He's concerned that the Resistance may attack, but his main focus is on you."

"If something happens to me, please tell her I love her and wish we were together again as a family."

"I'll watch over her and make sure she is fed. Go with God, my son." The priest departed into the night.

At the hotel, Hoffman ate a small meal and slept well. The following night, June 29 at 1:00 a.m., he snuck into the seminary through the basement window unlocked by the rogue priest. He needed to contort his body to make it around a garbage chute and slide down to the floor. He walked slowly around the dark room, found the hats and folded cassocks using a flashlight, and made his way to the main floor. One lesson drummed into him from his years in the army: do your own reconnaissance whenever possible. Don't rely on another's intelligence, especially reports coming from your own side.

He moved through corridors, veered into the chapel that had one small light bulb lit by the side door, and stood quietly to see if guards were present. He moved to the altar and located the door key. The shadowy insides revealed that the chapel held expensive furniture and tapestries. At the rear was wooden scaffolding used by repairman to fix a broken cornice on the sixteen-foot ceiling. He saw various chemicals they used; some were flammable.

Silently, he moved into the foyer and discovered the office section. One door had a sign that read BISHOP and the other doors went unmarked. He opened the bishop's unlocked door and scanned the desk, phone, closet, and a large steel safe. Then he probed the other office, conference room, and hallway that led to the kitchen and dining area.

When he moved from this section, a distant tap of boots announced a guard's entrance down the hallway, so Hoffman jumped behind a curtain, smacked his body against the wall, and flattened his cheek against the cold stone. As the sound of approaching boots grew, Hoffman sweated and recalled the danger in the dark Argonne Forest in 1918 and the massive tree trunks that enveloped him. After the German passed the curtains, the clack of boots faded into the chapel. Hoffman's body remained rigid as he gasped for air.

He was angry that his visions appeared in this perilous moment. The fright almost caused him to yell at the mirage to leave, but instead he stifled his voice and willed the hallucination to disappear. As the panic slackened, his composure returned; he scolded himself for behaving in a nonmilitary manner. A soldier on a mission, a very personal one, needed to function with purpose and calmness.

When the SS guard returned to his post, Hoffman mopped his brow, took a deep breath, and scurried to the rear of the building near the storage room where Caroline was held. When another guard suddenly entered the hall from a different location, Hoffman stepped into a closet and kept his poise. He estimated that each guard made their rounds every fifteen minutes.

Hoffman continued down a passageway for ten more minutes, but a guard, who came from yet another direction, entered the corridor and took an alternate route near him, so Hoffman hid under an adjacent table. The guard opened a door across from Hoffman's hiding place and went in. Hoffman peered under the tablecloth and saw that the room contained maintenance items like mops, rags, and cleaning solvents, but it also stored rifles, pistols, ropes, grenades, and what appeared to be dynamite. Grenades and dynamite in a seminary?

After the sentry returned to his post, Hoffman entered the room, glanced around, stole a handgun, and checked the box of dynamite to confirm that it was the real thing. It was, but he didn't see any matches. Still on the alert for guards, he moved to another wing to check the ceiling, windows, stairways, doors, and hallways as best as possible given the minimal light.

Next, he plotted a possible escape route. He went outside and surveyed the parking lot on the left side of the chapel. Under the waning light of an outdoor bulb, he found three Kubelwagens with swastikas on the sides. Two sedans plus one limousine probably belonged to the seminary; only the seminary vehicles had keys in them. Apparently, the priests didn't expect anyone to steal from the church or risk life and limb against the SS. The military vehicles were clean and appeared to be well maintained. The church cars, however, were older models, showing dents and scrapes on the side.

From the parking lot, Hoffman walked around the building to get the lay of the land, seek escape paths, and to proceed to the driveway where he crossed the road and reclaimed his bicycle.

Chapter 32

June 29-30, 1944
Meersburg, Germany

Encouraged from his reconnaissance, Hoffman returned to his hotel room and knew that his plan, whatever it was, would require a diversion. He arranged with Sky Hawk to have the German Resistance fire rounds of bullets at the church's exterior in the early morning, which would occupy the SS and pin them down away from Caroline's location.

With information from his recon and cooperation from Sky Hawk, Hoffman was primed to develop a strategy, but no matter how hard he tried, ideas would not appear. Instead words from the priest filled his head about the German soldiers who experienced shell shock from the Great War. This knowledge gave him little satisfaction since he considered the Jerries brutal and without any conscience.

The priest advised him to confront the nightmares and feel them. Didn't Hoffman do that with the pastor already? In the safety of his hotel room, he thought about those bleak moments in the Argonne Forest with death strewn everywhere, and death terrified him. He stood up, paced around the room, and noticed his rapid pulse.

When he returned to his bed and sat down, he recalled the fright that took him to 1918 while he hid behind the curtains in the seminary. Why did the trauma kick in at that moment? I live in 1944, not back then. Hoffman contemplated this phenomenon for many minutes without understanding. He couldn't save Caroline if he had to compete with multiple realities. His feelings took him to the ambush, and afterward he experienced the sensation of his presence in the hotel room. Neither had any charge. He asked his dead comrades for guidance, and they came out of the ethers but withheld their comments.

"Come on, men. I need help." But they just looked at him.

Finally, he tried a new idea. He felt his existence in the hotel room plus let the feelings in the Argonne Forest roam around, a double dose of perception. As he surrendered control over both sensations, the awareness calmed him. The experience reminded him of watching a movie. He sat on the bed aware of being in a room in 1944 but observed action from long ago. He could still feel fear as if it came from a scary movie like Frankenstein, but knew he wasn't in danger. When he treated his nightmares in a similar fashion, the Argonne trauma lost its intensity. The dead bodies were dead bodies, and even if the corpses were gruesome, they couldn't kill him. He viewed them as objects akin to looking at a tree or hotel table. When he saw the death masks of his men and the serenity on their faces, his anxiety subsided. His clenched muscles relaxed. Vitality returned and his shoulders felt lighter.

However, he still felt the knot in his stomach. He went to the bathroom, looked in the mirror, and reflected. Would this mission be his last? Either he'd die or he wouldn't. He had no choice. Fathers come to the aid of their children.

After he faced his mortality, the terror dissipated. Then Hoffman noticed the table, the paper, and pencil. He touched the sturdy tabletop and felt the wood of the pencil as his thoughts returned to the mission. With a refreshed mind, he addressed his strategy. The plan called for him to enter through the window in the front and reach the basement. Hoffman agonized over the next part since no matter what he did, the risks would be massive. He considered the possibility that he could be caught early and never see his daughter again. He wouldn't dwell on this prospect.

His inspection of the seminary showed openings as well as obstacles. He ran his hand through his hair, rubbed his eyes, and walked around the room in a struggle to devise an escape. Finally,

Hoffman came up with a scheme that entailed igniting chemicals on the scaffolding and wearing the priest's cassock as a disguise.

Hoffman counted on the element of surprise, but since all plans never go smoothly, he weighed alternate options. Short of a frontal assault by a battalion of infantry, acting as a priest provided certain advantages. If an SS soldier stopped him, he would shoot him. The off chance of bumping into Konrad he hoped would not occur.

He planned to soak the wooden planks with chemicals and to ignite the scaffolding at 5:15 a.m., which would allow flames to build. He had directed the Resistance to provide sweeping gunfire at 5:25. Once their firepower commenced, he would find his way to Caroline's locked door around 5:30 or 5:35.

Hoffman was nervous as he tried on the clerical robe over his clothes. He noticed that the hem of his cassock did not have any fancy stitching, which meant he rated as a junior priest. He put a matchbox in his right pocket and dropped the key to Caroline's cell in his left pocket. The gun he purloined from the maintenance room went into his belt hidden underneath the robe.

He stuffed his other pistol, Gebauer's Luger with silencer, into his pants' waist on his left side underneath the robe and his shirt. He found he could move easily wearing a cassock, so with his preparations concluded, he removed his robe and accessories. He rested, took a breath, and wished he were driving to Konstanz with Caroline in the passenger's seat without any Nazis around. Disregarding his daydreaming, Hoffman sobered to the reality of the present and eliminated any thoughts of failure.

He tried to take a nap without success so decided to start early. He gathered his gear and reached the seminary at 3:00 a.m. Even though he planned his mission for 5:15 a.m., he wanted to sneak inside and give himself large swaths of time to scout and adjust to the darkness. Hoffman reached the basement, put on the cassock, went into the chapel, and probed the first floor to double check the guards' recon schedule. The guards adhered to their routine of fifteen-minute intervals and yawned while performing their patrol.

In between the guards' rounds, Hoffman hid his supplies near the scaffolding, found the flammable chemicals, and buried them near a corner under a tarp. As he sat back and rechecked his equipment, Hoffman noticed ghosts slowly approaching him from the altar. As they converged, he saw that they were his buddies. Hoffman tried to beat them away with his arms. Get away. Not now. Come at me when I'm in Switzerland. Their visages drifted nearer, smiled, raised their diaphanous hands showing the V for victory sign, and disappeared into the shadows. Hoffman nodded.

When the 5:05 guard finished his route, Hoffman poured oil and paint thinner on the planks, grabbed his box of matches from his pocket, and lit them. They burst into flames, and Hoffman dashed out of the chapel to a spot behind the curtains.

At 5:20, the new guard smelled the smoke, ran to the scaffolding, and saw the blaze. He alerted other guards who awakened a priest who roused thirty other priests to put out the blaze. At 5:35—ten minutes late—the German Resistance from a position in the hills, fired their rifles into the seminary's rear walls.

With many clergy and soldiers scurrying around, Hoffman dodged them, raced through the chapel, past the foyer, into the hallway, and stopped at the oak door of the storage room that kept Caroline as prisoner. He had the extra cassock and hat for her under his arm and drew his pistol that he stole from the maintenance room. He slid the key into the lock, and turned it slowly. The lock opened, and he walked into the lighted room. It was empty.

Chapter 33

Panic set in as he turned to depart, then another door in back of the room opened and Caroline with a frightened look lurched forward with a gun barrel jabbed into her neck. The gun was held by Bachmann. Two SS soldiers accompanied him aiming their rifles at Hoffman. As they made their way to the middle of the room, Hoffman backpedaled and noticed that Major Konrad Frolich and a priest brought up the rear. Hoffman spotted the fancy needlework on the robe's hem.

The guard said, "Raise your hands and drop the gun." Hoffman threw it across the floor. The priest, who in fact was the bishop, said, "I forgot to tell you that a back door opened to an office occupied by Major General Bachmann." He smirked.

Caroline had tears in her eyes and said, "You knew my rescue was hopeless. Why did you come?"

Bachmann said, "We watched you ever since you entered the building. You took your sweet time getting here." In his dark SS uniform, he looked at Hoffman in his clergy outfit. "You look so pious. I have a confession to give you." Bachmann paused. "Father, I will sin. And after I kill you, I will sin again." He looked at Caroline and laughed.

"Okay, you made your point. You captured me. Now let my daughter go."

"Oh, I'm not done with her, but first, you and I need to settle up."

Caroline interrupted and spoke to the bishop. "Father, can't you help? This is outright murder."

Bachmann said, "Caroline, dear. The bishop rigged this whole thing. You're wasting your breath."

Caroline's face twisted and stared at the bishop. "What do you mean?"

At that moment, the gunfire from the Resistance stopped. Bachmann looked at his watch. "Right on time." He grinned at Hoffman. "Let me provide the introductions." He turned his head in the bishop's direction. "Colonel, this is Bishop Ernst Gruber. You spoke to him two nights ago."

Hoffman's nostrils widened and eyes glared at the Catholic clergy. "So, you're a bishop and set this meeting up. Jesus would be proud. You should replace your cross with a swastika."

Bishop Gruber said, "Herr Hoffman, your mission was doomed from the start. You expect me to go against my country?"

"I expect you to honor your vows and follow the Commandments." Bishop Gruber ignored Hoffman and turned to Bachmann. "I should leave now and make that deposit you requested."

Bachmann watched the bishop leave the room and then gazed at Hoffman. "It's time for biblical vengeance. You know, an eye for an eye."

Konrad said, "I'll take Caroline from the room."

Bachmann nodded. "And call Sky Hawk. We won't need him anymore. We'll take care of Stork now."

As Konrad was about to leave the room, Hoffman raised his voice. "You're a hell of a son-in-law. You can't fool me. You're going to the maintenance closet and getting dynamite to blow me up, right? Well, let me help you." Both Caroline and Konrad were dumfounded at these comments as Hoffman reached into his pocket, which prompted the two SS thugs to step forward and push their rifles at Hoffman's chest.

Hoffman raised his right hand, slowly opened the pocket in his cassock, and brought out a small box. Looking away from the guards, he thrusted the box at Konrad. "Here's some matches. Or do you want me to light them for you?"

Konrad took them with a dazed look. Bachmann said, "That's a good idea. But first, I have other plans."

Caroline through her tears said, "You shouldn't have come."

Hoffman said, "I couldn't help myself. You are such a blessing to me, sweetheart."

Bachmann shouted, "Shut up, you two." He looked at Caroline and said, "Take a last look. You'll never see him again." He ordered Konrad, "Take her out of here."

As Konrad grabbed her by the arm and pulled her toward the door, she said, "Dad, I love you."

Hoffman said, "I love you, Caroline."

Bachmann got in the last word, "Isn't that touching." He looked at Hoffman, and exclaimed so everyone in the room could hear, "Don't worry about her. We have plenty of men to keep her company after you go."

Chapter 34

June 30 1944
Meersburg, Germany

Caroline didn't want to be separated from her father, so she grappled with Konrad as he dragged her out of the room. When they reached the hall outside, Caroline snapped at her husband while still in his grasp. "Are you a spy? You must do something. You must save him."

Konrad searched and found the maintenance closet and pushed her inside.

Caroline said, "How can you go along with the murder of my father?"

With his arm around her waist, he located the box with the dynamite inside, then seized her shoulders. "Caroline, honey, I need you to help me right now without any questions."

"Why should I?"

"Remember why you married me?"

"Yes." She paused. "Because I can trust you."

He looked into her eyes and said, "For that reason, stay here. I'll be right back." He took two sticks of dynamite and left the room.

With people inside the castle struggling in the chaos of the fire, no one noticed that Konrad slipped out the back door that took him to the exterior of the storage room. Sunrise had commenced fifteen minutes ago at 5:41 a.m. and provided some light. He looked around, didn't see anyone, and dug a small hole under the outside wall followed by the placement of the dynamite. Using a match from the box Hoffman had given him, he lit the fuses and ran back to the closet. Upon his return, he hugged his wife and together they crouched on the floor. "I hope this works."

After Hoffman watched his daughter leave, Bachmann approached and slugged him in the mouth and in the gut. Hoffman bent over but remained standing, so Bachmann pushed him down and kicked him in the ribs. "This is going to be fun, you ass." And then he kicked him again.

Hoffman had one chance. He was an excellent judge of character and hoped his intuition was right about Konrad. Would Konrad risk his position to help? Hoffman guessed yes, but it was a long shot.

As Bachmann came near him again, an explosion obliterated the far wall and caused both SS soldiers to fall on the floor stunned by the force. Bachmann was knocked near the chairs as blood trickled down his face, but he had the presence to creep out the back door and let the guards deal with the chaos. Hoffman staggered, but because he anticipated the blast, he withstood most of the impact although he strained to stand up. He retrieved his pistol from the floor, put it into his pocket, went to one dazed guard, and snatched the rifle and two clips of ammunition. He also grabbed the extra clerical robe and biretta where he dropped them.

As Hoffman fled the room, three other SS soldiers ran from the corridor. Hoffman ordered, "Help the guards." The soldiers rushed inside and ignored Hoffman since they thought he was a priest. He saw Konrad and Caroline at the doorway of the closet and motioned them inside. "Thanks. You've restored my faith in Germans."

Konrad said, "How did you know I'd help you?"

"From MI6. I'll elaborate later."

"Clever how you provided matches for me."

"You told me you took a demolition class." Then Hoffman said to Caroline, "Put this robe on, and tuck your hair inside the hat." Turning to Konrad, "I'll divert their attention and meet you at the gate in the private parking lot. Steal a car and let's get out of here." Hoffman kept the pistol and gave the rifle and ammo to Konrad. Hoffman moved into the hallway and searched for an escape path through the firefighters.

The two bloodied SS guards had recovered from the impact and were helped up by three fresh soldiers. All five exited the partially destroyed room and recognized Hoffman in his priestly robes as he ran down the hall and scrambled to the left passageway into the chapel. The guards took up the chase. When it was safe, Konrad and Caroline took the right corridor.

Hoffman evaded the other clergy while they doused the fire. The aisle that stretched to the altar provided an opening, and he veered right and opened the door to the basement. The SS soldiers had a more difficult time through the cluster of priests but glimpsed the fleeing Hoffman as he slipped into the basement. The location of the light switch remained a mystery, so Hoffman felt his way through the dark and around the furniture as he had on two previous occasions.

The SS entered the unlit room and did not know the location of the switch either, so they bumped into furniture and cabinets. They stopped to hear any noise that Hoffman might make, but he didn't move.

In the silence, Hoffman waited near the shaft that would take him outside but realized that moving into the narrow access would create a racket and make him an easy target. He grabbed his pistol, not the Luger, and flung it across the room. The five soldiers heard the thud on the far wall and fired their rifles repeatedly. Hoffman sprang into the space and crawled upward into the hollow passageway that took him to the small utility door that led to the outside. The guards heard sounds from Hoffman's movement and pumped lead in that direction.

When Hoffman exited, he scanned the area and saw the taillights of the seminary limousine that headed north and thought the bishop was in it. He ran to the parking lot to locate

Konrad and Caroline but did not see anyone. Hoffman proceeded through the gate and cautiously moved through the bushes on the right side opposite the parked vehicles.

With the silencer attached to the Luger in hand, he went under an arch, around a ledge, and kept within the shadows amidst hedges, but could not spot anyone. The entire lot seemed deserted. Where were Caroline and Konrad? He took three careful steps forward and an SS guard stepped out from a column into the dim light. "Halt, Colonel."

Overcoming his initial shock, Hoffman, partially shielded by shrubbery, furtively placed his pistol on the ledge and said, "What do you want, my son? My name is Father Trautman."

"I know every priest here including the bishop. We have captured your friends over there so let's join them. It'll be a pleasure to kill two Americans."

Hoffman withheld his surprise and thought, Now what? and said to the guard, "The bishop knows me. He'll verify my identity. Where is he?"

"Too late. He just departed for Switzerland. I'm sure General Bachmann will recognize you."

"By all means, let's go to Bachmann."

"But first, let me search you."

Hoffman anticipated being frisked, so he spread his arms out, looked straight ahead, and kept his awareness of the ledge holding his pistol. The guard felt around Hoffman's body and legs. "All right. You're clean. Let's go." The guard, with his rifle aimed at his enemy, backed up to give Hoffman room to make it through the brush. Still in the shadows, Hoffman pretended to trip over a root and with this distraction, he grabbed the gun from the ledge. Using his body to shield the weapon from the careful gaze of the SS, Hoffman asked, "Which way do you want me to go?"

The SS guard motioned with his rifle by pointing the barrel to the left. As he did so, Hoffman's right hand came from behind, and he fired two shots. The silencer muffled its usual blast with phfft-phfft. Hoffman clutched the soldier and eased him onto the ground at the side of the building. He kept the rifle. Next, he quietly slipped down the covered walkway. As he neared the side door, he overheard Konrad. "I am an SS major. Release me before I report you to Major General Bachmann."

"We are under Major General Bachmann's specific orders to capture you and your wife."

Concealed by the foliage, Hoffman observed two guards pointing their rifles at the captives. He stepped around the plants and approached the sentries from the rear, aimed his pistol, and phfft-phfft. Konrad and Caroline were surprised to see the guards fall and jolted when Hoffman appeared. He said, "Did you find a car?"

Konrad said, "Not yet." He picked up a rifle from one guard and bolted across the lot to a parked car. Hoffman gathered the other rifle and passed it to Caroline. "Let's get to Switzerland."

Caroline said, "Glad you have that silencer." Konrad got into the sedan, started the engine, and backed up so Hoffman and Caroline could get in.

Konrad said, "I'd gun it, but I don't think the transmission would last." The auto, with its lights off, left the seminary and headed north. Hoffman said, "Can we catch the bishop?"

"Maybe. He doesn't drive, and the priests that do, drive in an unhurried manner, but the condition of the bishop's car far surpasses ours. I'd bet on the bishop." One mile later, Konrad turned the car lights on. Two miles later, he said, "We have company. Lights are gaining on us. Military vehicles are in excellent condition. Also, our gas is low."

Chapter 35

Four SS soldiers, a squad leader, and three young riflemen jumped into a Kubelwagen in the seminary's parking facility and bolted after the old sedan.

The driver, a private from Wiesbaden, said, "We should catch them within minutes."

The squad leader ordered, "Get your weapons at the ready. As we get close, we'll shoot out the tires and kill them."

Another rifleman from Sandhausen, a rural parish near Heidelberg, asked, "Are you sure we're supposed to shoot an SS officer and two priests?"

"They're spies, you dummkopf. They dynamited the seminary."

Konrad pressed on the accelerator of the rickety sedan and the engine gasped, belched, and did not speed up. He kept a vigilant eye in the rearview mirror and said, "Their vehicle is a Kubelwagen and more powerful than ours. And it's fast. What do we do when it catches us?"

"How much time do we have?"

Konrad said, "About five minutes if not sooner."

Hoffman waited until he saw a curve in the road. "Go past the bend and stop on the right side before those boulders." After braking, the car skidded on the dirt and came to a stop with a

191

shudder. Hoffman grabbed the two rifles taken from the guards at the seminary plus the ammo magazines and gave one to Konrad.

Caroline said, "Now what?"

Hoffman pointed to the field. "Sprint to the forest. The trees will protect you and force the Nazis to expose themselves as they look for you. They should be prime targets."

The four SS riflemen followed the arc of the road until they spotted the parked sedan. They slowed down and coasted next to it with rifles pointed outward. Once stopped, they noticed two people — a man holding a rifle and a priest — running to the edge of the forest almost fifty yards away.

With dust scattered around their vehicle, the squad leader said, "You two chase after them and finish them off." He then looked at the driver. "Stay here and cover me."

The first two SS soldiers ran to the clearing, aimed their rifles, and fired. Because of their haste and gasping for air, they lost stability in their arms and the barrage missed. They continued to run after the fugitives, fired their rifles on the way, and continued to miss.

Konrad and Caroline reached the edge of the forest when bullets flew past them and hit tree branches. "Just keep running and keep your head down. We'll be fine when we get into the forest."

"I hope you're right. These are SS and we're not battle-hardened," said Caroline.

"These are young kids and haven't had much training. We'll find a way." They made it into the woods and Konrad pointed, "Go to the left behind that big tree and be quiet." He went to the right behind another tree.

The driver and squad leader remained by the Kubelwagen, wary of an ambush and scanning the vicinity to locate the third person who they suspected hid behind the rocks.

As the squad leader searched the area, the driver approached the sedan to check if anyone was in it. His eyes then swept the rocks and road. "No one is here."

Both glanced at the other two SS soldiers running in the field. The two soldiers neared the forest, slowed down, and stopped short of the trees. They didn't know where the enemy went and so fired at two openings in the thicket. The SS soldiers advanced inside of the tree line, and side by side slipped deeper into the foliage and fired at any noise.

The driver watched intently and wondered if his comrades had killed the escapees. After the initial shots, no other sounds erupted except for birds chirping and insects' shrill grating. Thirty seconds later, six shots were discharged followed by silence. The two guards by the vehicles worried and kept their eyes focused on the forest. One yelled to his comrades, "Is everything all right?"

More silence.

The driver shouted again. "Hey, are you okay?"

At that moment, Hoffman popped up from a big rock on the far right and blasted four times. After his first flurry missed, he fired again and killed one and wounded the driver. Hoffman expected Konrad and Caroline to have won the skirmish and waved his arm for them to return. Hoffman heard Konrad's voice. "We're okay."

In the meantime, Hoffman disarmed the wounded soldier who shook at the prospect of a bullet about to come to his head.

"Where's your first aid kit?"

"In the car."

Hoffman returned and bandaged the driver as best as possible, laid him near the field, and left a canteen of water for him. He dropped the rifles and ammo into the faster and better maintained military vehicle, and the trio departed to pursue the bishop in their new car.

Hoffman asked, "No problems with the SS in the forest?"

Konrad replied, "It went just as you predicted. They never saw us behind the trees. Have you fought in a forest before?"

"Years ago." Hoffman moved away from this subject and said, "How far to Konstanz?"

"About forty-five minutes. We have to go around the lake and should be able to overtake the bishop."

The three relaxed from the SS encounter and felt euphoric since they fought off death once again. Caroline faced her father. "Why didn't you give me the rifle? I'm a better shot than Konrad. Or is it that I'm a woman? Or you don't trust me?"

"You're a better shot than I am, but if you had the weapon, you'd have to live with the killing."

Caroline wondered how she would feel if she took a life. A few moments in thought passed and then she asked her husband, "I'm confused. When did you become a spy?"

Hoffman said, "You work for MI6, right?"

"How did you figure it out?"

Hoffman said, "When MI6 told me that the SS suspected Caroline was a spy, they added that their contact came from inside Bachmann's group. I knew it had to be you, Konrad. Who else? You were in the Wehrmacht when you married Caroline and probably cherished Prussian traditions and not the insanity of Hitler. Being an agent is tricky, but I imagine that part of your personality for risk-taking appealed to my daughter even if she didn't know you were a spy."

Caroline asked, "When did you become a British spy?"

Konrad still kept his concentration on the road but said, "A few months after our wedding in November 1938."

"You mean Kristallnacht, the Night of Broken Glass?" asked Caroline.

"When the Nazis torched synagogues, destroyed Jewish businesses, and killed and arrested thousands of Jews, I signed up and eventually became part of MI6. My great-grandmother was Jewish."

Caroline said, "I understand, but then why did you order the SS at the safe house to kill us?"

Konrad said, "If they captured you, I couldn't intervene. I didn't want you to suffer a gruesome death by Gestapo torture. Can you forgive me?"

She gave him a kiss on the cheek, sat back, and said, "What other secrets have you kept from me?"

"Believe me, you would worry frantically if you knew this one."

She changed the subject. "I didn't know you saved Bachmann's life. When did that occur?"

"About one year ago. I needed to secure Bachmann's confidence. I planted dynamite near his office, and when the American planes dropped their bombs near the building I set a timer and physically pulled Bachmann out of his office. When the dynamite exploded and we suffered minor injuries instead of death, he was convinced of my loyalty. He even awarded me an Iron Cross."

Hoffman said, "So intelligence school taught you well."

"I didn't plan on acquiring that skill, but it turns out that I gained more from the demolition phase than any other part of the class."

Caroline said, "Why is the bishop going to Switzerland? He inferred that his trip was assisting the SS."

Konrad said, "He's going to make a deposit. I've even gone there a few times for the same reason."

"Deposit? What for?"

"Bachmann confiscates gold and convertible currency— mainly British pounds—to hide in Swiss banks. They plan to fund escapes to South America for the SS after the war."

"Why don't they deposit Reichsmarks?" Caroline asked.

"It's not convertible. No one outside of Germany will accept them. The ships will accept Swiss francs, British pounds, and American dollars for passage to Buenos Aires."

Hoffman said, "Why use the seminary? Can't the SS cross the border with the cash and visit the Swiss Bank?"

"Bachmann trusts no one, so keeping it confidential takes priority, and he trusts the bishop to store the currency in the large safe, to deposit it, and to minimize questions and searches from the border guards. No one would suspect the seminary as part of the government. By the way, the castle is not a seminary. It's a cover for the priests to prepare fake identification cards and passports for escaping SS. This effort has the blessing of the Vatican because Hitler supported the church despite the fact that he and the SS murdered many priests who didn't go along with the Nazi program. The Vatican is more afraid of Communism — which is anti-God and anti-church — than Nazism."

Caroline said, "So how much money is stuffed into the bishop's trunk?"

"Not sure. The money this time was taken from the Central Bank of Romania."

Caroline asked, "So, what will be Bachmann's reaction when he finds out we stole his money?"

"Bachmann will erupt. He will throw things around the seminary and will shoot Jesus and the cross in the chapel if he gets mad enough."

She said, "But he can't do anything to us in Switzerland, can he? Switzerland's neutral."

Hoffman said, "If they let us in?"

Konrad thought about the status of neutrality. "Switzerland will cooperate with Bachmann if money changes hands. Besides, Switzerland depends on Germany for the bulk of its coal and other items. Germany relies on the Swiss for its currency and for precision instruments for its weapons. They worked out an understanding years ago to avoid a German invasion. Once we enter Switzerland, the rules of neutrality dictate that we can't leave until the end of the war. Neutrality laws prevent soldier repatriation to their home country."

"Suits me fine," said Hoffman. "I've had enough fighting."

The vehicle picked up speed, and its occupants looked forward to catching the bishop's car.

Chapter 36

At 7:30, with the morning sun gleaming in a cloudless sky, Konrad raced around the lake to Konstanz and sighted a vehicle ahead. "There's a car, and I think it's the bishop's. I can draw level with them shortly."

Caroline said, "How do we stop them?"

Hoffman picked a rifle from the back seat. "This should persuade them."

"Sir, he's a Catholic bishop."

"Caroline, have you forgotten that he set us up so the SS could kill us? Forgive me if I don't give a damn about his religious title." Caroline tensed upon hearing her father's anger.

Konrad said, "We could bluff them."

Caroline regained her composure. "Sir, I agree with that suggestion."

Hoffman said, "Your mother raised you well. You are a kind person."

"She didn't want me to be a soldier."

"Since we're at war, it's fortunate that I became one. My goal is to get you to Switzerland, for you and for Kaye's sake, and I'll do whatever is necessary to accomplish that."

The bishop's sedan was three car lengths away, and Konrad said, "Colonel, are you ready? I'll pull alongside and motion for them to pull over. Don't shoot the tires."

Colonel Hoffman's indignant glare and his rifle persuaded the driver to slow down and park on the shoulder. The driver, a young priest with shaky hands, complied. The bishop lowered his head in the back seat and wondered if he'd survive the confrontation.

When both cars stopped, Hoffman exited and aimed his rifle at the driver. "Get out."

The occupants followed the command, their bodies trembling. Hoffman, still dressed in his cassock, looked at the bishop adorned in his fancy robe. "Hitler kills Catholic priests who disagree with his inhumanity. What should I do with you? My finger is so ready to pull the trigger."

Caroline intervened. "Sir, don't do it. You'll regret it. What would Mom say?"

The bishop muttered, "If you kill us, you'll rot in hell."

"But it's saintly to have us killed, huh? You make me sick. Take off that robe."

Caroline tried to speak, but Konrad hushed her. "Honey, it's all right." He saw that Hoffman was letting off steam and trying to unnerve the bishop.

Hoffman said, "Konrad, check out the sedan. Are the keys in it? Does it have enough gas? And examine the trunk."

The bishop said, "You are interfering with God's work. Let us go."

Hoffman said, "I don't like it when your God wants you to kill me."

The bishop reluctantly removed his robe, and Hoffman laughed when he saw the ratty underwear and shirt underneath. Picking up the bishop's embroidered robe, purple biretta, and valise, Hoffman folded up the garments.

Konrad returned and said, "I've never seen so much cash and gold in my life. What a haul."

The bishop said, "That belongs to God, donations for the church."

Hoffman countered, "So, you deposit these donations in Switzerland all the time?"

"Well, not all the time, but frequently."

"So, the banks and border guards know you?"

"Of course. I'm a bishop. They respect me and my position in the church. You, however, show how rude and crass Americans can be."

Hoffman fumed. "Please forgive me, Father. I didn't know the Central Bank of Romania cleaned out its vault to give you and your forgers a large donation."

Caroline said, "Sir, let's go. Leave them alone."

"I can't let someone get away with trying to kill me. Think of all the dead people killed by Nazis because this bishop and other clergy support the Führer."

The bishop started to sweat. "I'm a man of God. How dare you?"

"But you don't act like a man of God. You act like an executioner during the Reign of Terror. You and the Nazis kill dissidents, Slavs, and Jews. You are killing the children of God. Do you think God is happy about that?"

The bishop said, "If you kill me, you will be like the Nazis."

"My, how you turn the tables. It's acceptable for you and the Nazis to kill, but not acceptable for me to act like a Nazi. You have sure found your calling in life." Hoffman walked away in disgust and went to the sedan. Curious to see the riches, he opened the trunk, looked in the bags, and nodded at the sight of so many bills. He took ten one hundred-pound notes and stuffed them in his pocket.

Caroline said in a soft voice, "Sir, let's get out of here."

"Bishop Gruber, the only reason I won't kill you is because you gave me good advice about my shell shock. Maybe you should reread your vows and follow your own advice. You can be a helpful servant of God if you wanted to." Hoffman looked at his daughter. "All right, I'm ready." With that, he walked over to the military vehicle and shot the tires.

Hoffman put on the bishop's cassock, got into the back seat with the valise, and sat next to his daughter who remained in her robe and hat. Konrad in his SS uniform resumed his role as chauffeur. He placed one rifle in the front seat and one on the floor in the back.

When the fancy German limousine departed, the young priest who served as the bishop's driver exhaled deeply, grateful that he wasn't shot. The bishop swore at losing his robe and being harassed and humiliated. He hated Americans.

Inside the car, Hoffman said to Caroline, "Forget the 'sir' stuff. Call me Dirk or Father."

"How about Dad?" Her smile was only exceeded by her father's.

As the sedan gained speed, Hoffman asked, "How far to the border?"

Konrad said, "I think twenty minutes or so."

"Will we have problems with the border guards?"

Konrad said, "I don't think so. How can they detain a German bishop? And I am an SS major, and Swiss army soldiers don't want to upset the SS."

After enduring torture, obstacles, duplicity, betrayal, and within miles of Switzerland, Hoffman knew his plans could still be derailed if he lost concentration of his goal. He looked in the bishop's valise and found a passport and other documents. Caroline's documents remained confiscated at the seminary, but Konrad had plenty of ID.

Hoffman said, "The bishop has crossed into Switzerland plenty of times, so we shouldn't experience too many difficulties."

Konrad asked, "Won't the guards see that you're not Bishop Gruber?"

"I'm visiting from a neighboring diocese and helping the SS. If I'm not convincing, I'll excommunicate them." He arched his eyebrows, and the others grinned. Hoffman added, "Let's proceed."

Konstanz was founded by the Romans in 40 AD and later named after its emperor, Constantius. Located on the western edge of Lake Constance adjacent to Switzerland, the city ignored the blackout requirement and kept its lights on at night thereby fooling Allied pilots who thought the city belonged to Switzerland. As a result, it wasn't bombed, and the effort saved historic neighborhoods including prominent Renaissance and Gothic buildings as well as the Konstanz Cathedral, which was completed in 1378.

The three reached the city of Konstanz about 8:15 a.m. and were greeted by little traffic. People on the sidewalks looked up as Konrad drove through town. The locals stared at them and thought the occupants must be important since they had a big car plus gas to drive it.

Hoffman marveled at the beauty and color of the buildings built in late medieval times. His previous travels through Germany showcased bombed-out areas in Berlin, Munich, and Friedrichshafen. But Konstanz went unscathed, and the intact structures awed him. He didn't dwell long on their magnificence because he needed to focus on crossing the border.

Konrad said, "I haven't had too many problems in the past, and I assume they will recognize the car."

Hoffman said, "Is everyone ready?"

"I guess so," Caroline said nervously.

The road funneled the cars into a protective sector that ended with a traffic gate similar to those at railroad crossings, a manually operated arm that swung up and down. Seven German guards stood in front of the gate.

On the one-lane road to the gate the German soldiers recognized it and waived it forward. When it stopped, one sergeant, who appeared to be the leader, came to the driver's side. The others left. "Good morning, sir." When the window came down, the sergeant noticed the driver wore an SS uniform. He looked into the back seat and saw two clergy, one he assumed was the bishop.

The sergeant asked the driver, "Where is the other driver, sir?"

Konrad said, "We have a special meeting, and the bishop needed me to assist."

"Oh, okay. You may pass." The sergeant motioned to two men to raise the gate.

Konrad passed the guards, and Bishop Hoffman blessed the soldiers when he gave the sign of the cross with his right arm.

"Our next hurdle is to get past the Swiss guards," said Konrad. "They require proper paperwork or we'll be sent back."

Hoffman said, "We can call the American legation, and they'll help."

Caroline worried. "I don't want to be sent back to Germany."

Konrad drove one quarter of a mile, approached the Swiss border, and crossed into the city of Kreuzlingen. The auto stopped, and the guards recognized the bishop's car. The Swiss only had three guards posted. The sentry came to the driver's side. "Good morning." Konrad put the window down, and the Swiss soldier looked inside and saw the clergy in the back seat. "Show me your papers, please."

Chapter 37

June 30, 1944
Kreuzlingen, Switzerland

Konrad said, "Here's mine. The bishop and his friend don't have theirs. We have an appointment in Zurich."

After the guard reviewed Konrad's passport, he said, "You can go, but I can't allow anyone to pass without proper identification." Konrad looked at the back seat and asked, "Can we speak with the manager?"

The guard saw that the driver was an officer in the SS, and so proceeded with care. "Pull your car over to the side."

As Konrad parked he said, "We should level with them." Hoffman agreed and took off his robe as did Caroline. The guard escorted the three into a small room. They sat down and impatiently waited for twenty minutes. Finally, a portly man about fifty years old strode into the room. His posture was rigid and the look on his face stern. "I am Gottfried Rechsteiner. So, you don't have papers?"

Hoffman stood up and said in German, "Mr. Rechsteiner, my daughter and I are Americans and have just escaped the Nazis. The major is my daughter's husband. We seek asylum in your country. Can we call the US Legation? They are expecting us."

With his cautious demeanor, Mr. Rechsteiner spoke in English, "How could the legation know you are coming?"

Hoffman replied in English, "The Resistance informed them after we escaped." He didn't want to reveal too much. "We've endured near-death situations to get here, and if I can call Mr. Allen Dulles at the legation, all problems will be solved."

Mr. Rechsteiner said, "I'll make the call then." They all went to the manager's office. After a few minutes, he got through to a secretary.

"May I speak to Allen Dulles please. I am the manager at the Kreuzlingen border station." Mr. Rechsteiner waited and kept his eyes on the three. When someone spoke on the other end, he said, "Is this Mr. Allen Dulles?" Mr. Rechsteiner informed him about the two wayward Americans without passports, and Mr. Dulles asked to speak with them.

"This is Dirk Hoffman."

"What is your code?"

"Stork."

Mr. Dulles said, "I'll handle everything. Welcome to Switzerland." Hoffman provided the name, phone number, and the location of the border station. The three returned to the small room. Twenty-five minutes later, Mr. Rechsteiner returned and even smiled. "You three can cross." He shook his head in disbelief. "Your friend has big-time connections in our government."

With the border guards' blessing, the three got into the sedan and departed for the freedom of Switzerland. Hoffman finally let out a big smile. He reached his goal: Caroline was free, and Kaye will rejoice and not suffer. The only negative: Konrad will no longer serve as a valuable spy for the Allies, but he and Caroline can resume their marriage without wartime risks.

"Where are we going?" said Caroline.

Konrad answered, "To Zurich to visit Schweizerische Kreditanstalt, or known in London as Credit Suisse Bank. They have a huge, four-story office building on the Paradeplatz. Usually, Bachmann selects an SS officer to deposit gold to the Swiss National Bank, the central bank. I've done it a few times but for this transaction, I prefer to keep away from the central bank and deal with a large private one."

Hoffman asked, "Do Swiss banks do business with the Allies?"

"Certainly. They have bought more gold from the United States than any other country."

One hour later, they arrived at the bank's four-story headquarters, and Caroline was awed by the classical building's size and grandeur. Konrad, in his SS uniform, went in and mustered four men with two carts. The bags of British pound sterling and gold were loaded, and the group pushed the carts inside the first-floor corridor past the colonnaded atrium and into a luxurious office.

A distinguished man wearing a dark blue suit with a pressed white shirt and silk tie came out. He was reserved in manner and appearance, and Caroline thought he could double as a spy. "My name is Jorgen Wurgler. I understand you want to open an account."

Konrad introduced himself and his cohorts. Everyone spoke in German.

"Mr. Wurgler, I wish to open a new account with three of us as signers."

The bank processed the deposits without any questions, which was normal procedure when receiving large amounts of gold from the SS. Two women brought coffee and pastries. Since the three hadn't eaten in what seemed like two eternities, they welcomed the food and downed the coffee to stay awake.

The main difficulty in this transaction was counting the sterling, which was in bundles of one hundred-pound notes. The gold commodity team arrived and quickly weighed the bars, which totaled 345,000 pounds sterling. The operations group sat down and tallied the currency which was valued at 450,000 British pounds. Hoffman took a few more loose bills for himself and converted them to Swiss francs equal to US $2,000. They needed cash for living expenses.

Caroline said, "What's the total in dollars?"

Konrad thought. "About $1.6 million."

She needed to sit down. "I didn't know that much cash existed."

Mr. Wurgler returned to the office with some papers. "Sign these, and we're all set." After shaking hands, the trio left the bank, and Mr. Wurgler returned to his office to make a phone call to the German embassy.

Hoffman, Caroline, and Konrad were relieved that their funds resided in a large Swiss bank and not the trunk of their car. Next, they traveled to Bern, the capital of Switzerland.

Caroline asked, "Now where are we going?"

Hoffman said, "To find the United States Legation."

"Doesn't the US have an embassy here?"

Hoffman continued, "The legation is a small embassy, and the head of it is called a 'minister' who is considered to be the personal representative of the government. He differs from an embassy head, which is called 'ambassador,' who acts as a personal representative of the head of state."

Caroline said, "I don't know why they can't make it an embassy and quit playing semantics."

After two hours of driving, Konrad parked in front of the US Legation. Upon entry and inquiring after Allen Dulles, a lean man with thin brown hair wearing a dapper double-breasted blue coat, gabardine slacks, Oxford black shoes, a pressed white shirt, and red silk tie walked up to them. Hoffman thought that this man must be a clothes model for Esquire magazine or else the Americans brought a tailor for the legation's staff.

"Welcome to Bern. You made it. What a relief. I've been following you since you arrived at the seminary." He shook hands with everyone. "I am Winthrop Endicott, Mr. Dulles's executive assistant. Come with me. His office is nearby at 23 Herrengasse. Remember that address."

Endicott joined the group in the bishop's sedan and directed them to the address and a parking place in back. "Everyone uses the back entrance since we want to keep Mr. Dulles's business and conversations confidential."

Hoffman felt that Endicott tried too hard. He had a slight frame, pale skin, thin lips, and a pointed nose that pinched when he smiled. He didn't hesitate to remind everyone that he graduated from Princeton.

Dulles's four-story apartment building, designed in northern European Baroque, was erected in 1756 and in need of painting, but the façade projected strength with its sandstone exterior. Dulles's group rented the entire first floor, and he used it both as his residence and office.

Endicott said, "Dulles is on an important call but asked that I interrupt him. I'll get him," and left them in the living room. The sparse décor reflected the wartime shortages as the old sofa showed worn fabric and rips in the pillows, but it was comfortable.

Allen Dulles, aged fifty-one, held his pipe with his left hand and entered at a brisk pace with Endicott following. Hoffman, Caroline, and Konrad stood. Dulles wore rimless glasses, looked like a college professor in a ruffled white shirt, tweed jacket and bow tie, and possessed a cunning toughness.

"I don't have much time at the moment, but glad you finally made it to Switzerland. I imagine you need plenty of items including a place to stay. Winthrop will take care of your needs. Let's meet tomorrow after lunch, say, one o'clock here."

His exit was faster than his entrance. The three new arrivals watched his departure with disappointment because they wanted to inform Mr. Dulles about their hair-raising adventures in Germany and how they bested an SS general.

"We escape death, can offer insights about Germany, and he runs away as though we have leprosy." Hoffman spread his arms out in frustration.

Endicott said, "You must excuse him. He has a few emergencies." After an awkward pause, he continued. "Let's get you settled."

Hoffman said, "I need to send two telegrams, one home and one to MI6 in London. Then a hotel, hot bath, and a relaxing dinner. New clothes would help. I want to burn the outfit I'm wearing."

Endicott arranged for their rooms in the Old City part of Bern at the opulent Hotel Bellevue Palace, then drove them to a shopping area and wrote down Hoffman's messages. "I will wire both when I return to the legation. We've already alerted MI6 about your arrival."

Endicott departed, leaving Hoffman to get new wardrobe — which was difficult because of his size and scarcity of clothes. Konrad wanted to lose his uniform as quickly as possible, and Caroline, armed with Swiss francs secured from her father, reveled in the delight of shopping. She looked at the women's clothing department at two stores while her husband and father leaned against the wall and chatted about Bachmann.

The fancy Hotel Bellevue Palace astonished Hoffman with its luxury in the middle of a war. Built in 1865 and renovated in 1910, the 230-room art nouveau structure served as the guesthouse for visiting heads of state, diplomats, intelligence agents, and legislators since it was located adjacent to the Swiss Federal Assembly. From its magnificent lounges, one enjoyed superb views of the Alps and the Aare River. The dining room had wood-paneled walls, and half the space hosted Allied guests and the other half seated Axis patrons. The bar area facilitated many secret meetings between agents and was a haunt for Allen Dulles and his ubiquitous pipe.

Dulles's title was Special Assistant to the US Minister, but everyone including the one hundred German spies that prowled around Switzerland knew that he served as the OSS station chief in Bern, and Bern served as a caldron of espionage activity from all sides. Even a reporter for a Swiss newspaper wrote that Dulles was the personal representative of Franklin Roosevelt and was America's spymaster. Dulles collected intelligence about German activities from his contacts and spy networks inside Germany, and this effort took most of his time.

The next day at 1:00 p.m., Hoffman, Konrad, and Caroline waited alone in Dulles's living room. Twenty minutes later, he and Endicott strode in and sat down without any apologies for their lateness. Dulles made it a point to shake each person's hand as Endicott, dressed in a white shirt and tan cashmere sweater, stood in the background.

When Dulles came to Hoffman, he said, "I was so worried about you. I didn't know where you were after Berlin. You did a great job."

Hoffman didn't show his shock about Dulles's comment, which differed from Endicott's. Maybe he just forgot. Ignoring the awkwardness, Hoffman asked, "What's happened on the Western Front? We've been away from the news."

Dulles said, "After some initial delays, our troops have plowed through France and caused the Germans to fall back in a slow retreat. General Bradley plans to recapture Paris in August." He paused and changed the subject. "Colonel, you've had quite an adventure. MI6 didn't think you'd last past the torture."

Caroline interrupted. "Torture?"

Dulles smiled and said, "You'll have time later to update your daughter about your courage. Well done, Dirk. MI6 would like to debrief you."

"Can we leave Switzerland?"

"The Swiss government considers you to be an 'evadee,' similar to an escapee. You walked into the country, so the Swiss will allow you freedom to live here or leave whenever you want. Allied pilots, when they ditch their damaged planes in Switzerland, are considered internees and are kept in internment camps that have guards watching them. So far, about twelve hundred pilots are housed in camps."

"Why so rigid? Don't they have compassion for the Allied air forces and all they have had to bear?"

"The Swiss follow strict neutrality laws primarily because they are under constant threat of invasion. Surrounded on three sides by the Nazis produces paranoia. They don't want to give the Nazis any excuse to attack."

"Is there a way to get to London?"

Dulles said, "A weekly flight exists from Zurich to Lisbon followed by a British flight to London, but it is hard to get a seat. If you wait three or four weeks, the Allies will have taken southern

France, and then you can travel to Lyon and catch a military transport. With your recent knowledge about Germany, you can do more good here than you can in London, and we can sure use you."

Chapter 38

July 2–20, 1944
Bern, Switzerland

Bachmann did not reveal to his chain of command that Hoffman eluded him once again. Gossip circulated that a sedan was stolen, but nothing else happened in the seminary. Dulles assumed that SS silence served to deceive the OSS about a future commando raid into Switzerland, but as the weeks passed, the Americans discarded this possibility.

Hoffman took advantage of this break to rest and to write letters to Kaye. Caroline did the same. She missed her mother and the gossip about Fort Knox. In a neutral country, letters were delivered more quickly as opposed to mail from the Allied nations with its censorship delays.

After four days in the Bellevue Palace, Hoffman moved into a one-bedroom unit paid with his Swiss francs. Konrad and Caroline found an apartment about a ten-minute walk from Hoffman's place. No one complained about the sparse rooms and few amenities since housing was difficult to obtain. Despite the scarcity of clothes, new and used, the three managed to outfit themselves and blend into Switzerland as civilians.

They often ate dinner together, and Hoffman enjoyed these meals since he got better acquainted with Konrad, not to mention a deeper bond with his daughter.

Each day, Hoffman walked to the legation to meet with Endicott who gave him OSS and MI6 telegrams to read. Sometimes Dulles would meet privately with Hoffman at the colonel's apartment to discuss issues and arrive at a strategy. Dulles preferred the tranquility of Hoffman's place instead of his own to avoid interruptions, phone calls, and visitors.

After a wait of sixteen days since he mailed his first letter, Hoffman received a letter from Kaye. He ripped it open.

Dear Dirk,

I can't tell you how happy I have been to know that you are alive and not missing in action anymore. A huge burden was lifted when I received your letter. But to tell the truth, I knew you would be all right. After your experiences in the Argonne Forest, I knew the Nazis couldn't capture you. Caroline's letter was most welcomed, too. Thank you, my darling, for bringing her from Berlin to Switzerland. I slept for twelve hours last night knowing everyone was safe.

To hear you speak about the new relationship you have with Caroline is a dream come true. She is like you in so many ways — smart, clever, stubborn, and talented. Now both of you can use these traits together and not against each other. Oh, there is a God. He has given me so much happiness.

Love, hugs, and kisses, Kaye

At the legation, Hoffman asked, "Don't you think I should go over these telegrams about the SS with Allen? They seem to be important and may be helpful to him."

Endicott said, "Allen has a full plate. He avoids the legation and is always late to meetings since his schedule is disrupted constantly, and each intrusion wipes out his daily agenda. If Allen doesn't have time for you, don't take it personally. He doesn't have time for himself."

"I understand that he has many masters."

"At night he hangs out at the bar in the Bellevue Palace to confer with spies and diplomats on both sides. It seems surreal to talk to our enemy, and I often occupy a bar stool to watch and listen."

Around 3:00 p.m., Hoffman was viewing cables when Endicott sprinted through the back door out of breath, a telegram clutched in his hand. "Dirk, come with me." Endicott and Hoffman raced to Dulles's office.

"Allen, look at this." Endicott bent over using one arm to steady himself on the desk pulling for oxygen and began to read.

"At 12:42 p.m., 20 July 1944, a bomb exploded in the Wolf's Lair, Hitler's Eastern Front headquarters in East Prussia. Hitler was not killed but only received leg wounds, and now the Gestapo are on the rampage to execute the guilty parties. We'll know more tomorrow."

Dulles read the telegram and almost chewed his pipe stem off. He said, "This is disastrous."

Endicott said, "Did you know about it?"

Dulles stood up and looked out the window. "We've worked with a few groups, but I didn't expect it to happen since three other plots had failed."

Hoffman said, "I bet Bachmann will interpret that he failed to protect his Führer. He will suspect your involvement, Allen. You need to take precautionary measures."

"I had no part in it."

"Doesn't matter. In his mind, the OSS orchestrated it. The SS and Gestapo will go after many in the Wehrmacht and in the Resistance."

Dulles said, "I've got to help some German friends who may be in danger."

Hoffman asked, "Would Bachmann dare to cross into Switzerland and seek reprisal?"

Dulles said, "It's possible he might send an assassination squad, but it's too risky for him to come personally."

Hoffman replied, "According to Konrad, Bachmann holds grudges forever. He takes revenge for small and large infractions. This bombing is personal, and if he suspects that you arranged it, you are a likely target with me right behind you."

"Why you?"

"I stole money from him and escaped his capture. Plus, his subordinate, my son-in-law, spied for the British. That in itself would prompt a huge temper tantrum."

Endicott said, "What can we do?"

Hoffman replied, "We need to put a watch on the German embassy."

Dulles added, "We can't cover the embassy and its leaders since our manpower is limited. The Nazis have more resources in Switzerland than we do."

Chapter 39

For two weeks, the US Legation mobilized its military guards and requested assistance from the Swiss armed forces to protect the American staff, especially Allen Dulles, Winthrop Endicott, Hoffman, Caroline, and Konrad. Border guards were put on alert, but as each day progressed without trouble, the guards relaxed their vigilance and fell into an easygoing routine.

In the early afternoon, Hoffman met with a smiling Winthrop Endicott, dressed in a gray cotton suit and blue silk tie, who said, "I received a message from one of our agents. He saw Bachmann in Hamburg."

"In Hamburg? What's he doing there?"

"I don't know. He must be rounding up top Wehrmacht officers who were involved in the assassination attempt." Endicott leaned against the desk. "You know what that means?"

Hoffman said, "Go on."

"It means that he's not in Switzerland."

Endicott looked for an expression of joy at the good news. Instead, Hoffman's face became serious, and he paced around the room with his eyes cast downward and his hands clasped behind his back. After several minutes, Hoffman turned around with his eyebrows arched. "Do you believe your source?"

"He's been consistently reliable. So, pressure's off for a while." Endicott's tone was calm. He looked out the window at the

215

summer's bloom of geraniums. "What's the matter, Dirk? You worry too much."

"We need to be cautious."

As an afterthought, Endicott added, "Oh, I forgot. Allen wants to meet at his place tomorrow at one and include both Konrad and Caroline. The staff will vacate, so we'll have complete privacy."

"Subject?"

"Allen and I have gone over intelligence reports and want your input. These are very sensitive reports."

The next day, Hoffman arrived early and waited alone in Dulles's living room that doubled as a reception area. Figuring that Dulles would be late again, he sat down and waited. He wore his usual tan slacks, sports shirt, and a blue jacket. He kept his Luger in the left side pocket and the silencer in the right. A few minutes later, he heard a knock at the door. When Hoffman opened it, he saw a soldier wearing an American army uniform with a rifle. "Yes?"

"Colonel Hoffman?"

"Yes."

The soldier pointed the rifle at Hoffman. "Move back."

Hoffman widened his eyes and moved away from the front door with his hands up. Another soldier dressed in an army uniform came in, followed by a man in a gray suit whom Hoffman recognized as Bachmann. He took off his coat and handed it to the soldier.

Hoffman said, "Lost your way, General? This is Switzerland."

Bachmann motioned for the guards to watch his captive and said, "Where's your gun?" Hoffman pointed to his jacket's left pocket. Bachman said, "Underhanded, carefully throw it away."

Hoffman lifted the handle out with two fingers and a thumb and flung it across the floor. It landed on the hardwood and skidded under the skirt of the couch fifteen feet away with half of the handle showing. The soldiers and Bachmann ignored it. With the drop on the American colonel, the German general was confident. "Nice of you to come to my meeting."

Hoffman said, "It takes three Nazis to kill me?"

"I have four guards outside dressed as Swiss police. No one will interrupt us. You won't get away this time." He looked around the room. "We'll wait for the others."

"What others?"

A guard at the door said, "Two people are coming."

When they knocked, Hoffman suspected Konrad and Caroline. He yelled, "Run! Get away from here!"

Bachmann hit Hoffman in the face and he fell to the floor. The guard opened the door and his rifle welcomed Konrad and Caroline, and the barrel waved at them to come inside. Despite their shock, they obeyed.

Seeing her father on the floor with blood on his lip, Caroline cried, "Dad, are you okay?"

From the floor, he stared at the pistol by the couch, but it was too far away. Konrad followed Hoffman's gaze and saw the weapon but couldn't move with the rifle barrel poked in his chest.

"I'm fine." But Hoffman stayed down.

Bachmann sneered and said, "Get up. I didn't hurt you." He looked around at his captives, then walked to a large table in the rear and picked up a report, sat down, and crossed his legs. As he filed through the papers, he said, "We will wait for one more."

Bachmann looked at Hoffman. "While we're waiting, you can tell me what happened to Gebauer."

"I haven't seen him."

"I don't believe you."

"Want me to make up something?"

Konrad said, "Who's Gebauer?"

Hoffman said, "I'll tell you later."

The phone rang twice and then silence. Ten seconds later, it rang again and Bachmann answered but did not speak. He nodded his head, then tightened his jaw. "Okay. We'll start." He hung up and said, "Mr. Dulles will not be able to join us. So, let's begin."

Hoffman said, "Begin what?" He wondered what happened to Endicott.

"I want the number of your account in Credit Suisse, and I want you to sign this withdrawal slip."

How did he know about the bank? thought Hoffman. Only two people, the manager and the operations specialist, knew about it besides his daughter, Konrad, and himself. Hoffman pulled out his wallet and fumbled for a folded paper with the number, wrote it on the bank slip, and signed it.

Bachmann snatched the slip and slid it into his coat pocket. "And you thought you could steal my money and get away with it, but instead, you and your family will pay." His eyes riveted to Konrad's. "As a special treat for my former SS confidant and to you, Colonel, you both will witness the main event, which will star Miss Caroline."

Bachmann gloated and led the guards past their prisoners toward the back of the room. With Bachmann standing between them, the guards faced the front door and aimed their rifles at the three who remained ten feet in front of the couch.

Bachmann ordered his sentries, "Keep an eye on them." He stepped to Caroline and yanked her away from her family to a place between the guards. "Now we'll see how your daughter performs on my stage."

Hoffman said, "So, the master race can't get women without force."

Konrad's face flushed red. As he moved toward Bachmann to protect his wife, Bachmann drew his gun with its silencer and shot him in the abdomen. Konrad clutched his belly, his face distorted in pain. He felt an electrical wave flow to his ribs and lost his breath. As he fell, he tilted his body in order to fall near the couch. His legs landed near the couch's skirt, and his ankle fell on Hoffman's gun. Resting on his stomach, he grimaced as he turned on his right side and faced Bachmann. Konrad used his right leg to shield the gun and moved it with his left foot slowly against his right leg upward toward his calf, then nudged it behind his right knee. This location made it easier for Hoffman, who was five feet away, to grab. He observed Konrad's maneuvering and gave a slight nod that he saw the gun's new position.

Bachmann said to the colonel, "Are you right-handed or left-handed?"

"What?" yelled Hoffman.

"Right or left? A simple question."

"Right." With that, Bachmann shot his right upper arm. Hoffman writhed in agony as the bullet pierced his muscle.

Chapter 40

August 4, 1944
Bern, Switzerland

Hoffman's left hand covered the wound as he clenched his jaw from the sudden pain.

Bachmann said, "That's only a scratch. It will hurt more in a few minutes when another bullet comes into your body. I will watch you suffer and soon you will see daddy's little girl suffer." He laughed. "This is your reward for humiliating me in front of the High Command."

Konrad put his hands over his own wound to stanch the bleeding but without success. Hoffman saw the problem and bent down close to Konrad to help him. Bachmann yelled, "Leave him alone!"

Hoffman said, "I'll tell you what happened to Gebauer, but first, get me a shirt or a towel."

Bachmann nodded to the guard. In a moment, the guard returned with a white shirt and tossed it to Hoffman. He caught it with his left hand and applied pressure to stop the flow of blood on Konrad's wound. His left hand was two feet from the hidden pistol, but seeing the rifle barrels pointed at his head, he played for time. The two SS guards watched Hoffman tend to his son-in-law and could not see the gun behind Konrad's pant leg.

Bachmann twirled his Luger and said, "Tell me about Gebauer."

"Gebauer was a stupid man. He tried to rape a young nurse. She reminded me of Caroline, so I killed him with his own gun." Caroline stared at her father upon hearing that he killed yet another German.

Bachmann said, "I'm smarter than Gebauer. I'm keeping you alive to witness the violation of your daughter before I kill you."

Hoffman's eyes darted from the gun against Konrad's leg to Bachmann. "So, if you're so smart, why did you select Gebauer? I used him to give you false information."

Bachmann said, "He told me about your friend and your platoon in the Great War and that you cried and cried. Just like a baby."

Hoffman's heart beat faster.

Bachmann elaborated. "Your buddies weren't clever enough against our Aryan soldiers, were they? The Germans killed your friends easily. They fought like girls just like you with your crying." Bachmann laughed. "What a warrior you are."

Hoffman's eyes narrowed and blood rushed to his face.

Bachmann said. "We are the supreme race and destined to purify the world. We will exterminate the weak races."

"I am German on both sides. Why murder me?"

"You're American and a crybaby."

Hoffman loathed Bachmann. He was evil. "You have no honor."

Bachmann smiled. "Honor makes no difference in war. A bullet reaches its target whether one has honor or not."

The mention of bullets and the throbbing of his arm reminded Hoffman about the lifeless body of his friend Zach, in 1918, lying on the floor of the Argonne Forest. Hoffman couldn't do anything against Jerry then but could do something now. He glanced at Bachmann and pressed the shirt on Konrad's wound, mindful that as he leaned forward, he was closer to the gun.

As the guards focused on Hoffman, Bachmann shifted to Caroline and stroked her cheek. She bit his finger and turned away in disgust. He encircled her throat with his other hand bringing blood to her head. "You will obey me or I will kill your husband." Bachmann turned and shot Konrad in the right leg, then shot Hoffman in the left leg and said to Hoffman, "I am a marksman. I will kill you slowly, one bullet after another. You'll cry in agony while seeing me ravish your daughter."

Hoffman's leg buckled and he fell on his left side, winced in pain at the new wound, but had the strength to ease himself up on his knees — his hand itched to clutch the pistol nearby.

With more pain in Konrad's right leg, he kept it immobile so that his left leg could protect the pistol that was lodged underneath it.

Caroline shouted, "You peasant! You wear a uniform but you're still an ignorant peasant."

Bachmann slapped her, which caused Hoffman to shift his head toward Bachmann but stopped when a guard's rifle wacked the side of his face. Hoffman fell on his back.

The guard said, "Go ahead. I haven't shot an American for a while."

Hoffman seethed as he tried to tolerate the pain in his arm and leg. Bachmann jerked Caroline back to the area between the guards. She glared at the SS general with fire in her eyes.

Hoffman raised up and said, "What kind of weakling picks on a woman?"

Bachmann said, "If we're so weak, why are you unarmed and only have a few minutes left to see your daughter perform?" He shot at Hoffman's left rib cage as he again dropped back to the floor.

Bachmann holstered his Luger and pointed his finger at the colonel. "Now watch your little girl, old boy. See what a real man can do. After I finish, I'll let the guards take their turn. This show will be better than Jodl's birthday party."

Next, Bachmann swung around to face Caroline, grabbed her blouse, and ripped it open revealing her bra. She held onto the cotton material, which prevented Bachmann from removing it, so he pulled it over her head causing her arms to elevate. She had the presence to wrench it away from Bachmann's grasp and cast the ripped cloth over the head of the nearest guard. The second guard turned from Hoffman to assist his comrade.

With the confusion of the Germans and fighting the pain from his ribs and leg, Hoffman shifted his body and leaned toward Konrad and with his left hand grabbed the gun behind Konrad's leg and fired one shot into the head of the closest soldier. When the other guard removed the garment off his head, Hoffman pulled the trigger and saw an explosion of red over the guard's forehead. He shouted at Bachmann, "I lied! I'm left-handed and a marksman too, you ass."

Bachmann clasped Caroline's upper arm with his left hand, drew his pistol with the right, and thrust the barrel next to her skull. "If you kill me, she dies."

Hoffman raised himself on his right knee and swayed slightly from the loss of blood yet kept his gun pointed at Bachmann. "Leave her alone, and I'll let you go unharmed."

"No chance. She stays with me." Bachmann noticed the quantity of blood on Hoffman's clothes and floor as his injured body teetered back and forth as he tried to remain balanced. "Besides, I'll just wait while you bleed out."

No one said anything; the two men locked their eyes in silence. Then a smile crossed Hoffman's face.

"What's so funny?"

Hoffman said, "This impasse reminds me of a game called *Incoming* that Caroline and I played when she was a child. Remember?" Hoffman looked at his daughter. "We pretended that mortars were falling on us?"

Bachmann said, "What do mortars have to do with anything?"

Hearing the word incoming, Caroline ceased resisting and slackened her muscles, and Bachmann relaxed his grip around her arm but kept the pistol next to her jaw.

Caroline gave a slight grin and Hoffman said, "When we played the game, I cried out, 'Incoming'!"

With those words, Caroline's hand bumped Bachmann's gun hand upward and she quickly dropped to the floor, sliding her arm out of his grasp. He was surprised and exposed. Hoffman fired and hit Bachmann's wrist, causing the gun to fall to the floor. The general clutched his bloody hand and looked for his Luger.

Caroline picked up the pistol, stood up, faced him, pointed it at his face, and shrieked, "You animal!" She fired two shots into Bachmann's groin. He fell to the floor and screamed in pain as Caroline bent over him and thrust the barrel into his forehead. "You monster. I'll turn your brain into pulp."

Hoffman struggled to his feet, hobbled to her side and quietly said, "Caroline, give me the gun."

Bachmann, on his back holding his privates, whimpered as he viewed his bloody groin. "Don't do it. Don't shoot," and wept.

Caroline thundered. "So, is this show better than Jodl's birthday party?"

Hoffman repeated, "Caroline. I'll take over now. Don't do it." He paused. "Call the legation for an ambulance and soldiers. Quickly."

Caroline's nostrils flared as she stared at Bachmann. "Your life is over."

Hoffman spoke softly, "Caroline. He's not worth it. Let it go."

She held the gun tightly, her hand shaking. She didn't speak but breathed loudly between her clenched teeth. Seconds passed. Bachmann shuddered.

"You can thank your lucky stars that my father has more honor and integrity because he's stopping me from shooting you."

Bachmann snarled and cried out, "You bitch."

Slowly Caroline lowered the gun. She looked at her dad, "I really want to shoot him."

Hoffman said, "I know."

She gave the pistol to her father and kicked Bachmann in the genitals as another wave of pain radiated throughout his body. Bachmann curled up on the floor and sobbed like a baby.

Hoffman leaned against a chair to hold himself upright and said, "Call the legation, tell them about four Germans dressed as Swiss police, and look after Konrad." Caroline saw her bleeding husband and burst into tears. She took hold of her blouse to cover herself and went to the phone and dialed the legation. She returned to Konrad, knelt at his side, and pressed the shirt to his wound. She held Konrad and spoke in a low voice, "I love you. I love you."

After more hugs and tears, a shot startled her. She turned and saw her father peer down at the lifeless figure. Hoffman, wobbling back and forth, said without emotion, "He tried to escape."

Caroline looked at the carcass lying in a pool of blood. "You didn't let me kill him."

"I don't want you to live with it."

They waited in silence as his words sunk in. She said, "He deserved it."

Hoffman responded, "But you didn't. Death never leaves you."

She slowly nodded and turned to her wounded husband. Hoffman turned over Bachmann's corpse, reclaimed the withdrawal slip, and fell onto the sofa.

Chapter 41

On the following day, the city of Bern sparkled in the sunshine. The Old City, with its diverse architecture of Romanesque, Baroque, and Gothic influences, retained its medieval character and serenity despite the bloody war that surrounded landlocked Switzerland.

Caroline ignored the beauty of the town as she hurried to the hospital, worried about Konrad and recalling the doctor's comments, "Your father was lucky as his wounds are not serious; however, Konrad's injuries are deeper and require more attention. His recuperation will take longer."

After she arrived at the front desk and received clearance to proceed, Caroline dashed down the corridor to the patients room shared by her husband and father. She entered and saw Allen Dulles and Winthrop Endicott standing by Hoffman's bed. They parted to allow Caroline to rush to a sleeping Konrad and hold his hand.

Dulles said, "I can't believe that Bachmann attacked you in my own apartment."

The nurse hushed Mr. Dulles, who spoke more softly and looked to his assistant. "Winthrop, meet with Hoffman when he's better and get a full report. I'm pressing this matter to the Swiss government for their lack of border security."

Endicott said, "Sure, Allen." Then he turned to Hoffman. "When do you want to meet?"

Hoffman's ribs and leg were bandaged and his right arm rested in a sling. Still groggy from medication, Hoffman said as he glanced at his wounded son-in-law, "How about tomorrow? We can do it here tomorrow afternoon while Konrad is in surgery, so it'll be the two of us. How about four?"

"Make it four-thirty."

Caroline looked at Konrad as he opened his eyes and gave a tired smile. "Hi, honey. I pulled through."

Fighting back tears, she said, "I was so upset."

"Why? I'm the one that got shot." They laughed although Konrad cringed in pain since laughter pulled on tender muscles.

Hoffman held onto his sling and sat up, looked beyond Dulles and Endicott and said to Konrad, "Thanks for getting me the gun."

Konrad said, "Anything for my father-in-law." He smiled and changed the subject. "Any fallout inside Switzerland about Bachmann's attack?"

Dulles said, "The government is embarrassed and suppressed the story. I complained to the foreign minister who sidestepped my questions."

Caroline asked, "Do you think another attack might occur?"

Dulles said, "I don't know, but the legation directed its security team to monitor my office, your room here, and Hoffman's apartment."

"I will be staying with Father when he is released until Konrad is discharged."

Endicott said, "Because Bachmann is dead, I don't think the SS will pursue. Bachmann's obsession focused on Hoffman."

The nurse interrupted and said, "Can you leave for thirty minutes? We need to do some tests on Herr Frolich. Herr Hoffman can use a wheelchair and go outside with you, if you wish."

Caroline said, "I'm hungry. Does the hospital have a dining room?" She leaned over and kissed her husband's forehead, snatched her purse from the side of the bed, and pushed the wheelchair containing her father to the corridor.

In the hallway, the four talked briefly; Dulles pulled Caroline aside while Hoffman and Endicott continued in front of them. In a low voice Dulles said, "Caroline, I need you to go to Zurich's newspaper, Zürichsee-Zeitung, to pick up some files. Ask for Emma Schwegler, the manager of the archives. The files will be ready tomorrow. A legation car will pick you up at one o'clock. Bring the files to me at my office, and tell no one." He glanced at Hoffman and Endicott and repeated, "No one."

Caroline narrowed her eyes and simply said, "Sure, Allen." She wondered what the files contained.

Dulles and Endicott departed, leaving Caroline to propel Hoffman down the hallway to the dining room. They sat at a small circular table and gave the waiter their orders. Caroline said, "We can finally relax. That monster is dead."

"Other Nazis may come. To be safe, can you bring me my pistol? And don't mention it to the nurses."

"I'll bring it at dinner, but you heard what Endicott said. Only Bachmann was obsessed with killing you. I doubt if others will have the same fixation."

Hoffman held his daughter's hand. "How do you know he was obsessed?"

"He told me in the seminary. You really upset him, and he wanted revenge."

"What else did he say?"

Squeezing her father's hand before pulling it away, she said, "He was surprised that I married Konrad. He felt I could do better, get a more virile man, probably referring to himself." She blushed.

"Anything else?"

She thought for a moment. "He said that even if we reached Switzerland, he'd find us." She rubbed her eye. "Now that I think back, he implied that we weren't safe in Switzerland, that he had a contact here."

"The Nazis have one hundred spies in Switzerland. Did he give names or places? Any clues?"

"No. I didn't see him again until yesterday."

Running his hand through his short hair, Hoffman looked away in a remote gaze.

"What's bothering you, Dad? Ever since I arrived, you seem preoccupied."

Hoffman checked out the open dining area with its few patrons and said, "What do you think of Endicott?"

"Why?"

"I don't trust him. He has a stupid smile. I know that doesn't make sense, but it bothers me as though he's hiding something."

"Dad, a stupid smile doesn't make him a bad guy. What's this about? He's been helpful to us."

"I've had time to think and review past conversations." He paused. "He lied to me."

Caroline sat straighter in her chair. "About what?"

"I don't know. Something's not right."

Caroline gave a big sigh. "He works for the OSS. They're supposed to lie. He can't reveal everything."

Hoffman moved more closely to his daughter, and said softly, "Endicott admitted to me that he had monitored us during our escape to include our time at the seminary. Dulles told me in a separate conversation that he didn't know our whereabouts after we left Berlin." Hoffman viewed the dining room's front door and said, "Something's wrong. These two men work closely together and would pass along any information about us, so Endicott's reference to the seminary puzzles me."

"Maybe Dulles forgot. After all, he has a huge workload."

"Endicott's told so many lies, he can't remember what's true and what isn't."

"So, what are you trying to tell me? Is he under suspicion for something?"

"The answer is yes, but I don't know for what."

The next day, Caroline left at 1:00 for Zurich to pick up files for Allen, arrived at 2:45 in the lobby, and was taken to the office of Emma Schwegler. Emma, wearing a plain print dress with her gray hair tied in a bun, had a friendly smile and welcoming personality. Her reading glasses rested at the tip of her nose that remained in place as she escorted Caroline to the basement. Known affectionately as The Librarian, Emma had spent twenty-three years in this position. She was the most well-informed person at the newspaper because she filed the clips either by the topic, photograph, or journalist, and knew where to look when a request came from the editor or a reporter.

"It took me a while to compile the information, but I'd do anything for Allen," she said with twinkle in her eye. "I found very little but put the items in one folder," which she handed over.

Caroline looked at the tab that said Francois Genoud. She recognized the name that Dulles mentioned when she first came to Switzerland.

Emma said, "It contains three small newspaper articles and five photographs with the date of January 29, 1943, on the backs. They were not published because the camera man said to keep them for reference."

Caroline looked at the articles briefly and then the photos. After looking at the first four, she came to the fifth picture and gasped. Then she looked more intently at the four men talking in a bar and zeroed in on two of them. "Emma, these are very helpful. Now I must get back to Mr. Dulles. Many thanks."

The legation driver picked her up and motored to Bern as Caroline ignored the scenery to examine each picture. The first four photos showed a bar with many men drinking beer and laughing. She couldn't make out any signs or recognize any person. The last photo showed four men talking at the end of the bar unaware that a camera had snapped them. She recognized two.

After another hour and forty-five minute drive, Caroline entered Dulles's office and found him on the phone. She waved the folder in front of him and mimicked an explosion with her outstretched arms. Dulles tried to turn away, so Caroline shouted, "Hang up." He continued to talk.

Giving a big sigh, Caroline took out the fifth photo, slapped it on his desk, then pointed to one of the men. Dulles said to the caller, "Just a minute." He stared at it, looked at Caroline, his eyes widened, and spoke on the phone, "I'll call you back."

Dulles viewed the other photos and returned to the fifth one nodding slightly and said, "These shots are incredible."

She waited for a moment and said, "Who are the other two men?"

Dulles positioned the photo for Caroline to see. "The man on the left is Francois Genoud, who oversees Hitler's personal finances. He sells and deposits gold stolen from Jews to the Swiss National Bank, the country's central bank. We're talking millions of dollars. The bar in the picture is called the Oasis. It's a nightclub in Lausanne owned by Genoud and known to be a hangout for Nazis and the SS."

Leaning on her elbows to see the images more precisely, Caroline asked, "So who's the guy on the right?"

Dulles grinned. "I bet Konrad knows him. He's SS General Karl Wolff. He's Himmler's adjutant and the one that receives the gold and cash in Berlin. He established a finance channel to transport the wealth to Lausanne for Genoud to deposit. You know the fourth person very well. I can't believe Endicott let someone catch him on film with these three Nazis. The photographer must have had a hidden camera."

"Endicott is meeting with Dad right now. Could he be in danger?"

"We can't waste any time. Let's go." Dulles made a phone call.

"Should we bring guards?"

"They'll meet us at the car."

Chapter 42

August 6, 1944
Bern, Switzerland

Endicott entered the hospital room at 4:30 p.m. and Hoffman said, "Come in." He felt more alert than he did the previous day. He chuckled as he marveled at Endicott's exceptional taste in his wardrobe and admired the navy-blue cotton suit, tailor-made white shirt, and the red-and-blue silk tie. Hoffman gingerly got up from the bed wearing pajamas and a robe. Despite his right arm in a sling and bandaged ribs and leg, he shuffled over to a chair at the small table and gestured for Endicott to sit at his right.

Endicott took his coat off and grabbed a pad of paper and pen from his bulging valise. Hoffman kept adjusting his arm sling, and Endicott, seeing the colonel's discomfort, said, "Are you all right?"

"The sling keeps rubbing against my wound and I need to adjust it. I'll be okay."

"Bachmann took a huge risk to sneak over the border to kill the three of you. I guess the German embassy paid off the Swiss border guards."

Hoffman said, "I was shocked when I saw Bachmann and surprised that German soldiers wore American uniforms. It was eerie to shoot them." Hoffman leaned back in his chair. "Allen's lateness to meetings benefitted him this time." They both laughed. "Weren't you supposed to attend it as well? What happened?"

Endicott said, "I got called away for an emergency from one of my networks. My German spy saved me from Bachmann, and I should thank him."

Hoffman didn't say anything but waited for Endicott to resume.

"So, Dirk, let's get started. Give me all the details, and I'll put them in a report for Allen."

Hoffman rearranged his sling, described the events of the gun battle, and opted for brevity, but when Endicott wanted more details, Hoffman supplied them. After he finished with his story, he said, "Three things bother me about the attack: first, how did the SS get over the Swiss boundary; second, how did they know the time and date of the meeting; and third, why didn't our legation's security patrol come by at noon?"

Endicott looked down as he rubbed his hand, twisted his head around to look at the front door, reached into his pocket for a handkerchief, rubbed his nose, and put the handkerchief back. He turned to Hoffman and said with his stupid smile, "As for your third point, I pulled the patrol off since I didn't want the meeting disturbed. As for the first two, I share your concerns."

At 5:10 p.m., Allen, Caroline, and two guards jumped into the sedan and headed out. Her eyes widened and she looked straight ahead while Dulles chewed on his pipe as they sped toward the hospital.

Caroline said, "How long have they been in the meeting together?"

Allen said, "Over thirty minutes."

"Do you expect Endicott to avenge Bachmann's death?"

"He won't jeopardize his position, but if Hoffman pushes, no telling what Endicott will do."

Hoffman yawned after completing his report about the ambush and said, "Well, Winthrop, that's all I can tell you about it. Any other questions?"

Endicott dropped his pen and stretched his arms. "What an incredible adventure. To think you outwitted an SS general in Dulles's office. In fact, your entire journey through Germany was miraculous to include surviving the torture. How did you outfox Major Gebauer? He's known to be one of the best Gestapo interrogators."

Hoffman sat up, eyes sharp. Twisting his head slightly, he stared at Endicott. "Who told you about Gebauer?"

"I don't remember. Must have been Bainbridge at MI6."

"Are you sure?"

"Had to be. I heard it from somewhere."

Hoffman sat back, grinned, and crossed his arms. "I have an addendum to my report since everything now fits together."

Endicott wondered what Hoffman meant.

"You gave yourself away when Bachmann showed up to kill us; the general planned his revenge so carefully. No one in the legation knew the time for the meeting except you and Allen, and Allen was delayed and you didn't attend."

Clenching his fists, Endicott said, "All explainable. Others could have known the start time. Allen could have said something. I'm not responsible about how it was known."

"Yes, you are, because you set up the meeting, the time, and the location."

"The Nazis have an extensive spy network here. They could have found out."

Hoffman's eyebrows narrowed. "Winthrop, Bachmann knew my code name, Stork, and that of the German Resistance head."

"Sky Hawk?" He stared at Hoffman. "Then one of their spies obtained it. The German Resistance is full of leaks, you know that. Just because someone knows a code name shouldn't direct your suspicions to me. Dirk, maybe the doctors gave you too much medication. Your allegations make no sense."

Hoffman took a few breaths. "Allen told me that he called you about 1:00 p.m. to say that he would be hours late to the meeting. Bachmann received a phone call around 1:05 p.m. informing him that Dulles would not attend. How do you rationalize this one when Allen said to keep it a secret?"

"He could have told others that he would be away. You are making a fool of yourself. All circumstantial. It wouldn't hold up in court." He smirked.

Hoffman seethed at seeing Endicott's self-satisfying smile. Hoffman continued. "During the past two years, as Allen linked up with German networks and coordinated with headquarters about OSS matters, you were all alone and unsupervised. You could deal with any spy or German friend and pass along American secrets with ease."

"All conjecture." Endicott faced Hoffman but couldn't hold eye contact.

Hoffman scowled. "You met with spies at the Bellevue Palace bar where you passed and received classified information. It's a perfect cover."

"Allen accompanies me to the bar and meets with the same people. Does that make him a spy, too?" Endicott's face was getting redder.

"It's impossible for someone in the civil service to buy expensive tailored suits and custom-made leather shoes. Did your father buy them for you?"

"My father didn't buy me anything."

"Then the SS bought them. You wear nice clothes and enjoy the good life, but the expense goes beyond what you make on a bureaucrat's salary. You sold out the country to look like a dandy."

"You're crazy. I work for the OSS. We're on the same side. I paid for everything. My wife's family has money."

Hoffman sat back and swallowed. "Winthrop, you are correct." Endicott opened his mouth and tried to follow Hoffman's logic. "I stand corrected. Another person could have revealed my code name as well as the meeting time of 1:00 p.m. I grant you that you could be innocent despite overwhelming odds and coincidences to the contrary. And your wife could have financed your wardrobe. You made good points."

Endicott's fingers poked at the tabletop. "Thank you, Dirk. I knew you'd be reasonable and see other possibilities. The war has brought pressure to all of us, and you have endured an incredible amount during your escape."

It was Hoffman's turn to project a greedy smile. He waited a few seconds as both men settled down, and said in a quiet voice, "Winthrop, no one knew that Gebauer interrogated me except the High Command and Bachmann. Is that who told you?"

Endicott's smile disappeared. "Then Konrad told me. He was Bachmann's intelligence officer. He had to know."

"He didn't know either." Hoffman noticed Endicott's rapid breathing. "I couldn't figure out why you would betray your country but realized that you must have been recruited when you lived in Berlin in the twenties, right? You're the mole who relayed information to sabotage the German Resistance and the OSS."

Endicott looked over the room and squirmed. He was cornered. Then he took a deep breath, sat erect in the chair, relaxed his facial muscles, and said, "It's amazing you're still alive. The SS should have killed you at least five times." He pulled the pistol out of his valise and nonchalantly pointed it at the American colonel.

Hoffman said, "And you killed two friends who were trying to help me at the safe house in Berlin. Unforgivable."

"I hate the British and the French. They're so vindictive. They screwed Germany with the Treaty of Versailles and wouldn't listen to President Wilson and his Fourteen Points. The Weimar Republic was a joke."

Hoffman listened in silence and then said, "Of course. I see the link. Wilson was president of Princeton at one time. A Princeton man, same as you and Allen."

"Wilson was the only sane person at the peace table."

Hoffman said, "But Germany is now fighting America."

"Hitler has good ideas about restoring German pride, but you are correct. They pay me a handsome sum. My finances needed bolstering."

Hoffman twisted slightly to his left so the back of his right arm in the sling faced Endicott. Hoffman put his left hand into the sling and scratched his ribs but did not remove it. As he tilted his head back, he said, "If you shoot me, everyone will know you did it. It's over for you and over for Germany."

"Allen will accept anything I say. He's too busy to make any inquiry."

Hoffman looked at the barrel aimed at him. "Winthrop, I've been scratching my arm to adjust the pistol in my sling, which is now in my hand and aimed at your heart. Drop your gun."

Endicott reacted with a start, relaxed with his nervous grin, and said, "There isn't much room for a gun inside the sling."

Hoffman's body tensed, ready to spring out of the line of fire. "Give me your pistol."

Endicott looked at the sling. "I underestimated you, Colonel. You're a smart guy, but so am I." He gave a forced smile. "I think you're faking. I went to Princeton, remember?"

"Don't make me show how dumb you are."

"I admire your guts in the face of death, but the smart ones need to go on with their lives. Besides, even if you have a gun, I'll be executed for being a spy, so my odds at calling your bluff look favorable."

Hoffman focused on Endicott's eyes as he learned from army training: In close quarters with an enemy, look at the eyes and when the corners start to squint, react in a split second. It is a sign that the person is pulling the trigger. Hoffman saw terror in Endicott's eyes. He was not going to drop the gun. Perspiration glistened on Endicott's forehead.

Opposite from Endicott, Hoffman's face was relaxed and his eyes were calm and steady.

As both men faced each other, Endicott said, "Colonel, you're quite the soldier. You should have been in counterintelligence."

Endicott's eye muscles twitched. He pulled the trigger while at the same instant, Hoffman bolted backward and fired just as Endicott did. Endicott's bullet found Hoffman's left shoulder, and Hoffman's bullet pierced Endicott's heart. Endicott jerked into the back of the chair, his jaw dropped, and his eyes lost their gaze as his body lurched forward onto the table and then rebounded onto the floor.

Blood splattered on Hoffman's robe and sling, and his facial muscles tightened as he recoiled in pain as his body received yet another wound.

Hearing the shots, Allen, Caroline, and the two guards raced through the lobby to Hoffman's room, opened the door, and gaped at Endicott's body on the floor. Caroline and Dulles followed, breathing hard, saw the body, and approached Hoffman. Caroline wanted to hug her father but didn't know how since blood covered his upper torso and his limp left arm.

Allen said, "Sorry we're late. Caroline showed me the photo of Endicott and Genoud at a Nazi bar and guess who stood at his side but an SS general none other than Major General Bachmann. We worried about you. Glad you're the one standing."

"Me too, just barely. Endicott confessed to being a spy."

Caroline called for a doctor.

Hoffman rested in the hospital bed as both arms were put into slings, which limited his activity—especially feeding himself. "I have enough problems managing my other wounds, so how do I handle not using my arms?"

Konrad had returned from minor surgery and glad he missed the gunfight in their hospital room.

Caroline spoke, "The doctor said Endicott's bullet only glanced off your shoulder, and it will heal quickly."

Once Hoffman got comfortable with pillows propping up his shoulders, Konrad said, "I hope we're finally rid of Nazis for a while."

Chapter 43

October 1944–August 1945
London, England

On August 15, 1944, the Allies, which included a large contingent of French forces, invaded Marseille under Operation Dragoon and pushed the Germans northward. Hoffman followed the progress from the US Legation offices and vowed to get to an army airbase as soon as southern France was liberated.

After the US Army captured, repaired, and reopened the Lyon airport in early October 1944, Hoffman, mostly healed from his wounds, went to Geneva, hitched a ride on a military convoy to Lyon, and flew to London. His arrival at Supreme Headquarters shocked everyone especially Major General Joe Machinski, the man who approved his sojourn to Berlin.

When Hoffman entered his boss's office after a five-month absence, Machinski bolted around the desk and shook hands with his missing subordinate. "Who would have thought a supply jockey would go undercover and return? Can I buy you a drink?"

"I gave up drinking last May, remember?"

The general laughed. "Quite so."

Technically, Hoffman still belonged under Machinski's command, so he reinstated Hoffman to his old job in supply except instead of landing craft, he focused on food and materials with the added responsibility to streamline the distribution system. Caroline remained in Bern to tend to Konrad's recovery, but her father promised they would reunite after the war.

Seven months later on May 7, 1945, generals from the Western Front and from Berlin converged on a century-old farmhouse in Reims, France, that served as Eisenhower's headquarters. For almost one thousand years, twenty-five French kings were crowned at Reims's majestic Cathédrale Notre-Dame. The town also served as the unofficial capital of northeastern France's champagne wine-growing region.

The people of Reims took extra pleasure with the Germans signing an unconditional surrender since the Boche almost destroyed their town in the Great War. The belligerents sat in a conference room that had maps spread all over the walls. General Alfred Jodl, German military chief of staff, signed the capitulation agreement. The war in Europe was over.

When the world heard the news, millions rejoiced, but Hoffman did not have that luxury. With economies destroyed and twelve million exiles crisscrossing Europe, supply difficulties had compounded, and the most intractable problems landed on his desk.

Refugees dominated the devastated European countryside as German troops escaped the Soviets; other countries kicked out panicked German civilians; and displaced persons—who had no country—required life-saving attention. So the Allies, principally the United States, had to feed the weary, the destitute, and the haggard. British, French, and American forces set up camps to address this mayhem. Because human needs competed for limited resources, intense pressure mounted to address the shortages while millions died from starvation, cold, and suicide.

As he did in Switzerland, Hoffman continued to write to Kaye on a regular basis. The letters recounted his happiness that he had reconnected with Caroline, and he told her about the progress he had made against his demons. Periodically, he apologized for his past behavior but wouldn't elaborate beyond his regrets.

At the end of May 1945, he picked up his pen and wrote:

Dear Kaye,

The army won't release me since we have Herculean supply problems, and they need me to deal with them. I will be relocated to the headquarters of the American Occupation Zone and was thinking if you could travel over here, we could set up a new household in Frankfurt. The army will pay for you as long as I commit to two years. I can get a two-bedroom house. Caroline and Konrad will travel there soon so our family will be reunited. I will transfer in July and will set things up, and if you could arrive in August, I would welcome your presence and maybe we can start over.

Love, Dirk

Two weeks passed and each day brought worry to Hoffman. His mind raced over the myriad possibilities about the reply to his letter. Maybe Kaye didn't want to start over. Maybe the letter never arrived. Maybe she had a boyfriend in Fort Knox. He didn't blame her but did have hope. Maybe she can see how I have changed from the tone of my letters.

After sixteen days of waiting, Hoffman received Kaye's letter. He held it to the light and wondered if he should open it, afraid of her answer. Gently, he unsealed the back flap and unfolded it. His eyes were riveted to her words.

Dear Dirk,

I would love to be with you in Frankfurt and set up our new house. Maybe we can do a better job of it this time. These past three years have been difficult for all of us and especially you in a war zone. I will enjoy being with Caroline again and will be there when you want me.

Love, Kaye

A big smile crept over his face and soon his eyes moistened. He got a second chance.

In the middle of July 1945, Caroline and Konrad made their way to Frankfurt and moved in with Hoffman until they found a place of their own. The hiring of ex-Nazis in Germany was prohibited although officials relaxed this rule since cities needed to fill openings.

For municipal government positions in Frankfurt, Hoffman endorsed Konrad to the city manager. Hoffman couldn't say that Konrad was a British spy but hoped his words might carry weight. With so many reconstruction projects, a US Army colonel's recommendation lent credibility and persuaded the city manager to hire Konrad as a planner.

The army employed Caroline to assist in the administration of three hundred refugee camps. Caroline filled the slot because she spoke German, and her dad had a high position in army supply that they hoped to tap for their camp needs. A stigma attached to Caroline because she was married to an ex-Nazi, but when Hoffman revealed that his daughter housed American and British pilots on their escape route out of Germany, the stain was erased.

Hoffman had the presence of mind to get a gift for Kaye but didn't know what to buy especially since few stores had goods to offer. He wandered near a commercial area with rubble strewn over the street and buildings. Women crews worked with old carts and old tools to clear the debris. Emaciated civilians approached soldiers begging for cigarettes, chocolates, or food or offered to sell family valuables for a pittance.

As Hoffman strode past the masonry fragments, a middle-aged, gaunt woman dressed in rags solved his problem. She targeted American officers and said, "Do you want to buy a precious bracelet?"

Hoffman's first instinct was to walk past her, but he saw the sparkling piece of jewelry. "How much?"

"It's been in the family for two generations, but we need food." She took a deep breath. "Cost is a pack of cigarettes."

He stared at the deep red stones. "What are the jewels on it?"

"Garnets."

Hoffman studied her face and assumed she didn't want to part with it especially for such a low price of a few cigarettes, yet cigarettes and chocolates were used as currency on the black market to buy food. The Reichsmark was worthless. Many women offered sex for cigarettes. Hoffman carried cigarettes and chocolate to serve as barter.

"I'll take it. Here's the pack." He gave her cigarettes that Americans easily and cheaply bought at the post exchange. She didn't say anything but dropped her eyes and turned to leave. He stopped her. "Where do you live? This is only a down payment. I'll bring you food to cover the rest of the value."

She stood looking at him and could not find the words to express her gratitude. Later that day, he cleaned his shelves and put everything into a duffle bag. When he dropped the food off, he saw that the woman's dilapidated house sheltered three grubby children. Hoffman said, "If you will allow me, I'd like to assist until things improve." She burst into tears.

Chapter 44

On August 19, 1945, Hoffman, Caroline, and Konrad waited fifty minutes at the Frankfurt Hauptbahnhof, the main station, for Kaye's train. Caroline and Konrad were excited about her arrival. Kaye had spent months in 1938 chaperoning her daughter on her singing tour and knew Konrad during that time, which included their wedding in November of that year, so mother and son-in-law were close.

A dejected Hoffman walked around the station, touching his pocket for the fiftieth time where the jeweled bracelet rested, and reached the platform's edge.

He practiced a small speech but gave up after two tries. Given her reservations about him, he would move cautiously and wait for her to decide how she greeted him. When the train whistle blew in the distance, he rejoined Caroline and Konrad. Caroline said, "She's here. Oh my goodness. I can't wait." Hoffman looked downward.

When the train slowed and finally stopped at bay number eight, the crowd migrated to the railcar doors and waited for the passengers to disembark. As Kaye held onto the railing and stepped down, Caroline charged through the crowd with Konrad right behind and rushed into her mother's arms. Both laughed loudly as their bodies twirled back and forth. After a few moments, Konrad squeezed in and threw his arms around his mother-in-law. Hoffman trailed with a hesitant grin. He longed for her but was afraid to make the first move.

Kaye saw him and disengaged from her daughter, looked at her husband with tender eyes, and said softly, "Dirk. It's been so long." He was surprised when she wrapped her arms around his neck and pulled him to her. After the embrace, they pushed back to look at each other. She had tears in her eyes, and so did he.

"Kaye, you look magnificent. I've missed you so much."

"It's good to see you and see you safe."

They resumed their warm hugs while Caroline cried at seeing them together, but Hoffman felt that Kaye held back. They had issues to address as well as time for reacquaintance.

In an army truck borrowed from his unit, Hoffman drove the group to the Officers' Club for a celebration dinner. Many officers who worked with Hoffman witnessed his smile at being reunited with his wife, and as he guided the party to a table, the dining area erupted in cheers and applause.

"Welcome to Germany!" "We're thrilled to have you here!" Kaye, surprised at the outpouring, blushed, waived, and then put her hand to her mouth in embarrassment.

Drinks were served at the table and army colleagues intermittently dropped by with their wine glasses to toast Kaye and welcome her to Frankfurt. Hoffman acknowledged their good cheer and returned the toasts with his water glass. Kaye accepted an invitation to a wives' tea party, and a major's wife said, "We have lots of shortages, so don't expect caviar or much wine, but we'll offer some interesting hors d'oeuvres."

At this heartfelt celebration, Hoffman's group settled down to hear about Kaye's trip. Caroline asked questions about the States, and Konrad mentioned the excursions he'd planned for her. Hoffman remained at a distance enjoying the chatter, but mostly he gazed at Kaye, recalled her mannerisms, and loved hearing her voice.

Hoffman dropped off Caroline and Konrad and drove to their small house. He turned off the engine but stayed in the car.

Despite sporadic honks of distant car horns, the street was quiet and dark. Kaye lingered in her seat, looked at her husband, and soaked in the serenity of the moment.

Hoffman leaned back, faced his wife, and said softly, "It's so nice having you here."

"I loved how you and Caroline enjoyed each other. It made me so happy."

"She's a great kid. You did a wonderful job." He lowered his head. "I feel so badly that I didn't contribute."

"When Caroline was in Switzerland, she wrote that she would be dead if it wasn't for you, so I think you made up for it. I have my daughter. That's what matters."

After her comments, Kaye leaned over and rested her head on Dirk's shoulder. "This has been a memorable welcome, but I'm fading fast." She gave a loud yawn. "I hope I have energy to make it to the house."

"Are you ready to start a new home in a new country . . . on a new continent?"

"I'm ready. I bought a new apron. Does the stove work? I want to bake your favorite cookies once I get some rest."

Hoffman took her hand and kissed it.

Chapter 45

When they entered the house, she leaned on Dirk's arm to make it inside. The dinner festivities and seeing his wife again caused Dirk to forget that he had a present. "Kaye, just a minute." He reached into his pocket and gave her a wrapped box.

Kaye's eyebrows went up, and she stepped back to look at him. "A gift for me? What is it?"

"You need to open it."

She unwrapped it with wide eyes. When she saw the bracelet, she sniffled and put a hand over her heart. "It's beautiful."

"The stones are garnets, your birthstone."

"I don't know what to say. I don't have anything for you."

"Yes, you do. You're here. I can't thank you enough."

She said, "Honey, I want to talk, but it must wait until tomorrow. I'm exhausted."

"I need to talk to you, too . . . later."

That night, they slept in the same bed for the first time in ages and fell asleep quickly. She did feel his kiss her on her forehead before she conked out.

The next morning, a groggy Kaye woke up and noticed that Dirk was gone. She looked at the clock and was astonished that it read 10:30 a.m. She had slept for eleven hours. Her head fell back into the pillow and she tried to remember the previous day's events. Seeing Caroline and Konrad again was a blessing. Dirk was so thoughtful. He even laughed. Has he changed? How do I feel about him making love to me? He didn't seem interested when we lived at Fort Knox, but he appears interested now.

She showered, dressed, put on the bracelet, and inspected her new home. It was clean and sparsely furnished, but as one wife told her at the O Club, "You'll adjust."

Dirk did an excellent job of stocking the kitchen. She checked the old stove, pots and pans, the icebox, and concluded that she could cook dinner without too much trouble. By the sink she noticed two bottles of her favorite kind of red wine, pinot noir, which brought a smile. He remembered.

At noon, Caroline dropped by. "Mom, Dad asked me to give you a brief tour of the neighborhood, so let's go."

The expedition included lunch at a local café. Despite the limited menu, they dined on the delicious entree. Mother and daughter caught up on girl talk, such as Caroline's experience in wartime Berlin, her marriage, her stay in Switzerland, and her job.

"Mom, you won't believe this, but Dad saw me sing and enjoyed my performance."

"Where did he see you?"

Not wanting to worry her mother about the perilous journey to Switzerland, Caroline said, "That's not important." She signaled the waiter for more water. "He actually liked my singing and said he should have paid for more lessons."

Kaye said, "Did you perform at your house?"

"I'll tell you later. When we traveled through Germany, I was shocked at the devastation." Caroline suddenly became serious. "I saw Dad in his military bearing, saw him handle danger against the Nazis. He stopped me from shooting a bad guy. I didn't think about the burden one carries when you kill someone, but Dad did."

"I didn't realize you had a gun. Were you in combat?"

"A Nazi snuck into an apartment and tried to shoot us. Dad and Konrad saved the day. I got so angry that I could have killed a

German. In the heat of the fight, I didn't think about morality, but afterward, I hated myself."

"Were you in any serious danger?"

"No, just a few scrapes. We stayed in Switzerland for the rest of the war and away from those horrible Nazis."

"But you're married to one."

"Well, he's not a real Nazi. He didn't kill people." Caroline raised her voice. "Mom, Konrad had to work for Nazis, otherwise, they would have killed him."

"But you'll tell me all about it later, right?" Kaye pressed her daughter with her eyebrows raised.

Caroline changed the subject. "Mom, I have a job for you and hope you'll be ready next week. We have so many needs and too few Americans around."

"What will I be doing?"

"We need help with overseeing the refugees. There are so many people in the camps, and we have so few reserves. Dad is helping with the supplies, but more people arrive beyond the limits of our provisions."

Kaye said, "I am so pleased that you and your Father get along so well."

"Mom, you don't know the half of it. It wasn't easy talking to him at first, but we became a team. With you coming here, I've never seen him so excited and nervous."

"Nervous? I'm the one who's nervous. I don't want to live through his nightmares again or his quick temper. To tell the truth, I wasn't sure I wanted to come, but the chance of seeing you convinced me."

"Give him a chance. I did, and you saw the results."

"He's a good man and gave me a wonderful child. I'll be open, but I can't believe he is nervous."

"I'll let him explain."

Chapter 46

Kaye returned from the outing with Caroline at 3:00, which gave her time to prepare the kitchen and put her own stamp on it. She wore her new apron, put a cloth over the table, and arranged the utensils, glasses, and plates.

At 6:15, Kaye heard a noise on the porch. She quickly took off her apron, checked herself in the mirror, and waited in the living room. Dirk entered clad in his army uniform and gave Kaye a half smile. His eyes looked left and right, and he took a deep breath. "Did you and Caroline have a good lunch?" He fidgeted, kept his hands at his side, and tried to think of something to say.

Kaye said, "Are you all right? You look wrung out."

"I need to talk to you about some awkward subjects."

"I think I need to hear them."

They walked to the frayed sofa and sat down, but he sat away from her, to give her room and himself space.

He looked at the ceiling, swallowed, and said, "When I returned in 1919, I promised myself not to say anything about the cruelty of war and all the killing. My family didn't need to get their brains messed up with the gore."

Kaye said, "You certainly kept your promise because you walled yourself away from us. You occupied a space in Fort Knox, but mentally you remained in France. It was an awful experience to see you this way."

"I'm breaking my promise now."

"I can't promise about how I'll react, but I'm ready to listen."

Hoffman nodded. "You asked for it, but first I need to apologize. I behaved badly in our marriage. Getting Caroline to Switzerland showed me how little I knew about her and how much I missed out."

He bent forward and brought his two hands to his chin and tried to speak. His left knee shook as he looked straight ahead. "Back in 1918, the Germans surrounded our battalion and killed many during the six-day battle, and the experience shut me down and I couldn't stop it. I talked to two Germans about my nightmares, and they encouraged me to let my emotions out, to talk about my feelings and fears, so here goes."

Kaye's heart beat rapidly.

"My problems started before going on patrol. When we were cut off from our lines, I lost thirteen men plus more who were wounded. The Germans kept firing during the night, and I thought we'd be overrun since we had little ammunition and food. I hadn't slept or eaten for two days. They even yelled and urged us to surrender. I was so scared.

"For two nights in a row, the Nazis rushed our defenses and without ammo, we fought them hand to hand and used our bayonets. I killed two by sticking my blade into their bodies. When we held our positions and the Germans retreated, I felt sick. I couldn't throw up since I had nothing in my stomach. I had to deal with my remaining men who were wounded and drag the dead to another area.

"When I looked at my dead comrades, I wanted to leave the battlefield. I was a coward. In the morning, a few of my men formed for a patrol and I was crying."

As Kaye heard the story, she wanted to cradle her husband's head in her lap, but she sat still and listened attentively.

His lips quivered and his eyes stared at the rug. "I feel the battle even now, I can smell it." He gulped. "When the sun came up, we were ordered to scout and look for a way out. I didn't want to go. I wanted to quit. I had no energy. I exhausted my reserves three days before, burned up my adrenalin two days prior, no water to help my dry throat. My stamina was stretched, my tears evaporated, and fear spread through my body like a power surge. Nothing mattered, not family or friends.

"My sergeant and close buddy, Earl Zachery, saw me and volunteered to handle the squad. I don't know where I got the energy, but at that moment, all that counted were my men. I couldn't shirk my responsibility, so somehow I stood up and joined them. Five minutes into our recon, the Nazis caught us in a small open space. The noise of rifle fire and mortar rounds was so loud. Shrapnel flew in every direction and smoke spread over the bushes." His head tilted upward. "I thought my life had ended. I saw others in my squad die or fall wounded. I saw no way out.

"Amidst the bullets, Zach crouched next to me beside a tree. As we searched for a retreat, a Nazi bullet pierced my ribs and another found Zach's heart. It killed him instantly, and he fell on top of me. His sightless eyes stared at me, and his blood splattered over my shirt. I pushed him off and found that my blood-soaked clothes stuck to my skin, Zach's blood. I kept pulling the drenched shirt away from me but could never unstick it."

Kaye said, "So that's why you always pulled your shirt or uniform in the States."

"I guess so. I didn't realize it before. Zach didn't have to come on this patrol but did it for me. He saved me. He saved a coward. I should have died instead of Zach. I made sure Zach got medals for his bravery." He hesitated, looked downward, his face flushed, and tried to speak. Kaye waited.

"I . . . I . . ." and he put his head in his hands and sobbed. He gasped for breath. When he looked up, he reached for Kaye, and she pulled him to her. His tears streamed over her shoulder and moistened her blouse, and she held him.

They parted slightly with their hands clasping and his breathing subsiding.

"How did you get away?"

"After I nudged Zach aside, I saw an opening. I fired my rifle so the Nazis took cover. Used up all of my bullets. This quick break allowed the five of us to slip into the underbrush. We were all wounded but crawled, hid where we could, and then finally ran for protection of the trees. Once together, we made it back to camp." Hoffman stopped, shook his head. "I left three dead buddies there."

Kaye felt so close to her husband and wished she could say something to comfort him but knew that silence would help him get through the reliving of his terror.

During the afternoon, I fell asleep in my foxhole and was awakened by a soldier who I thought was a German. I searched for my rifle until the man spoke English and said he was an American. I asked for water and that's the last thing I remembered. Troops from the 154th Brigade, our brigade, had broken through and saved us."

He cried again but this time he cried with his head resting on his folded forearms. "Sarge must be so disappointed with me." Hoffman took a breath. "I was taken to a hospital. I found out later that some unit rounded up all the dead. I wasn't there and never said good-bye. I don't even know where my men are buried."

Hoffman stopped, lost in thought. "I remained in the hospital for two weeks, and then the army shipped me home. On board a troop ship, Germany ended the war and signed an armistice. I had so much time to think about those six days and what a failure I had been. I failed my men. I didn't want anyone to know about this hell. This was my state of mind when you picked me up at the Fort Knox station."

Hoffman remained sitting and glared straight ahead. When the tension left his body, Hoffman looked at his wife. "Thank you, honey. It felt good to talk about it."

Kaye was crying too, for her husband, for his buddies, and for herself.

That night, they made love slowly and fell into a deep sleep.

On the third evening, Kaye said, "Caroline wrote in a letter that the Nazis kidnapped and tortured you, but you got away somehow." Kaye looked at her husband with raised eyebrows. "That must have been unimaginable." She waited. "Caroline admitted that she would have died if you hadn't come for her in Berlin. I guess that's the assignment you mentioned in your letter."

"I was prepared for the torture if one can ever be prepared, but afterward, my body was a wreck. Fortunately, a good German saved me, and his girlfriend, a nurse named Freya, brought me back."

"What's his name?"

"Axel Lichterman. He was a captain in the German army and assisted a Gestapo maniac who shot me up with truth serums. I would have died if Axel hadn't stepped in. He advised me to talk my pain out."

"Where did the interrogation take place?"

"At a Berlin hospital. I hope one day to thank him and Freya. She reminded me of Caroline."

Chapter 47

Konrad went to work for the City of Frankfurt Planning Department to aid in the cleanup and reconstruction. Germany did not have a national government until 1948, so rebuilding was approved at the local level.

Working with Caroline in the administration of German refugee camps gave Kaye enormous satisfaction to carry out American relief. Her limited German language skills that she learned from her German grandmother helped in handling 250,000 refugees. She compiled the weekly lists of new displaced persons in various camps and consolidated them into a new roster. Each day over the past two months she made her usual quick glance at the "L" category in search of Axel Lichterman. Despite not seeing the name, she continued just in case he might show up.

On this day, she blinked a few times and refocused when the name Lichterman appeared. The list said he was a captain from Berlin, and arrived at the Amberg camp, twenty miles east of Nuremberg, 260 miles south of Berlin. She saw a number of Freyas from Berlin but didn't know if any worked as a nurse.

That evening, an exhausted Hoffman returned home and was greeted with the news about his German friend. "I have to see him. I wonder if he'll remember me?"

Kaye said, "I checked with the travel desk. We could take a train from Frankfurt to Nuremberg and hitch a ride on military transport to Amberg. I'm friends with a secretary in the Transportation Department, and she can arrange the trip for us."

"Why do you want to come?"

"I'm indebted to them for saving my husband. Also my boss said I could go and evaluate the facilities. The administrators here know very little about that camp."

Two days later, the Hoffmans arrived at the Amberg office after six hours of travel and introduced themselves to the administrator. Upon hearing the story, he instructed his sergeant to bring Axel Lichterman and Freya, if she was with him, to his office.

As they waited, Hoffman said to Kaye, "I wonder what condition they are in. Will he be angry that he's in a dismal camp? I hope Freya is with him. He may not want to see me."

"Patience, Dirk. I'm sure he'll be glad to see you."

"So much has happened, and they lost the war."

Kaye patted his arm and looked out into the crowded yard. She saw the sergeant leading two ragged people, one with a hobble. They approached the back door and entered the room with downcast expressions on their faces. The sergeant stayed in the rear. The man and the woman were dirty, scrawny, and tired. Recognizing the limp, Hoffman said, "Axel?"

The man looked up. His eyes opened widely, and a smile crossed his lips. "Dirk?" Then Axel turned to the woman. "Freya, it's the American colonel."

Hoffman couldn't believe the changes that had come over them in one year. "It is so good to see you. This is my wife, Kaye."

Axel and Freya stood in an aloof manner embarrassed at their condition. Not sure if he should salute, shake hands, or remain in place, Axel said to Kaye, "Nice to meet you. Dirk has told me much about you."

Hoffman came over and excitedly shook Axel's hand. Freya couldn't talk. She shook and then cried. Kaye stepped forward and hugged her. She recognized similarities in appearance with Caroline and felt close to her right away.

Hoffman guided them over to a table and extended his arm suggesting that they sit down. Freya whispered to Kaye, "Thank you. We've been walking a long time."

Kaye said, "I imagine you are hungry, too."

Hoffman picked up the hint. "Sergeant, could you bring in some food for this couple?"

The sergeant saluted and said, "Yes, sir."

As the Germans consumed soup, bread, and coffee, Axel explained their journey. "The Soviets captured Berlin on May second and went on a rampage of killing and raping for days and days. No woman was safe. If anyone objected, the soldiers shot them."

Hoffman asked, "Did they reach the hospital?"

Freya said, "Yes, but Axel saved many women including me. He put women, some wounded soldiers, and doctors in a big room, sealed it, and posted a sign that said, 'Warning. Typhus.' He wore a mask and told the soldiers that three hundred patients have already died and gave it to the staff." Freya gave a small grin. "It worked because after that meeting, the gangs of Soviet outlaws avoided the hospital. The delay gave us and others time to escape."

Axel said, "I received messages about the harsh treatment of our patients by the Russians. Any captured German soldiers went to labor camps, and the severely wounded were ignored or killed. We had to leave."

Axel and Freya regained strength with the meal and became more animated.

Hoffman asked, "How is Helga? I thought she didn't like me, but she was the one who called the fake SS to take me away. I want to thank her."

Axel looked at Freya with sad eyes. "The SS picked her up three days later. Someone accused her of belonging to the Resistance. She died in jail."

"This is so sad." Hoffman paused and looked away. "She saved my life and was killed for it."

Axel said, "Everyone at the hospital felt so badly. She watched over the nurses and helped the patients. A huge loss."

Kaye said, "I don't even know her and feel close to her."

After one hour of catching up on each's experiences, Hoffman asked, "Did you two marry?"

Axel and Freya gave a small laugh of embarrassment. He said, "We've been engaged for a long time and never had an opportunity to see a minister."

Freya broke in. "Axel wanted to, but my parents, before they died, didn't like him because he was born on a farm and walked with a limp."

Axel replied, "Freya, your parents are dead. We don't need their approval."

She nodded and grinned. "I think it's time we get someone to marry us."

Axel's smile expanded. "I got tired of proposing to her, so now she decides to set a date. She proposes better than I do."

Everyone laughed, and Freya and Axel relaxed into their more natural selves.

Axel said, "It was so nice of you to see us. You must be very busy with cleaning up and feeding Germans. I don't know how you could spare the time, so Freya and I will release you to return to your many duties."

Kaye interrupted, looked at her husband with her pleading blue eyes, and then said, "The administrators don't have enough places to settle everyone. Getting placed somewhere could take a long time. You could stay in the camp for years. Why don't you stay with us? I know an understaffed hospital that could use you."

Hoffman was surprised that Kaye extended the invitation but heartily agreed. "That is if you don't mind living with Americans."

Freya burst out crying again. Axel put his arm around her. "The war brought many difficulties. Your kindness is the first we've had in many months."

The four managed well in the two-bedroom unit, and Hoffman got them jobs at an army hospital. Kaye celebrated with a dinner that included Konrad and Caroline that brought about special bonds among all six. Kaye coordinated with Freya to complete paperwork and a date for a wedding. The ceremony and reception were attended by Hoffman's friends and hospital coworkers. Hoffman paid for everything from his Swiss bank account including a honeymoon. Afterward with everyone's approval, he transferred the remaining funds to the refugee camps' account.

When the Lichtermans moved to their own quarters, Hoffman said to Kaye, "I have one more mission ahead of me. I need to say farewell to some friends."

Kaye understood.

Chapter 48

The trip to the Meuse-Argonne American Cemetery required three weeks of planning as it was located in a remote agricultural area named Romagne-sous-Montfaucon, in northeast France—160 miles east of Paris, 60 miles west of Luxembourg, and 25 miles from Verdun where the bloodiest battle of the Great War was fought. Hoffman found out where the Argonne Forest casualties were buried.

Most of the region was covered with endless fields of wheat. Within this expanse, a 130-acre tract was classically laid out as a sylvan oasis of grass terraces bordered by linden trees to honor 14,246 American soldiers who lost their lives at the Meuse-Argonne offensive. This major battle of the final Allied effort of World War I extended along the Western Front and was the second deadliest battle in American history. It began on September 26, 1918, and ended with the Armistice of November 11, 1918—death and gore for forty-seven days.

Kaye and Dirk caught the train at 8:00 a.m. from Frankfurt to Paris. He dressed in his summer khaki uniform and helped Kaye up the stairs to the railcar and to their seats. Her blue-and-white print dress with a modest simple tie at the neck, red beret, and gloves reminded him of social activities they did together before the war, and Kaye looked even better now than when he left Fort Knox three years ago. He was pleased that she wore her garnet bracelet.

As the train crossed the French border heading toward Paris, he became pensive and nervous. He crossed his arms and legs and looked out the window at the passing vineyards. He remained quiet for almost an hour, and when Kaye offered a sandwich, he put up his hand and turned to stare at the scenery out the other window.

From Paris, they caught a bus to Reims. Hoffman remained remote, fidgeted with his hands, and gazed at the back of the seat in front of him. Kaye watched her husband and touched his wrist. "Dirk, are you all right?"

His sad eyes met hers and he said, "Going into battle is easier."

"Would you prefer that we go back home?"

"Kaye, I don't know what to say to my men. I'm shaking inside. Do they really want me to visit them? They died following my orders."

"You almost died too, Dirk." Kaye paused then added, "It's war. Nothing else needs to be said."

"Kaye, we trained together, worked together, fought together. But I survived. Why did I live and they didn't?" He sat back and surveyed the ceiling. "I've carried them with me since 1918. I did my best in the Argonne Forest, but it wasn't good enough."

Kaye swallowed. "No one knows why some soldiers live and some die."

"When I set about to rescue Caroline, I spoke with a German bishop about my problem. He said that my dead comrades want me to stop torturing myself. All is well with them." Hoffman pursed his lips. "The bishop suggested a remedy: that I should be with them, feel them, and let them go, that I have the power to do it. I tried to be with them in the hotel before I went after Caroline." Hoffman arched his eyebrows as he remembered. "I felt awful and even cried." He looked into Kaye's eyes. "After Caroline's rescue, I haven't had any nightmares."

Kaye covered his hand on his knee with hers. "The bishop sounds like a wise man."

"Yeah, except he turned out to be a Nazi and tried to kill me."

"Then he wasn't a man of God." Kaye looked at him for a long minute, then put her head on his shoulder.

The bus pulled into a station at Reims and they made their way to the street and met a two-and-a-half-ton army truck arranged by Hoffman. The two passengers and driver crammed into the cab. The driver, a corporal from Georgia, delivered supplies to rural areas and felt nervous about having a full bird colonel in his truck.

After a bumpy two-hour ride from Reims, the corporal drove to the front gates of the cemetery, and Hoffman and Kay climbed out. The driver gave a salute to Colonel Hoffman. "I'll be back in three hours, sir."

As the two started toward the entrance, Dirk stopped. "My legs are shaking. I don't think I can take one more step."

"Let's wait a moment and take our time," she said.

"Kaye, remember when you said I had a disease, and I said I didn't? Well, you're right. They called it shell shock in the Great War and in this war, they call it battle fatigue. I am so weak. Look at me. I shake, had nightmares, and cringed at loud noises. What kind of soldier does that? I don't deserve to lead men. They are the strong ones."

Kaye took both of his hands into hers and looked him in the eye. "I don't think shell shock is a weakness. You had the strength to lead men in dangerous situations when others feared to do it."

Hoffman cried silently. His breathing was irregular. Then he mumbled, "Thanks, honey."

Kaye put her arm around Dirk's, and they walked up the dirt road and entered the grounds. Once inside, Hoffman focused on the acres of white crosses. They didn't see any other person in the cemetery.

"What a waste of brave men," he said as Kaye listened at his side. They walked farther and stopped. "It's so peaceful and so beautiful." He was struck by the manicured hedges, the rich green of the grass, and especially the quiet.

Kaye said gently, "Shall we go?"

Her husband nodded.

As they continued down the path, Kaye asked, "How many of your men are here?"

Hoffman said in a low voice, "Sixteen." His eyes looked at the ground. "Not quite half of my platoon."

"You never told me about your platoon."

"I failed those sixteen."

Kaye said, "More men would have been buried here had it not been for you."

He dropped his arm, pivoted, and looked directly at her. "What do you mean? You don't know what went on in the battlefield."

"I learned from one of your men a long time ago."

Hoffman said, "Who?"

"You expect me to sit back and accept your anger all those years? I had to know what happened, so I collared one of your drinking buddies, and he gave me the name of Alex Correa in New York City."

"Alex?"

"I called him." Hoffman's mouth opened, and Kaye continued. "Mr. Correa said that you protected the men during the entire six days of combat and led the remaining squad out of the ambush despite being outmanned and outgunned. A wound to your ribs didn't stop you as you dragged two men to safety and then, after you arrived at the camp, you took dressings off dead soldiers and bandaged your men. You acted as doctor since your medic was killed two days before."

"Alex said that?"

"He mentioned that at the end, you were the only able person in the platoon and went to your foxhole to protect the unit against an assault even though you lost blood and were weak. Mr. Correa said that after you went to the hospital, the men made sure the company commander knew about your heroism."

Hoffman stood in disbelief. "I can't believe with all of our dead comrades that he would say those things about me." He walked away from her in deep thought. He wiped his forehead with the back of his hand, looked to the sky, turned around and came back. "Kaye, why didn't you tell me?"

"I thought you would be mad at me contacting one of your men, and we'd have another fight." She took a breath. "I hoped you'd come out of your depression, but you never did. The same thing happened to my father after the Spanish-American War, so I waited and waited."

Dirk came over to her and wrapped his arms around her. They remained in the embrace, and Dirk asked, "Did your dad ever come out of it?"

Kaye shook her head. "No. I felt badly for Mom. So, what did I do? I married someone just like my father and suffered as she did."

Dirk looked at a nearby tree, tightened his hug, and said, "That's not going to happen anymore, Kaye."

She smiled. "Let's go to the office." She reached for his hand, and he took it.

They followed the path to the Visitors' Center located on the top of a gently sloped hill. Before entering, they turned back to view the crosses, finally pulled open the heavy doors, and went to the front desk.

Hoffman provided the administrator with sixteen names. After a few minutes, the man rifled through a large book and wrote out the grave numbers beside each name. He also presented a map with the locations of Hoffman's compatriots that were circled with his pencil.

The Hoffmans strolled down the path to Section C to seek out his men. Going to row twenty-eight and moving down to grave thirteen, Hoffman spotted the first marble gravestone.

As Kaye lingered in the background, he faced the cross and spoke to it. After expressing an apology and affection, Hoffman cried. Composing himself, he knelt next to the headstone, put his right hand on top of it, and bowed his head. Then he rose, stood at attention, and saluted.

Hoffman went to fourteen more grave sites, and after each visit, he repeated his show of respect followed by a formal salute. His shoulders sagged lower after each stop.

As he advanced to the last site on his list, Hoffman read the engraved marble headstone:

Earl Charles Zachery

First Sergeant   308 Regiment

North Carolina   Oct 5, 1918

He scanned the grave site while taking deep breaths and returned his focus to the cross. "I feel so bad that you got killed, Zach. I messed up." He spoke to the marble cross expecting it to talk back. "If only we could have lasted one more month, the war would have ended, and we could've celebrated in Paris." Hoffman recounted the good times they had together and started to cry. "I miss you so much."

As he recovered his poise, he didn't kneel and touch the headstone as he did at the other graves but instead turned and called out to Kaye. "Come here." Kaye walked over on the immaculately cut lawn, and Hoffman said in a shaken voice, "I want to introduce you to Sergeant Earl Zachery." Hoffman inhaled more air, clenched his jaw, and said, "Zach, this is my wife, Kaye."

He elaborated about how Zach saved his butt on bivouac and took care of him and the platoon during the fighting. Hoffman's lower lip quivered and tears ran down his cheeks. Kaye turned and embraced him. She cried too. Kaye separated from the embrace, looked at the cross, and said to Zach, "Thank you for watching over my husband." Hoffman sobbed openly.

When they released each other, Hoffman faced his sergeant, stood at attention, and saluted. After he lowered his arm, Hoffman put his hand on the top of the cold marble, said a prayer, and stepped away holding Kaye's hand.

As they strolled between the crosses in the direction of the entrance, Hoffman said, "I would like to be buried at a place just like this one. It's so peaceful."

Hoffman held Kaye, kissed her, and said, "Thank you for coming. No more withholding."

Kaye said, "I will keep you to your promise." They grinned.

When the military truck picked them up, the two again squeezed in, smiled at each other, and Hoffman declared, "Let's go home."

Two minutes later, Kaye elbowed her husband and asked, "Dirk, exactly where did you hear Caroline sing?"

THE END

Please consider sharing a review on Amazon. Thank you.
Go to: https://amzn.to/3viJjCI

ACKNOWLEDGMENTS

As a Vietnam veteran familiar about Post Traumatic Stress Disorder, I became aware that most veterans regardless of the war do not share their experiences especially the scary ones, even though communicating them would benefit many about the horrors of war and provide a release for the vets themselves. My novel, while fictional, parallels real life suffering of the soldiers and their families, and my heart goes out to them.

I am grateful to many people for the birthing of this book. I appreciate the contributions of Linda and Buzz Bernstein, Arlene Gooch, Dan Johnson, Dave Williams, Dave and Lonnie Hinckley, and Bruce Malone, Superintendent, Meuse-Argonne American Cemetery in France. Niki Faldemolaei provided guidance in many areas of publishing and marketing. Shelly Chung with her copy-editing skills endured a minefield of spelling, grammar, and other mistakes. Thank you all.

My sister, Hilary, who as a writer herself, served as a sounding board, provided suggestions, used vats of red ink in her editing, and encouraged me to go deeper. Thank you, Hil. Your insights have been invaluable.

Thank you to Gordon Jack, who was a fighter pilot in Europe and provided stories and knowledge which added to the texture of the story. I am also indebted to "CP", who at 98 recalled his assault on Omaha Beach on D-day. He never did tell me his last name in our conversations. I am awed by these two warriors.

Our son, Bill Hinckley, provided extraordinary assistance with Word and proof reading as well as keeping me sane after many hours in front of a computer screen.

Thank you to my wife, Sharon, a watercolor painter, author, and yoga teacher, who provides the light and has always encouraged me in all my endeavors to access the creative side of my brain and to enjoy life to its fullest.

Made in the USA
Columbia, SC
01 July 2021